THERUS VALAIR

Book 2: Shyn Esari, A Dragon's Quest

By

Robbin Rosalis

© 2021 Robbin Rosalis
ISBN: 978-1-7370321-2-0

Want to follow the author or Therus and Valair?
Facebook: Robbin Rosalis
Web page: http://rrosalisauthor.com

Dedication

Thanks go to my husband, Jack. I could not have written this without his support.

Cover Art
By

Dar Albert
www.wickedsmartdesigns.com

Table of Contents

Dedication 3

Map 6

Chapter 1 8

Chapter 2 16

Chapter 3 26

Chapter 4 40

Chapter 5 50

Chapter 6 58

Chapter 7 72

Chapter 8 84

Chapter 9 90

Chapter 10 98

Chapter 11 112

Chapter 12 122

Chapter 13 136

Chapter 14 144

Chapter 15 150

Chapter 16 164

Chapter 17 174

Chapter 18 180

Chapter 19 190

Chapter 20 202

Chapter 21 216

Chapter 22 224

Chapter 23 234

Chapter 24 248

Chapter 25 260

Chapter 26 268

Chapter 27 278

Chapter 28 290

Chapter 29 298

Chapter 30 306

Chapter 31 316

Chapter 32 324

Chapter 33 334

Chapter 34 348

Chapter 35 358

Chapter 36 368

Chapter 37 380

Chapter 38 392

Chapter 39 402

About the Author 415

Map

Shyn Esari, A Dragon's Quest

Chapter 1

Fallon, Spring 2979: After the Battle of the Thorn

The trip home to River Rest passed quickly enough. The trip was slow due to the large number of fighters and equipment. The roads were clear, and the Long Riders mainly aided by ensuring there were no stragglers or gaps in the line. Fallon had a lot of free time to reflect. The nagging feeling of restlessness had not gone away. She discounted it a couple of days as remnants of concern about the threat of Pax. Her brother, Elkon, just shook his head. "Ok, Fallon, you know what the answer is. It's not The Thorn. You need to decide what you are going to do about it." They spoke for a while the night before he left with the units traveling north on the River Road. Elkon spent the rest of his time that evening with them around their campfire. Elkon told Goron, Fallon, Theron, and Feron he was headed to the Warrior Camp to look for the White Fox female who had caught his eye. If he did not find her there, he was going to the White Fox homeland.

Fallon kept a watchful eye on the road and made sure there were no stragglers. The fighters did an excellent job of watching each other and staying caught up. The pace was not fast, and the scouts reported no problems ahead, and yet the feeling of restlessness was back, the same as it had been for now the past season. Fallon groaned. *"Shut up, foolish drive to find a mate. Go bother someone else. The Goddess knows I don't want a mate. I want to travel. Why can't I just do that?"* No reply came. So, she grumbled for most of the morning, fully committing to wallowing around in denial, exasperation with a dash of anger for an extra little bit of spice that makes for a perfect chapped ass. By the noon stop, she was utterly pissed off and no closer to solving her dilemma. She knew being mad about it would not solve anything, but she also could not seem to think past it, so she just went with it until it abated. At the lunch break, she attended to her duties and then found a peaceful place to think with her lunch about her current situation. She chewed and thought for a while.

"Hum....maybe I could take a lover? It might make the restlessness shut up. No attachment, just some pleasure...." It sounded like a good idea. She sat back and looked at the fighters around her. Really, looked at them. Some of the best warriors from the Owl, Wolf, and Boar clan were right in front of her. Short of the clan's Althing, where was she going to find a better selection than this? With new determination, she dusted her breeches off and mounted her horse. She called for Feron to watch the line as she set out to see what she could find that enticed her.

For the remainder of the day, she rode the lines of the units scanning the fighters. In her clan, she saw no one that tempted her. Most of them she knew. She caught a curious look from her father, so she rode farther back down the line where the Owl and Wolf clans walked. The Owl clan males tended to be tall, trim, and stately. While they were a peaceful people, if provoked, they were tenacious fighters who were fast with a long reach. Their clan was known for their beautiful living structures made from wood, stone, or a combination of the two. Fallon looked at the line of tall fighters. *"Yes, objectively, they are very handsome."* she thought. *"Who looks tempting………"*

Bodhran pulled along beside her. "Who are you looking for?" he asked.

"What?" Fallon startled out of her thoughts.

"Who do you seek? You have been riding the lines all afternoon. You look like you are looking for someone." Bodhran replied as he drew his water skin and took a long drink. "Who is it? I'll find them."

"Just checking the line," she replied as she muttered in her mind. *"Why didn't I get some of the Scaeva slyness?"*

Bodhran's nose tingled, indicating Fallon was not entirely truthful. He found this surprising; this was the first time she had not been candid with him. *"Maybe there is a problem?"* He looked up and down the line

10

of fighting units and wagons lumbering past. No, everything looked fine. There were no stragglers; the wounded were in wagons, the road was peaceful, and the scouts had reported no issues. He glanced at Fallon. She had stopped looking for whoever she was looking for and was watching the back of the line. If there was a problem, he did not see it. She pulled her horse to the left and headed down the line. Bodhran followed her, still checking the line and continuing to find that all was well.

"Bodhran, go check the wagons with the injured. See how the stock is faring. If they look tired, let me know." Fallon called out to him as she cantered off.

Bodhran watched her ride off with a puzzled look on his face. The wagons with the wounded were near the center of the line. She had just ridden past them. *"Hum, maybe she wants some time to herself?"* It didn't explain her seemingly looking for someone. Bodhran shook his head and went to check on the stock pulling the wagons.

Fallon cantered away from the Owl units and brought her horse to a walk when she came to the Wolf clan. *"Goddess, that was close. Why did Theron and Feron have to get all the stealth in the family?"* She pulled her horse up under the shade of a tree and watched the line pass. The Wolf clan males were more rugged in appearance than the Owl clan males. They had thicker shaggy hair in shades of brown and black.

Their bright eyes missed nothing. Those who were shifters had a little wilder look to them. They were a bold and passionate clan who formed firm emotional attachments with those they considered family whether they were related or not. If the comments by Lea, one of her long riders, were to be believed, Wolf Clan males were ardent and voracious lovers. As they passed, a couple of the males made eye contact with her. A tall black-haired warrior with light amber eyes flashed her a smile and a wink. Fallon noted it by returning the smile. Fallon nodded to those riding drag at the end of the line when the last wagon rolled by her before she trotted her horse back to her unit.

Theron was riding beside Feron, and they were speaking quietly to each other. When Feron saw her, he promptly shut up and broke eye contact with Theron. "Oh, hey sis, everything is fine here," Feron awkwardly announced.

"Yea, we got this; if you want to check the line or, you know, just enjoy the fine scenery." Then Theron hastily added. " 'Cause, it's a nice day for a ride." When he finished, Feron punched him on the arm.

"Ow Feron. What's wrong with you?" Theron exclaimed as he rubbed his left shoulder.

Fallon sighed and shook her head. She reasoned that by twenty-three, the twins would have been more mature. They were better now than when they came to be in her unit at twenty-one. *"Maybe in a couple more years, they will be there. Goddess, help their mates,"* she thought to herself.

Bodhran rode up and pulled alongside Theron. He had heard the exchange. He looked towards Fallon. "The stock pulling the wagons are fine. One or two have shoes that need to be reset tonight, but the rest are in good shape."

"Good," Fallon replied. She reined her horse around and headed back down the line.

When Fallon was out of hearing, Feron turned to Theron. "You had to say that?"

"What? Say what? Brother?" Theron plastered an angelic smile upon his face.

"You said, 'Enjoy the fine scenery.' Maybe she doesn't want everyone knowing." Feron stated, looking exasperated at his brother.

Bodhran looked perplexed. "Know what?"

Theron chuckled, "That all afternoon Fallon has been looking at all the male warriors like she does sweet bread."

"Theron! That's our sister you are talking about." Feron punched Theron on the shoulder again.

"Shite, Feron, stop hitting me. She is a grown-ass woman. She can do what she likes." Theron grumbled while rubbing his shoulder.

Bodhran thought for a moment. Then it dawned on him what Feron and Theron were talking about, and it made sense why she was acting as she did. "Oh.... Hum....Fallon has reached the age of majority and can do as she pleases regarding selecting a willing male or female for......" he stopped because Theron and Feron were staring daggers at him. "for.... um...aggressive cuddling or whatever........ I'm going to go and see how the supply wagons are doing." Bodhran turned and trotted his horse off.

"That grown-ass woman is our sister, Theron. She does not have interludes, well, except for Sirona, and that was almost eight years ago. What if she picks a bad one?"

"I don't know, Feron. What if she picks a good one?" Theron returned.

"It's just a fifty percent chance of getting a good one. 'Cause she might pick a bad one." Feron looked at him. "It's not like she has a lot of experience as we do."

"Ugh, Brother, I don't think I can continue talking about this. Let her make her own choice. What can we do anyway?" Theron replied, looking decidedly uncomfortable with the direction the conversation was taking.

"Do you have any silphion? I'm out." Feron asked.

"Yes. I have some, or I can ride by the healer's wagon and get some." Theron replied as he looked at his brother with his forehead wrinkled. "Why?"

"I've been thinking about that, and I have the perfect plan." Feron smiled, quite pleased with himself. Feron spent the next several minutes convincing his brother to go along with his scheme.

Fallon walked her horse down the line glancing at the fighters as she passed. *"Why can't the right one be obvious? Maybe their hair could stand straight up on their head........ I don't know, something."* It occurred to her; what if they developed feelings for her she did not return? The more Fallon rode and thought, the more she realized taking a lover would pretty much be the same thing she did with Sirona. She did not want anyone to go through that. Fallon didn't ride down the line to the Wolf Clan. She didn't want the male who caught her eye to get any more ideas. By the end of the day, when they made camp, she was tired physically and mentally. She tended her horses and checked with the rest of her crew. When she was done, she headed to their campfire. She just wanted to put this day behind her with some hot food and her bedroll.

Chapter 2

Fallon reached the campfire, and Feron met her with a mug of tea. She sniffed it. It was silphion and mint. Feron smiled at her. "I know you like mint in it. Why don't you sit down and enjoy your tea? You looked like you had a busy day running the lines. Gael and Ken will have the night meal ready soon." After he gave her the tea, he hot-footed it out of camp.

Fallon watched her brother with suspicion as he left. Something was up. She made a mental note to check her bedroll for a snake or other creature later. Silphion was generally drunk once a week by women who did not want to become pregnant on Gatherday, when families got together for food and activities with the clan. Today was not Gatherday. Theron was not at the fire. Fallon glanced around as she sipped her tea. Nothing seemed amiss. She spotted Goron walking across the camp towards her. He sat down on the log next to her. "Daughter, how are you this evening?" He spoke as he eyed her tea.

"I'm fine. Would you like some tea? Feron made some silphion and mint. I can make you some without the silphion."

He raised his eyebrows. "Feron made you some silphion tea? May I see the cup, please?" Fallon

17

handed him the cup. Goron smelled the cup. Yep, it was silphion and mint. The scent indicated it was the correct strength. He gave the cup back to Fallon. He didn't doubt Feron couldn't make the tea correctly. He and Ambriel had taught all their children how to gather the herb and how to brew it. He was just surprised Feron had made the tea for her. Their family tradition held that on the first Gatherday after the full moon, the males in his house harvested the herbs and made the tea for the women while the women did whatever women did when they were to themselves. Ambriel and Fallon generally gathered it other times. Goron had been taking his sons with him ever since they were old enough to walk. However, this was not Gatherday, and it was suspicious. He sighed; the twins could make anything normal suspicious.

Goron smiled at his daughter, "There is nothing more fragrant than mint tea. Yes, I would like some. If you could put some ginger in it, that would be good." Goron sat back on the log while Fallon put some herbs together in a mesh bag and prepared his tea. Something was off, and he would bet his last coin the twins were behind it. He looked around the camp for Theron and Feron and tried to get an idea of what their latest caper might be. Gael and Ken were preparing the evening meal. Usually, the twins hung around cooking food like vultures waiting for it to be ready. *"Hum…. Conveniently absent…What could they be up to that is more important to those two hungry hounds than food?"* Goron mused as he surveyed the area.

There was a large, heavy pot hanging over the fire with enough meat in it to feed several shifters and Fallon's unit. *"That's odd."* Goron called to the cooks, "Gael, Ken, you look like you have a big meal going on there." Goron finished with a smile.

Ken looked up from where he was prepping some bread and dried fruit. "Yes, Feron asked if we could make extra for a couple of friends he and Theron were bringing into camp. You should stay; there will be plenty of food."

"Bam! There it is. Now, what is it?" Goron mused before he replied, "Yes, I would enjoy that. I don't get to spend as much time with my children as I would like."

Fallon handed her father the hot mug and sat back down to finish her tea. Goron noticed she looked tired. He reasoned it was why she overlooked the giant stew being prepared. A short time later, Bodhran wandered into camp. He raised an eyebrow when he saw the big caldron on the fire. "Ken, Gael, what can I do to help?"

Gael replied as she stirred the pot. "Nothing, we have it. It just needs to finish cooking. It's almost ready. If you are hungry, I have some bread and fruit ready until the stew is done."

Bodhran jumped up, grabbed some bread, and slathered across it some fruit and honey puree. "Thanks. It smells great! It just looked like a big meal, and I wondered if I could help with anything." He replied as he took a big bite of the bread.

Gael laughed, "Goron just asked that. Yea, Feron asked us to cook extra as he and Theron invited a couple of friends to join us for late meal."

He glanced down to see Fallon was drinking some tea which smelled like silphion and mint. "You are drinking some silp...........um...mint tea?" He asked Fallon.

"Yes, Feron made it for me," Fallon answered as she continued to stare into the fire and sip what was left in her mug. Bodhran's eyes bugged out; he stopped chewing and shook his head. Goron noticed his surprised look and narrowed his eyes at Bodhran.

"I need to go and check with the drovers about the stock with the loose shoes. I ran into someone from the Warrior Camp when I was there. Will there be enough if he comes to late meal with us?" Bodhran asked.

"Sure!" Gael replied, smiling. "We probably have enough to feed an entire unit. It will be nice to have some visitors in camp since The Thorn is no more."

"Thanks," Bodhran shouted as he jogged out of camp.

Goron sat there a few moments as he tried to figure out what was going on. He patted Fallon on her knee. "I saw you were very busy today. You must be tired, daughter."

"Shite! He has eyes like an eagle shifter. Think fast." Fallon looked at her father and smiled. "I am a little. I just want to make sure everyone gets to their home safely."

Goron considered her words. "They will. There are eight long rider groups here, in addition to seasoned scouts, warriors, and drovers. We will be fine. Don't tire yourself out. We still have many more days of travel."

Fallon nodded her head and continued to stare into the fire. *"That is a large pot of stew. How many people are they bringing into camp?"* Fallon shrugged it off. Having guests in the camp was not a problem if they discussed it with the cooks. She considered it an excellent way to drum up business and to find out the local gossip. She rolled her shoulders and stretched her back. She was beginning to feel better. The stew was bubbling pleasantly in the cauldron as the scent of cooking meat and vegetables perfumed the evening air. Fallon pulled in a deep breath. It smelled delicious. Ken and Gael were outstanding cooks who kept the company well fed.

Goron shifted his weight next to her and murmured. "The stew is starting to smell about right. Theron and Feron will be here presently."

Fallon chuckled, "Yes, they always know when a meal is ready to eat."

**

When Bodhran jogged out of camp, he headed to the drovers and found them already resetting the loose shoes on the horses. He waived to the Wolf Clan Long Rider unit overseeing the job and headed toward the main Wolf Clan encampment. While Fallon may have had no idea why Theron and Feron were bringing guests into camp, he knew exactly why. They planned to help their sister out in the area of romance. Bodhran considered their "help" was not going to be very helpful. He had seen the females they had cavorted with, and frankly, to Bodhran, they were low-hanging fruit. Oh, they were fair enough for a one-night tumble, but Fallon did not strike him as the one-night type. Maybe, he thought, she did need to be amorous with someone. Goddess knows she hadn't been in the time he knew her. The more Bodhran considered it, the more he decided she could very well do with a good rutting with someone who was a cut above easy pickings. Bodhran had trailed behind her out of sight earlier today. He saw her make eye contact with the Wolf clan warrior. He stayed out of sight and watched her ride back to the front of the column. When the wolf units passed, he rode out of the woods and back up their line, where he pulled alongside the black-haired wolf male with light gray eyes. "Wolf Clan champion Lonan Cathair, it is good to see you again." Bodhran began as he reached over to clasp him by the forearm in greeting.

"Bear Clan champion Bodhran Fast Strike Gideon well met! It has been a fair number of years since the Warrior Camp. I swear by the Goddess, I think you have grown taller and packed on even more muscle if it's possible." Lonan grasped his forearm, smiling.

"You look well, Lonan. How did your unit fair in the battle with The Thorn?"

"We did well with no loss of life in my unit. Three of the other Wolf Clan units had a couple of casualties, but we were very fortunate overall. It was a good plan the Boar Chieftain and his second had. It saved many lives in the Ten Clans." He ran his hand down his horse's neck as looked back at Bodhran. "I hear you are in a Boar Clan Long Rider unit. If so, you are a long way from home, brother."

Bodhran nodded his head. "You heard truth. The leader of the Long Rider unit I am in is the daughter of the Boar Clan Captain, Goron Scaeva. Her mother is Ambriel Tulun from the Wolf Clan."

"I know the Tulun. They are a good den. Goron, yes, there are stories about him. He is a fierce adversary." Lonan nodded his head. "A Boar Clan female Long Rider chief was scanning the lines. She had short brown hair. Would that have been her?" Lonan looked at Bodhran with a slight smile playing at the corners of his mouth.

"Oh aye, it was her. The other Boar Clan Long Rider crew leader is male." Bodhran replied, wondering where this was leading.

"She was riding the line most of the afternoon. Was there a problem?"

Bodhran thought a moment. Shifters could detect lies, and he knew Lonan was a wolf shifter, so he gave a carefully crafted reply. "No, no problem. She takes her duties seriously. Making sure things go according to plan is her top priority."

Lonan nodded his head. "That is a good quality in a leader."

"She is a good leader. She is courageous and a hard worker. All in her unit consider themselves lucky to be in her crew." Bodhran finished with assurance.

Lonan could detect no lie or partial truth in anything Bodhran said, not that he would have ever thought Bodhran would be untruthful. Lonan thought it was a little unusual a Bear Clan champion would be in a Boar Clan Long Rider crew. He was intrigued with the female Long Rider he had seen earlier. Now Lonan had her name, and he wanted to meet her. Their conversation was cut off when a female warrior rode up to them with an issue about the supply drovers. He turned to Bodhran. "I must address this. We should talk later if you are free of your duties."

"Yes. It was good to see you again, Lonan." Bodhran trotted his horse back up the line to keep an eye on Fallon.

**

Bodhran jogged to the Wolf camp. When he thought back on the events of the afternoon, he did not know why Fallon was traveling up and down the lines or why her brief interaction with Lonan seemed important. Now, it made complete sense. Fallon was seeking a male for sex. She appeared to be interested in Lonan. From his conversation with him, Lonan seemed to be interested in Fallon. He congratulated himself on trailing Fallon and stopping to talk with Lonan. This was going to be too easy. All he had to do was get him to come back to their camp. Lonan would be vastly superior to anything the twins brought back, no matter how well-intentioned they were. He would introduce Lonan to Fallon and let nature take its course. Well.... not so much nature, but Lonan. Wolf shifter males were a passionate bunch when they set their sights on a female they liked, and Bodhran had the distinct feeling Lonan had Fallon in his sights.

Bodhran found Lonan's camp with little effort. They were just starting to prepare their late meal. Bodhran had only to mention "ready to eat meat stew," and Lonan put his second in charge to follow Bodhran back to the Boar clan camp. Bodhran smiled to himself. If there was one thing a shifter would not miss unless they could not help it, it was a hot meal.

Chapter 3

Goron refilled his mug with water. The savory smell of stew wafted through the camp. He inhaled and sighed contentedly. In only a matter of minutes, the twins would arrive. They were a constant as the seasons. When the food was ready, they always appeared. Then he could sort out what mischief they had planned. He didn't have to wait long. Theron, Feron, and two other males came into camp. One of the males he knew, Evrard Hardy, a Boar Clan warrior and metal smith.

Theron and Feron looked at him and quickly glanced at each other. "Father" Theron began as he entered camp. "We thought you would be in camp with Chieftain Woutan Bright Hammer Boar, but it is good to see you at our camp. Fallon, I brought Evrard Hardy to late meal."

Fallon stood up and grasped Evrard's forearm in greeting. "Welcome to our camp, Evrard Hardy."

Gael spoke up, "The meal is ready. Please wash up and get a bowl. There is cider, water, and some ale. The mugs, bowls, and spoons are on the trestle table."

"Yea, those two haven't changed. They still know when supper's ready, and something is going on."

Goron thought to himself. He nodded to Evrard. Goron knew Evrard to be a solid Boar Clan member. He was a skilled fighter. His metalwork was durable, and he treated his customers fairly. He attended warrior practice and worked in his shop. That was it. Goron had never heard anything negative about him. He did not know Theron and Evrard were friends. He did not seem to be the type of male with whom Theron would be good friends. Evrard was reliable, respectable, very predictable, and did not seem to have much variety in his life. Besides being reliable, and with Theron reliable meant finding mischief, Evrard and Theron were complete opposites.

"Evening Father," Feron spoke as he headed towards Fallon with the other male in tow. "Fallon Tulun, this is Kaymeronn Leiko of the Hart Clan."

Fallon stood up and grasped Kaymeronn's forearm in greeting. "Welcome to our camp, Kaymeronn Leiko."

"Thank you, Fallon Tulun. It is a pleasure to be in a camp with beautiful women, and if the smell of the stew is any indication, some of the best cooks in all Therus." He slid his hand down her forearm, gently grasping her hand, and brought it to his lips before releasing it.

Fallon raised her eyebrow and smiled. "Gael and Ken are very talented cooks."

"A camp where such talent and beauty can be found; I am happy Feron invited me to late meal." He smiled and walked to the trestle table and began to ladle a bowl of stew.

Fallon blinked her eyes, and it struck her; something was off. She had been so wrapped up in trying to resolve what was her body's mate quest she had not noticed what was going on in her camp. She shook her head, admonishing herself. This was not like her. She stayed on top of her crew. Fallon glanced around. The cooks had used the large cook pot. The trestle table had bread, cheese, and a fruit spread. Her father was here. He had his arms crossed, and the look on his face, she knew all too well. It said, "What are the twins up to?" There were guests in camp. It occurred to her; she had no idea how Theron or Feron knew the men they brought to camp. *"Shite, something's up. One day, I drop my guard for one day, and they decide to pull something.....But what? I swear sometimes it's like they are tempting me to kill them."*

Fallon surveyed the camp. She caught Evrard staring hard at Theron as Theron shrugged his shoulders. Kaymeronn flirted shamelessly with Gael and made her blush, which was a feat considering Gael was accomplished in that area. Ken was staring daggers at Kaymeronn. This was understandable since Ken had been trying to woo Gael for the past two seasons. It appeared at first glance Kaymeronn was oblivious to the murderous looks Ken was sending him. A moment later, he saw the lethal gaze Ken was sending him, smiled, and continued his teasing banter with Gael. When she gazed in Theron's and Feron's direction, she discovered they were focused entirely on getting their food and avoiding any eye contact. Before she could put any more thought into figuring out what they were conspiring to do, Bodhran sauntered into camp with a male, and not just any male, but the stunningly handsome Wolf Clan shifter warrior who winked at her earlier today.

Bodhran walked up to her. "Fallon Tulun, leader of the Boar Clan Long Rider Crew, I have brought Lonan Caithair, Wolf Clan champion and Commander of the Crimson Company, with me to late supper."

Lonan grasped her arm in greeting. His amber-colored eyes were bright as Fallon spoke. "Lonan Caithair welcome to our camp. Late supper is ready; please get some food."

"Thank you for extending to me the welcome of your camp." He looked to the older male standing close to Fallon. Their hair coloring was the same, and they both had a similar scent. He determined this must be her father, Goron Scaeva, who Bodhran had mentioned. He addressed him. "You must be Goron Scaeva, Captain of the Boar Clan."

Goron nodded his head. "You are correct."

Lonan clasped his arm in greeting. "It is good to meet the warrior who worked to craft the clever plan which caused The Thorn and the Scorpions their downfall."

"Thank you. The Wolf Clan warriors did a fine job of closing the trap behind The Thorn's renegades. The army of Therus was skillful and disciplined. It enabled us to win the day with relatively few deaths."

Lonan nodded his head. "Putting us to meet the White Fox warriors to close the trap was a good strategy; we are both quick clans in battle."

Goron grunted. "Let us hope it will not be needed again for a very long time. You should eat. If you wait, the twins will clear out the entire caldron."

Lonan grinned, "You are a wise male, Goron Scaeva." He turned to Fallon. "Long Rider, you put in a lot of work today, assuring the line moved smoothly. Please sit. I'll bring you a bowl."

"You are a guest in our camp......" Fallon spoke to his broad back as he had already crossed to where the food was laid out.

"I've got this." He said with a wink.

Fallon felt her cheeks heat up as she spoke. "My thanks to you, Lonan Cathair."

"Just Lonan." Lonan picked up two bowls and began to ladle the thick stew. His wolf brushed against his mind.

"The Tulun den female is toothsome, but she is not our mate. It's a shame. She is a pack leader from two strong dens, the Tulun and Scaeva."

"And she is beautiful, Sable," Lonan thought back to his wolf.

Sable stretched shook out his fur. *"The other two males want her. We can easily defeat them."*

Lonan bristled. *"Which two males?"*

"The foolish one flirting to the cook while her potential mate wants to stab him with the big knife. He is trying to make it seem as though all women want him. The quiet one across the fire has been staring at her and not eating much."

Lonan glanced at them while he picked up two mugs. True enough, the one flirting with the female camp cook was cutting glances at Fallon so much he was missing the murderous looks the male cook was giving him. The male by the fire was so wrapped up staring at Fallon; he dipped his bread in his cider instead of his stew.

Sable wrinkled up his nose and scoffed. ***"Bread dipped in cider?"***

Lonan had to admit the competition did not look formidable. He thought back to Sable, *"There is no need to challenge them. They will defeat themselves."* Sable laid back down with his head resting on his paws.

Lonan skillfully carried the bowls and mugs back to where Fallon sat. He gave her a cup and bowl then went to sit by her father, where he struck up a conversation with him. When he glanced at Kaymeronn, he had gathered up some food and sat down on the log right beside Fallon. The male then began to pick up his relentless flirting with Fallon, who parried his advances with adroit skillfulness. Lonan divided his attention between Goron and listening in on the conversation between Fallon and Kaymeronn. He waited patiently as Kaymeronn flashed big smiles, feigned attentiveness, and crested up to display his chest and shoulders like a stallion in breeding season. Sable, who had been watching the display, rolled his eyes and sighed. ***"Fortune has wasted too much male good looks on that undeserving creature. If his aspect shaped his visage, he would be a warty toad."*** Lonan choked back a laugh.

33

Ken had pulled the cauldron off the fire and scooped the remains into a bowl. He went around to give out seconds to whoever wanted them. As he put more into Lonan's bowl, Lonan observed Ken's eyes were a little narrow, and his hand gripped the spoon like a sword. A discrete sniff determined Ken was still furious.

Fallon had dealt with pushy males in the past, but Kymeronn was worse than most. She was diplomatic to visitors to her camp, but this Hart male was exasperating. He might have been considered attractive by many women, but as soon as he opened his mouth, all his self-absorbed small and ugly, came out. Ignoring him did not work. Veiled insults were met with what looked like attraction from Kaymeronn. Fallon concluded he must be dense. If she needed to step up her game, then so be it.

"Hey, beautiful, feel my tunic. Know what it's made of? Stud material." Kaymerron finished looking quite pleased with himself.

Fallon sighed, *"You asked for it."* She thought to herself.

Before she could make a retort, Kaymerron, who took her silence for acquiescence, spoke. "What do you say to a threesome?"

"By the goddess, he did not say that!" She thought as the curling tendrils of anger raced through her body. She graced him with an icy smile. "A threesome, really? With whom?"

Kaymerron grinned, pleased with the direction the conversation was headed and oblivious to the frosty look Fallon was giving him, continued. "You and the camp cook, or your preferred female friend." He spoke as he flashed her a wink.

"Really? That sounds good. Who is the third person?" Fallon asked.

Kaymerron looked confused. Surely, she knew what a threesome was? "Um….well..with me," he finished.

"Oh. Then no," Fallon quipped

Goron and Lonan who had been listening to the conversation between Kaymerron and Fallon and getting increasingly more and more angry, burst out laughing when Fallon snubbed him. They were laughing so hard they missed Ken putting down the bowl of stew. After roughly setting the bowl on the ground, Ken strode over to where Kaymerron sat and smacked him across the head with the ladle he was holding and proceeded to yell profanities at the man as he lay sprawled out on the grass. Many of the obscenities had to do with Kaymerron's flirting with his intended lifemate, Gael. Fallon reached to stop Ken from continuing his attack but was knocked back as Kaymerron leaped off the ground and started throwing punches at Ken. Lonan grabbed Fallon and pulled her out of the range of the two men who were fighting. Goron hopped up and moved out of the combatants' way. Despite calls from Fallon to stop fighting, Ken and Kaymerron battled on exchanging punches and kicks. Armed with the stout ladle made by Evrard Hardy, Ken landed several well-placed shots.

"Only the lowest of tavern servers would fight with that piece of slag you are welding," Kaymerron yelled as he dodged a nasty swipe to his face by Ken.

"Slag! By the goddess' sweet tits! What do you mean slag?" Evrard bellowed.

Kaymerron glanced at Evrard. "Fuck you. Stay out of this."

And that was all it took for Evrard to join in the fray after throwing his plate down. Theron looked to where his father stood next to Bodhran. Goron glared at him while Bodhran calmly drank from his mug. Goron motioned with his head at the fight. Theron sighed and elbowed Feron. "Come, Brother, let's break up the fight."

Feron grunted in agreement. They made their way over to where the two were throwing punches. Feron grabbed Everard to pull him out of the brawl. Evrard twisted away, and Feron was left holding the remains of the iron worker's tunic. Kaymerron threw a punch at Ken, who jerked to the side, causing the blow to land squarely in Theron's face. All thoughts of breaking up the fight were tossed aside as a now provoked Theron waded into the fray. Evrard turned towards Feron to see who had grabbed him from the back. Feron put his hand out to stop Evrard from hitting him. He wrinkled up his face; there, on Evrard's chest, was a tick. "Brother, hold up. You have a tick." Feron stated while he reached over and before Evrard could stop him, Feron had plucked at the thing.

Evrard yelped and swatted his hand away. "Shite Feron, that's not a tick. That's my nipple."

"What?" Feron glanced down and counted. " 1, 2, 3….Evrard by the goddess, you have three nipples. Hey, Theron," Feron yelled, "did you know the male you brought for Fallon has three nipples?"

Theron solidly punched Kaymerron, sending him to the ground where he lay unmoving, replied testily. "No, Brother, I was not counting nipples. The male you brought cannot take a punch." He reached to grab Ken, who intended to hit the unmoving Kaymerron again with the hefty serving piece. They looked at each other and had a moment of clarity when they realized the entire camp had heard their comments.

"Oh shite!" The murmured in unison.

Fallon stomped over to where they stood. "Yes, Oh shite indeed. Clean this mess up. See your guests to their camp. I'll discuss the events of this night with you later."

Evrard scratched his head for a moment. "Theron, what do you mean 'the male you brought to camp'? Wait. You both brought mates for your sister to camp?

Theron looked at the ground, embarrassed. "Um....well...you see." He stumbled around a bit, trying to find the right words, then threw his hand up in the air and blurted out. "Yes. Yes, we did. We did not know who she might like."

While he was stumbling around finding the right words, Kaymerron got to his feet. "You asked me to come under the claim she was looking for a life mate!" Evrard yelled.

"I think the female is frigid. If she doesn't want me, she must be frigid." Kaymerron declared as he rubbed his jaw.

Feron stepped forward and punched Kaymerron straight in the face while Evrard went at Theron. The fight erupted anew, with Ken joining in to take more savage swipes at Kaymerron and Theron with the indestructible ladle that was still in pristine shape.

Fallon signed as she rolled her eyes, "Bodhran sort this out."

"I'll take care of it." He said with a straight face while his eyes twinkled with laughter.

Lonan had followed her and stood beside her. "Fallon Tulun, I find sometimes a long walk is a good way to clear the mind. Would you like to vacate the camp for a little while?"

Fallon thought about it. She was furious with her brothers and the stunt they pulled. She sighed. "Just Fallon. Yes, Lonan, it would be a wonderful idea right now." Fallon picked up her cloak and gave Theron and Feron one last murderous look before stomping out of camp.

Lonan stopped by the trestle table on the way out and grabbed an ale bottle. He held out his arm. Fallon placed her hand on him, and they left. Behind him, Lonan heard Bodhran wade into the fight to try to separate the combatants. His comments were dimming the farther they walked away. "Kaymerron, you do not want to fight me. Ken, I swear by the goddess if you hit me with that big damn spoon....." He also caught Goron warning Bodhran, "Oh aye, you'll be wanting to avoid getting hit with that mucking club of a spoon. Evrard, fine job on the serving piece! I'll be by to purchase one when we get back home......" Their voices faded and were overtaken by the noise of the other camps they passed. They walked further and turned off onto a path that forked off into the woods.

Chapter 4

Sable pricked his ears and scanned the woods. *"The forest animals are absent tonight with the war camps here. The moon is full, and she should have no problem seeing the game trail."* He smiled a toothy grin. *"I like their camp the food was good, and there was a fight….well…not much of a fight, but a fight just the same. We should come back and revisit their den. We could fight the next time."* Sable seemed quite pleased with the prospect of a meat-laden meal and a feisty scrap.

"Brother, I think the female may be embarrassed. She may not want us to come back. Her brothers brought those males into camp. She might see the fight as something she should have stopped herself without help. She may think others might see that as her not running a smooth camp."

Sable cocked his head for a moment and replied. *"That's silly; males warriors will sometimes fight. Yes, those were not the best males. She should only be embarrassed her litter mates brought them back to her. She needs a better male. Someone like us but not us."* Sable wisely advised before turning to watch the forest as they walked along.

Fallon strode along beside Lonan, breathing in the woods' clean smell with the faint whiff of smoke from the campfires. The night was cool, and the moon was bright enough to cast shadows on the ground. The farther she got from camp, the better she felt. Lonan's strides were long and quiet as they slid through the woods. She felt safe with him, and the forest felt oddly soothing. It had been a long time since she had spent much time in the woods alone or had any time alone; now, she thought about it. The duties of a Long Rider of late did not afford her much free time. She realized how much she had missed roaming the wildwood. Going dragon-watching was looking better and better all the time. She would have to find a place away from Theron and Feron so she could enjoy the peace and quiet.

She slyly studied Lonan. He was a handsome male. He was tall with broad shoulders that narrowed down into a trim waist. Like most of the Wolf Clan, he had black hair. It was neatly pulled back into a low ponytail. His eyes were the color of a wolf's eyes, a beautiful rich amber. Lonan felt her eyes on him, and he fixed his gaze on the trail ahead. Like all shifter males, he was pleased to have a female he was interested in look to her heart's content.

Sable brushed up against his mind. ***"The pond is not far, just up the trail. There are a couple of our brothers running and enjoying the moonlight. The***

Wardens of the Argent Woodland watch to safeguard this grove. All is well."

"Fallon, there is a small spring-fed pond close. We could go there and enjoy the ale or walk some more."

"The ale was made by Wenna Pallin and her mate, Artos Pernel. It is excellent; it would be a shame not to drink it." Fallon replied as she gazed steadily into his eyes.

"Indeed. How could I say no to excellent ale?" Lonan chuckled. A few minutes later, Lonan veered off to the left down another trail. The path soon widened out and opened to reveal a beautiful pond surrounded by large trees. Fireflies flickered between the trees around them, and the air no longer had the tang of wood smoke. It was now filled with the sweet scent of night-blooming flowers. Fallon drank in the view as moonlight danced off the ripples that gently caressed the sand where they now stood. "This feels like a place of old magic." Fallon began as she pulled in a deep breath of the perfumed air.

Lonan surveyed the forest around the pond. "Yes, it is. We are in the northern part of the Wolf Clan territory, but you know that." He grinned as his eyes flashed. "The Moon Pond is the heart of the magic for these woods. We do not hunt here. This place is a sanctuary for all animals and fairy. Novice warriors of the Wolf Clan patrol its borders to assure peace here as well as those who are called to the goddess's service to protect this place."

"It is close to the Wheel Road."

"It is, but there is an enchantment on the land here. Only a Wolf Clan member can find it and return to it after another clan member has taken them there. For others, they cannot find it again. The guards are here to escort them back to the Wheel Road." He touched her on the shoulder and pointed to a patch of ground covered in ferns. "Come, we will sit there and watch for sprites."

Fallon laughed, "Sprites? Is that what Wolf males use to entice women?"

Lonan feigned a melodramatic sigh with a boyish grin. "I have used it in the past with success in wooing a female, but it is also true."

"And tonight?"

"It is entirely up to you. The Wolf Clan warriors will separate from the army tomorrow, and we will each go our separate ways. We can simply watch for sprites and talk, or we can rut to your heart's content. While either is fine with me, I am hoping you will choose we pleasure each other. I'll warn you, though, I will spoil you for all other males." Lonan replied with a wink as he spread his cloak on the ground. He opened the bottle of ale and walked to a rock a short distance away, then poured a small amount of the ale into a depression in the stone. He came back and sat down on his cloak. He patted a spot next to him.

Fallon studied him as he lifted his head. His eyes glinted in the moonlight. Lonan's hair trailed down the gorgeous spread of his shoulders. Fallon's hands itched to stroke his chest, and her heart beat a little faster. He was a striking Wolf Clan shifter, and she needed a distraction. She weighed her options then decided. Fallon chuckled as she sat down beside him. "Aye, a claim made by many males."

"Ah, perhaps Fallon, but when a shifter male says it, he speaks the truth." He handed the ale to her. "Tell me, what were you seeking when you were riding the road today?"

Fallon took a drink and handed to bottle to him. Shifters could tell if you were lying, and she had nothing to hide. "My body is pushing me to find a mate. I do not want this. I have worked hard to be a Long Rider, and that is what I want to do. I love traveling and seeing new places." She smiled wistfully.

Lonan thought about her words before he spoke, "I did not know non-shifter clans felt the mate drive. It must be hard for non-shifters. Our animals let us know who the mate for us is. That part is easy for a shifter.

Sable, my wolf brother, has told me you are not our mate, but we both are attracted to you."

Fallon sighed, "Yes. That must make it easy. I was hoping the right one's hair would stand straight up on his head. That would make it easy for me."

Lonan was taking a drink of ale and burst out laughing and sputtering. Sable did his best wolf laugh in Lonan's mind. "I take it no one's hair stood on end?"

Fallon chuckled, "Unfortunately, no."

"A mate can sometimes take a while to find. I will start my mate search after I return home. Sable did not want to seek a mate until The Thorn was no longer a threat to our future mate and den." He shrugged his shoulders. "For some, it is easy, and for others, it is a quest to find them. I am an excellent hunter. No matter how long or difficult the hunt may be for a mate, I will prevail with Sable's help. You are a successful Long Rider captain, smart, hardworking, beautiful, and from a good pack. If you have not found your mate among the Boar Clan, and I suspect you have not, or you would not have been riding the road, you will have to quest to find your other half." Lonan smiled.

Fallon nodded her head. "I have begun to suspect as much."

"Your mother was from the Tulun Wolf pack. They are a den of tenacious hunters, very persevering. You are probably a skillful hunter too. Do not worry about the mating drive limiting what makes your heart happy. The one who is right for you and me will open some incredible opportunities for us, not limit them. I, for one, am very much looking forward to the hunt after my unit is safely back to their dens."

"My mother, Ambriel, has said as much about my other half; each is a good fit for the other."

"She was wise to tell you." Lonan stopped talking and turned his attention to the far side of the pond. Sable was pointed in that direction with his ears pricked forward, watching intently.

"The sprites are coming to the pond," Sable informed him.

Lonan motioned for Fallon to be still. He leaned over and whispered, "The sprites are coming to the pond. If we are still, they will drink the ale I poured into the depression in the rock."

Fallon could feel the warmth flow off him as it caressed her face and neck. He smelled of leather, cedar, and the woods after a summer rain. She settled against him and waited. Moments passed, and Fallon thought she saw a flash of blue light in the night in the

48

lower branch of an ancient oak tree. It was so fast she thought it was a trick of her eyes. Soon more blue flashes appeared that were met with lavender and teal blinking lights. The lights flitted closer to the rock where the ale was poured. A bright blue flash on the rock gave way to a tiny, male sprite no taller than her hand with delicate wings. He glanced at them before dipping his mug into the ale to drink. When he took the cup from his lips, he flashed his wings several times, and soon others appeared and eagerly dipped their tiny cups into the ale.

Fallon watched in fascination as, one by one, the sprites came to drink. She had thought sprites were the stuff of legend and fancy. Before long, the dip in the rock was emptied. The blue sprite flew toward them, stopped midway, then flitted back to the rock. He did it several times before coming back to rest only a short distance in front of them. Lonan watched curiously. He heard Sable laughing. *"The alpha of the sprite pack wants more of the ale you poured into the rock."*

"Hum, tell him I will give them much more of the ale if they sing a song for our guest."

Sable was quiet for a few moments before he spoke, *"The alpha agrees, but you must pour the ale first."*

Lonan nudged Fallon. "I'll be right back; it seems the sprites really like the ale."

Fallon laughed, "Wenna and Artos would be pleased they were fond of it."

Lonan stood and took the bottle to the sprites. They cleared a path for him and waited expectantly. Lonan poured half the bottle of ale into a deeper dip in the rock before he stepped away. The blue sprite nodded his head, and the wood filled with a soft humming that built into a melodious song. Fallon was incredulous. She marveled wide-eyed as the fairies flickered in time to the beautiful tune they sang while they skipped across the pond, in the trees, and danced in the grass. The song ended too quickly for Fallon. They watched as the sprites drank all the ale before they disappeared back into the woods. "Lonan, that was incredible! I have never seen anything like it. They were so beautiful." She shook her head. "I thought you were jesting about the sprites. I did not think they were real."

"They are still here in the places where magic yet lives. This place is a sanctuary for them we protect. I would not have brought you here if Sable did not like you. He is an excellent judge of character."

Fallon turned to him. "I understand and will keep the secret of these woods. Does my mother know?"

"Yes, most of the Wolf pack know and swear an oath to keep its secret. We can bring someone from our den or someone special to us here. If they are not a wolf shifter, they cannot find it on their own." He glanced down at the ground.

Sable brushed against his mind. ***"We cannot tell her it is another reason why our pack could not let any of the traitors who fought against us survive. A couple of the wolves who fought against us knew about the moon pond."***

"I know, Brother."

"I see this female's heart. She would protect the moon pond."

"I agree," Lonan sent back to Sable.

Fallon placed her hand on Lonan's bicep. "Now that I have seen the sprites, I would like to see for myself if the claim about the impressive ability for bed sport, that is a certain wolf shifter's boast, is true."

"Fallon, I would be happy to prove my ability to pleasure is just as real as the sprites." Lonan smiled as he lifted her hand to his lips and kissed and nibbled her wrist.

Chapter 5

The moon was far to the west as Fallon swam languidly in the Moon Pond towards the sandy beach where their clothes lay across bushes. The wolf shifter had made good on his boast Fallon decided with a grin. She wondered why she had denied herself a lover in the past. *"Right. Responsibilities,"* she sighed. With that thought, she waded out of the pond towards her clothes. Lonan had walked out and was drying off with his tunic. He reached over and began to dry her off with his top. "Your tunic will be very wet, Lonan."

"I'll be fine. Sable puts out a lot of heat. Besides, now I'll be able to have your scent with me on my tunic." He replied as he kissed her forehead. "I thoroughly enjoyed our time together. You may have spoiled me for only wanting a Boar Clan woman now."

"Your skill in flattery only surpasses your skills in bedding," Fallon teased.

Lonan chuckled, "Oh, is that so? Perhaps you need more convincing of my ability to pleasure?"

"Tempting, but the morning is about three hours away, and both of us have camps to attend." They dressed and headed back. Soon Fallon could smell the faint smell of wood smoke. Lonan guided her through the quiet camps. He stopped outside her encampment and stroked her hair as he kissed her. "I am very pleased you went on a walk with me, Fallon," Lonan said as his eyes twinkled in mischief.

"I greatly enjoyed the moonlight with you, Lonan," she chuckled.

He lifted her hand to his lips and kissed it. "Safe journey to you, Boar Clan, Fallon Tulun, Long Rider captain. Good luck to you on your hunt."

"Safe journey to you, Wolf Clan Lonan Cathair, captain and Champion warrior. May your hunt be successful." He dropped her hand, turned, and walked towards his camp. Fallon found her bedroll laid out and ready for her. She climbed in and slipped into sleep.

The noise of the waking camp dragged Fallon out of her peaceful slumber. She rolled over and debated briefly about pulling the covers over her head. She sighed and stretched before getting out of the warm blanket. The Long Rider camp was up and starting the day. Gael walked over, gave her a wink along with a bowl of porridge and a mug of hot tea. Glancing around camp, Fallon discovered Theron and Feron were not in the immediate vicinity. She scanned the camp perimeter and found them tending the horses. Fallon sipped her tea and savored the remaining moments of peace before the duties of the day took center stage. She smiled as she thought returned to the previous night. *"Lonan was right. I may not want another male who isn't a shifter. By the goddess, he had skills and staying power,"* she sighed contentedly. *"And sprites? They are real! Wonder what else of legend is real?"* She mulled it over and grinned as she remembered the gossip her female crew members had shared about the various shifters and their erotic talents. They had assuredly not been lying. She was smiling and in a good mood when she heard movement behind her. She looked to see Theron rolling up her sleeping covers.

Theron caught her eye as he glanced up from what he was doing. "Someone is in a good mood this morning." He quipped with a grin.

Fallon cut her eyes at him. She noticed he had several new scrapes, and his left eye was bruised.

"Um, well, someone was… in a good mood." He murmured as he finished folding the bedding and tied it off.

"I will be talking to you and Feron before we leave camp this morning." She stated as she stood up.

"We thought you might. Feron is saddling your horse for you this morning." Theron grabbed up her bedding and took it with him towards the picket line.

"Idiots," she thought. She might have to deal out some punishment for their actions, but they probably meant well. Besides, she was too blissfully content to be very angry with them.

She took her plate to the washstand, where she discussed her ideas for extra tasks for Theron and Feron, since they would now be assigned to the cooks. When she finished, she heard a rider entering her camp. She turned to see her father riding in. He stopped near where she stood by the camp wagon and dismounted. He looked a little tired, and he fidgeted with the reins to his horse. "Morning, Daughter. How are you today?"

I am well, father. Is there a problem?"

"I thought I'd let you know some of the Wolf Clan will start dropping from the march today. The chieftains discussed them riding at the end of the line since they will be leaving. I wanted to let you know there would be a line change. The Long Rider units which came with them will be at the front and back of the Wolf battalion. They oversee when the units leave." He was silent for a few seconds before continuing. "I did not know if you wanted to add your rider unit to assist them."

"They have three rider units with them. That should be plenty. I'll keep my unit at the end of the line behind the Owl Clan. We can ride drag when the Wolf

Clan starts to depart. I'll help them if needed unless my crew can be used elsewhere," Fallon finished.

"Good plan. I will come by your camp this evening. Be well, Daughter."

"The same to you, Father."

Goron mounted and rode his horse back towards the Boar Clan battalion that was forming up to leave. Feron and Theron walked up behind her, with Feron leading the horse that had been saddled for her. Her second mount was in place in the pack string. Feron saw their father riding away from their camp. "Dad was worried about you when you left. Bodhran told him not to worry, he knew Lonan well from the Warrior Camp, and Lonan was very honorable. Father stayed late and laid out your bedroll." Feron took in a deep breath. "Sister, I am sorry. Theron and I thought we were helping." Feron looked very contrite, and it was not the play-acting she had seen him and Theron use many times on their mother and father.

Theron patted Feron on the shoulder. "We are very sorry to have brought those men into the camp on false pretenses," Theron added.

"You two are not going to play matchmaker with me again. That is out. For bringing males into camp under false pretenses, the two of you are gathering wood for the campfire and helping with the camp meals until we are back home." She stopped to think for a second, and a realization struck her. "Was Bodhran part of this?"

They both shook their heads. Theron volunteered. "No, this was our idea."

Fallon narrowed her eyes at them. "I understand you thought you were helping, but don't do this again."

"Okay," Theron and Feron said in unison. Fallon took her horse from Feron and rode to the Boar Clan healer's wagons.

Feron nudged his brother. "Good thing you did not give Bodhran away."

Theron grinned. "Aye, we could have been uninvited from dragon-watching. Besides, no one likes a rat, Brother."

Feron chuckled, "True. I thought we would get in worse trouble."

"Me too. We will just have to be more careful the next time we play matchmaker," Theron added thoughtfully.

"Agree. It was harder than I thought it might be. It was easier sneaking in the Scorpion camp and cutting their horses loose," Feron replied as he mounted his horse.

"It does make for a good challenge and a fight, Brother. We are doing this again!" Theron promptly announced after he mounted up.

Feron grinned, "The fight was fun." He pulled his horse to face Theron. "You know, I think Ken needs some help charming Gael. We should start there."

Theron mulled it over. "Hum, you are right. He does. It will probably be easy to do. Besides, there is nothing else much to do while we are stuck being the kitchen help." They rode off to get the army moving homeward and spent the rest of their time plotting.

Fallon spent her day making sure there were no stragglers and wondering how she could not have known sprites existed. The thought of a mate crossed her mind, but she brushed it off. She did that already; it ended with a plot by her brothers that she missed and a brawl in her camp. Ok, it also included a fantastic night with Lonan, Fallon determined. Right now, she needed to put it aside and get her job done. Fallon reasoned there would be plenty of time for pondering when she was watching for dragons. Ever the pragmatist, Fallon decided she could take something with her and jot down a plan or some notes on how she would find a mate and what she was even looking for in a life mate. She nodded her head, problem solved. Now to get everyone home.

The rest of the trip went well. One by one over the next week, the Wolf Clan units peeled away from the main army headed home. Lonan's company was the first to leave the column. He caught Fallon's eye and gave her a nod and a wink. She smiled and nodded her head back at him. His unit turned off onto a small track off the Wheel Road. Ten days later, the Owl Clan turned south for home.

During the evenings, the camps were relaxed. The clans visited each other, playing games of chance, telling stories, or outdoing each other in weapon competitions. Bodhran had been excused from his duties as a Long Rider and spent a lot of time to himself. He meditated after late meal each evening. Lea had temporarily moved up into the position of second for her unit. The two new long riders to her crew were working out well. Goron came and had late supper with them each evening. Theron and Feron dutifully assisted the cooks, and from what Fallon could tell, they were subtly trying to help Ken win Gael's affection. All things considered, the little over four-week trip moving the army back home after the victory was pleasant.

Chapter 6

All of River Rest turned out to greet the army when they made it back home. Ambriel was waiting on them with the rest of the clan. On the way home, she told them Gita had given birth to a girl who they named Misty. Hector was home caring for them, or he would have been there to greet everyone. Once the horses were tended, the family gathered around the hearth to eat and share stories of their adventures.

The following day Fallon, Theron, Feron, and Ambriel gathered some food to take to Hector and Gita. They found Gita sitting in a comfortable chair nursing one-week-old Misty. While Hector tended the livestock, they visited with Gita and took care of the household chores. The grandparents alternated days helping the young couple. Gita's youngest sister, Aspen, stayed with them to lend a hand. By the time they left, the evening meal was prepared, a huge stack of firewood was cut, laundry had been washed, ample food put away, and the house was tidy. Fallon gathered the eggs as she tended the flock of chickens and ducks that searched the grass for tasty insects. She considered what it might be like to have her own family. Gita and Hector were elated with the birth of Misty. They both doted on her. Even Hallie and Terryl chipped in to help and were excited about their new sister. She thought about it, and to her, it all seemed very constraining. Her mom, Aspen, and Feron -to her complete surprise- all loved to snuggle Misty close and looked for opportunities to carry and rock her. Fallon had no desire to hold her, just as she had no desire to snuggle Hallie and Terryl when they were babies. Fallon did not dislike them; she just didn't particularly care for babies or feel any desire to have any of her own. At no point in her life had she ever wanted children. She sighed, *"That is going to make finding a mate harder."*

There were women in her clan who she knew who did not have children because they did not want to be mothers. It was a choice between the woman and the male. The elders advised life plans should always be discussed with your life mate well before things become serious. Honesty with one's life mate was viewed as paramount. Fallon made a mental note to stock up on silphion before leaving to go to the Bear Clan lands for dragon-watching. *"Who knows?"* she reasoned. *"I might find a mate there or on the journey. I might as well be prepared."*

Gita and Hector thanked them several times for their help. Ambriel shooed them off. "We are family; this is what family does. We help each other. That makes for a strong family and clan."

Theron and Feron had already left when Fallon and Ambriel were riding home. They met Goron on the way. "There are my beautiful ladies." He began as he pulled along beside them. "I thought I would ride out to meet you and take both of you to the Bronze Tusk."

"Mate, that would be a wonderful idea, but I am sweaty and dirty from helping with the grandchild," Ambriel stated as she pulled at her hair which had worked its way free of her braid.

"Good thing I brought you and Fallon both some clean clothes. I paid Dame Elyss for our baths." He leaned over and kissed Ambriel and loud whispered. "I asked her to ready the large private room. I told her I had an alluring siren I wanted to charm."

Ambriel blushed. "Sounds magical. The siren is definitely tempted, but you will have to catch her first." Ambriel kicked her horse, sending it racing down the road.

Goron laughed, "Daughter, we will see you later at the Bronze Tusk." He yelled as he took off after her. Fallon watched their playful banter. She hoped when she found her mate, they could be as happy as her parents were.

After a long peaceful hot bath and having her hair tended, Fallon made her way to the Bronze Tusk. Marjorie met her inside the door with a hug. "Fallon, I'm happy to see you. Goron had me set aside the table in the back corner for your family this evening. Feron and Theron are already there."

Fallon could see the twins already had mugs in front of them and a plate of cheese and bread. She walked over to join them. "Mom's not with you?" Theron asked as he passed her a mug of cider.

"She's with father. They should be along soon." Fallon supplied as she reached for the plate of bread and cheese. They talked until Goron and Ambriel arrived a short time later, holding hands and looking content. Not long after they were seated, a serving lad brought them plates and food.

The morning found Fallon up early and preparing breakfast. Theron and Feron joined her. "You know we need to tell mom today we are headed to the Bear Clan lands soon," Feron started.

"Agreed," Fallon said while she swung the hot kettle off the hearth and poured the boiling water into some cups on the table. "Last night at the tavern did not seem like the right time. We just got back."

"Yes, very true," Theron replied as he got the bowls and mugs down for the meal. "We will just tell her at breakfast."

"Tell me what?" Ambriel asked as she and Goron walked in on them.

"Um...well. We were invited to go to the Bear Clan lands and watch for dragons by Bodhran's uncle, Aren Gideon." Theron stated as he carefully looked to judge his mother's reaction.

Goron patted her on the back. "The whole family was invited. I did not know if you wanted to go or not."

Ambriel sat down on a chair, and Fallon handed her a cup of tea she had brewed. "So, tell me about this dragon-watching." Fallon recounted the tale about meeting Aren and being invited to the Bear Clan lands. Ambriel had sipped the tea while Fallon talked. When Fallon finished, she said, "It would be an adventure to go dragon-watching. However, with the new grandbaby, I can't leave. Who is going, and when are you leaving?"

"Theron, Feron, Bodhran, and I will leave in a week."

"So soon? All of you just got back." Ambriel replied as she set her cup down, looking disappointed. "I had hoped to have you three at home for a little while."

Goron passed Ambriel a plate with boiled eggs, bread, and sliced apples. He added to Fallon's statement. "Bodhran Fast Strike has some matters he must attend. He goes to his den to do it. Besides, how often does an invitation for dragon watching present itself?"

"True," Ambriel reasoned. "Fine. I know when I was your age." She pointed at the three of them. "I would have just about done anything to get a chance like this." She pointed at the table. "But today is Gatherday, and right now, we are going to eat breakfast together."

"The boys and I will collect the silphion after we eat."

"Good, then Fallon and I can go fishing. If we are lucky, there will be fresh trout for late meal."

Feron groaned, "I love your trout, Mom. I hope you both catch a lot."

After breakfast, Fallon and Ambriel gathered the fishing equipment and bait then rode towards the Fordwin river. An hour later, Ambriel had reached her favorite fishing hole. They cast their lines into the water and waited. While they fished, Fallon told her mother she felt driven to find a mate.

"Yes, you are twenty-six. If a woman will feel the mate drive, it is most common with those about your age. Have you seen anyone in River Rest who interests you?"

Fallon watched her fishing line twitch. She tugged it and set the hook into a nice size trout. "No, Mother, I have not. Neither have I seen any while being a Long Rider."

Ambriel thought for a while. "Fallon, there are a lot of things fishing and finding a life mate have in common."

Fallon chuckled as she thought about the males her brothers brought back to camp. "Yes, some of the fish you do have to throw back."

Ambriel nudged her and laughed. "You are right. Sometimes it is about finding a good fishing hole and being patient. I guess none stood out to you at the last clan Althing?"

"I was not beset with this matter at the last Althing, so I was not looking, but no, no one caught my attention."

"Hum, well, Daughter, I guess you will just have to be watchful and patient." Ambriel's line twitched, and she deftly jerked the line. She pulled in another fish to add to the one Fallon caught. She baited her hook, threw it back in, then sat back down.

"What do you think you might like in a life mate?"

"I have considered it. I have no idea. I thought I might puzzle it out while I was dragon watching."

"Good plan. You will have time to consider it while watching for dragons. I've solved lots of problems while hunting or fishing, like deciding to let a very determined young Boar Clan champion woo me." She smiled, "It's good to have a little time by yourself."

Fallon nudged her mother. "Father says he had a hard time convincing you. Sounds like you played hard to get."

"Of course, dear, I was not going to fall for just any old champion. I needed to see what he was made of."

Fallon chuckled and shook her head. They spent the rest of the morning fishing, and by noon they had a large catch. On the way back home, they dropped some trout off at Hector and Gita's cottage. Late meal on Gatherday was a feast of rosemary grilled trout, vegetables with herb butter, and flatbread. True to form, Theron and Feron made it home when the trout was nearly finished cooking.

The next few days passed quickly between helping with the new baby, visiting with friends, and duties at home. Two days before they left, they gathered items to take after speaking with Bodhran. They were checking their tack in the barn when Goron and Ambriel came to talk to them. Goron had a letter from

Elkon. "Elkon said the White Fox woman, Crystal Frost, was not at the warrior camp, so he is headed to the White Fox clan to seek her there. He will stay at the Indigo in Northpost while he looks for her. Your mother and I will send a message there for him to let him know you will be with Aren Gideon north of Cederton."

Fallon was standing by the fence with her saddle thrown over a rail, oiling it. "I hope he finds her there," she replied.

"We could go and help him after we spend a few weeks with Aren," Feron piped up.

Ambriel's eyes widened. She cleared her throat, "Oh. I don't think it will be necessary. I'm sure your brother can manage fine. If he needs us, he will let us know." Goron and Ambriel turned and walked back to the house. Fallon smiled. Probably the last thing Elkon needed was Theron's and Feron's assistance in locating and charming a life mate. She finished oiling her equipment and left the twins in the barn.

When Fallon left, Theron nudged Feron, who was cleaning a pack saddle. "Gael moved into one of the Long Rider cottages with Ken."

"Great! Our plan worked out," Feron returned as he repositioned the saddle to work on the other side. "So, who's next? This has been kinda fun. Kinda hard, but mostly fun."

"I don't know. We might have to think on it or just wait and see what the goddess throws in our path," Theron said.

"And I know the best place for thinking while we wait." Feron grinned.

"The Plowed Ox!" They both said at the same time.

They put away their gear and turned to find Goron leaning against the barn door. "Boys, you heading out to the Ox?" Goron said as he stared hard at Theron and Feron.

"Yes, Father," Feron replied.

"I was your age. I understand drinking and carousing. Both of you have reached the age of adulthood, and you have some coin to spend. You served Therus well. You deserve it."

"Thanks, Father." Theron knew there was a but coming, and he was waiting respectfully for his father to come to it.

"Your mother and I deserve to have a peaceful night. A night when we are not awakened by loud children coming home drunk. So how are you going to make this not happen?" Goron asked.

"We will stay at the barracks tonight, Father," Theron supplied

"Yes. And what are you going to tell your mother?" He asked, eyeing Feron.

"We are going to tell her we are staying at the barracks, and we are going to catch up with some friends before we leave, and that we will be back for breakfast." Feron hastily replied.

"Good." Goron stated as he moved off the barn's door and headed towards their home's back door.

"By the goddess, Father is quiet. I did not even hear him walk upon us," Feron said as he trailed Theron out of the barn.

"Yep, he's stealthy," Theron replied. "Let's grab our bedrolls; we can clean up at the barracks before we go to the Ox."

After letting Ambriel know where they were going, the twins headed out. Fallon had already gone to spend the evening at the Long Rider hall. She planned to gather any new information about the roads and to make sure her Long Rider unit would be handled while she was away. Luan had already made the changes, but Fallon wanted to confirm there were no complications. She found Luan at the Long Rider hall in her office behind a thick oak table piled with paper.

The door to her room was open. Luan stared up from the reports she was reading when Fallon entered.

"If this is a bad time, I can come back," Fallon began.

"No. I'm just finishing up for the afternoon before the rider's briefing. There was a lot of catching up to do with the Thorn resolved. What is it you need?" Luan pushed the papers to the side and gestured to one of the chairs by the table.

Fallon sat in the chair. "I wanted to make sure there were no hitches with my crew's coverage. I know having four people out of a unit is difficult."

"Normally, I would say yes, but it wasn't difficult. Ward's unit has two very seasoned seconds; one volunteered to be moved to your crew as the second. We discussed coverage for your unit and the two who wish to retire from being Long Riders in Ward's unit. Lea will be your crew's leader, and Savas will be second. We have several newly made riders who passed their apprenticeships and a couple of warriors who want to travel with them. The four of you leaving for a season or two, if you want, came at a good time." She waved her hand. "Don't worry; it's covered. Enjoy."

"Thanks. I'll be staying for the briefing this evening. We will be doing some traveling," Fallon replied as she stood up.

Luan grinned. "With the Thorn gone, now is the best time for a journey." She picked up a report. "I'll be in the meeting room in a few minutes after I finish reviewing this dispatch about the northwest section of the Wheel Road."

Fallon made her way to the meeting room and poured herself a mug of tart cider before joining Savas and Lea at a table. During the past seven years, Savas had matured. He was no longer the rash young male who had not passed the apprenticeship. Savas was now a measured and respected second. He and Lea would work together very well. They talked until Luan entered the guildhall. The room quieted as Luan approached the map of Therus. She lay a few papers on the stand, began the briefing on the roads of Therus, and gave details of the two unit's composition. Fallon listened. The routes were clear. There were no reports of thefts in the past two weeks. Barge traffic on the rivers had substantially decreased in the past several months due to spring rains, snowmelt off, and the Thorn. It was expected to pick up now the weather was more settled, and the rivers were returning to more favorable levels. It was the news Fallon had hoped to learn. The conditions in Therus were returning to normal, and their path to the Bear Clan lands would be untroubled. A few days later, Fallon,

Bodhran, Theron, and Feron rode out of River Rest headed north.

Chapter 7

Aren Gideon, Spring 2979: After the Battle of the Thorn, Bear Clan Territory

The journey home for Aren Gideon and the rest of the Bear Clan warriors took longer than he and Tyr preferred. They stayed with the rest of the army, traveling north along the River Road until they reached the Warrior Camp. From there, the Bear Clan left the main army and traveled northeast along lesser-traveled paths until they reached Ursa Minor. Departing the larger forces allowed the Bear Clan warriors to travel faster. The trek home gave Aren plenty of time to devise a plan for how he would look for the Fae female without his den discovering what he was up to. Looking for a Fae female would sound preposterous to his den. It even seemed a little strange to him when he thought about it, but he just could not get her out of his mind. So, he determined he would just have to be secretive about it. Getting Laith and Hearne in some clothes was going to be more challenging. Aren concluded if nothing else worked, as alpha of his den, he would simply order them to wear pants.

He was tired, hungry, and dusty when he and his fighting group made it to Irondenn. Aren decided he would take a couple of days in the city to rest while he gathered supplies to take home. While the small village of Cederton had basic items they could not or did not want to make themselves, Irondenn had much more variety. Aren hoped it also had a solution for naked bear shifters. It was nearly dark when Aren made it to Cooper's Inn. After a long hot bath and a hearty meal, he dropped into a deep sleep, dreaming of a buxom fairy with honey brown hair doing the most talented things with her strong hands.

The morning sun was well in the sky before Aren rolled out of bed. After breakfast, he shifted and let Tyr roam the large city park near the inn. Tyr waded into one of the park's ponds and paddled around for a while in the cool water. Occasionally he poked his head underwater and looked around. *"Brother, there are few fish in this pond."*

"Too many bears in the city. We will eat trout for late meal at a tavern tonight."

"Not as good as fresh caught." Tyr rumpled, sending him images of them fishing in the stream where they lived and landing a sizeable trout. *"That's tasty!"*

"Agree, we will have to go hunting and fishing when we get home. We will need to stock the larder since the Cub and his friends will be coming."

Tyr thought for a moment. **"Yes. We can look for the fairy female while we hunt. We should ask our den to help hunt too."**

"We'll do that."

Tyr roved through the park until the early afternoon when he lay down for a nap under a spreading chestnut tree. The late afternoon found Aren wandering the clothing merchant area of Irondenn on Texere street. With directions provided from a tavern keeper and a short search later, Aren was standing in front of the Sew Right Tailors' shop. The building was neatly painted and two stories tall, made of stone and wood. A sturdy bench was in front of the shop, and the business's door were flanked with two colorful flowerpots. A window displayed some of the wares. The goods in the window appeared to be finely crafted. A bell tinkled when he pushed open the door. The scent of wool, silk, and cotton wrapped around him when he walked into the building.

The shop's interior was well lit from a sizeable, charmed, bracketed fixture in the ceiling. The magical light cast the shop in a bright, cheery glow. A large mirror was in the back corner. Two men sat at a table in the rear of the shop sewing. One got up to greet him. "I am Vance Garsea, and this is my mate, Perry Sova. What can we help you find?" he extended his arm in greeting.

Aren shook it. "I am Aren Gideon. I need some clothing for a couple of males in my den."

Vance's eyes widened. "Oh! You are the champion warrior my mother, Shadin Kuma, spoke of when she came home from battle. She said you might drop by."

"Yes, I have two bear shifter males who don't like to wear clothes." Aren supplied.

"Yes, she mentioned it. It's not unheard of. Some bear males just don't like them." Vance mused.

Perry pipped up from the back of the shop. "Who can blame them? It can be disastrous to your wardrobe when you shift and rip them to shreds."

Aren sighed and crossed his arms. "That would be what happens, so I'm not sure there is a solution."

`"We may have a remedy for that problem," Vance replied as he gestured for him to follow him to the back of the shop. "My mate and I have been working on a garment design for shifters to survive a shift."

Perry explained as he set the piece down he was sewing on. He got up to retrieve a box from the shelf.

He pulled a couple of fabric bundles out of them, then unfolded one. "We wanted the clothing to be durable and handy for those who worked. It took a while, but we have a few examples of the garment we designed. We call it a breacan."

When he finished unfolding it, he lay it out on the table. The garment was made with a heavy, dark-brown cotton cloth and stitched with stout linen thread. It had loops for a belt. There was a flat panel in the front, but it had pleats around the sides and the back. Stitched to the breacan were several large pockets with closures. For all practical purposes, it looked like a stout, knee length shirt a female might wear. Not wanting to insult the tailors, he rubbed his chin for a moment to think.

"It looks like a tough garment. I'm just not too sure how the males of my den will like wearing clothes that are more of what a female might wear."

Tyr nudged him. *"We will tear the little naked pelt when we shift. We are a big strong bear."* Tyr looked at it again and continued, *"But it has sacks attached to it. We could fill them with nuts and berries to eat later.........Nut sacks. There are big, nut sacks on the small pelt."* Tyr chuffed in bear laughter.

Aren inwardly groaned; sometimes, Tyr's sense of humor was more like a teenage boy. While he considered how to respond, the shop's door opened, and a huge, hulking Bear Clan male with black hair streaked with silver ducked under the doorway to walk inside. He was wearing a sleeveless shirt and a gray breacan stained with coal dust and a couple of singe holes. The scent of a forge fire and sweat drifted around him. The male was larger than Aren, and his shoulders were nearly as broad as the door frame. His thick corded arms and legs were dotted with traces of soot. When he looked at Aren he grinned and strode over to him. "Claw Of the Clan!" He grabbed Aren by the right arm in greeting and cuffed his shoulder. "It is good to see you see in Irondenn, after the victory over the Thorn."

Aren had forgotten how massive Tarvos Kardos was. Even Tyr was impressed. ***"That's a big bear!"*** He thought back.

"Yes. It's good to be headed home."

"Will you be in Irondenn for a few days, or will you be heading out tomorrow?"

"I'll be in town for a day or two before I go," Aren replied.

"We will have to catch up if you have time." Tarvos nodded his head. "Hum…I believe Brenna is preparing trout tonight at the Hunter's Rest."

"Sounds good. I have a few things to do first, but I'll be there for late supper."

"Late supper it is then." Tarvos looked at the table where Aren stood. "You going to get a breacan?"

"I was considering it for a couple of males in my den. I haven't decided yet."

Perry flashed them a mischievous smile. "He was worried his den males might think they were female's clothes." Aren groaned inwardly.

Tarvos threw back his head and laughed, "Let me show you. These are handy."

They walked out the front door, followed by Perry and Vance to the green space which separated the tailor's shop from Darby Weavers. Tarvos pulled off his heavy boots, stood back, and shifted into a large, black bear with silver-tipped fur. The breacan, shirt, and belt flew apart. Vance collected the garments, then a few moments later, the bear receded to become Tarvos, the man. Vance held up the breacan for Tarvos to take. Tarvos turned it around for Aren to see. "The clothes are fine. See here on the side of the breacan. These are poppers. You mash them together like this." Tarvos pushed the two small metal pieces together, and they closed with a pop. "And your clothes are back together. The pants, shirt, and belt are just fine. When you shift, they pop open, so your clothes don't rip. Plus, the breacan is very breezy. Your mating hammer stays nice and cool. And by the forge fire, that's important to me."

Perry took the belt from Vance. "The only problem with the belt is it is not strong enough to hold a sword, or if you hang something else heavy from it, the poppers will separate. We are not sure if there is a solution for it." He connected the snaps and handed the belt to Tarvos.

Vance looked at Aren. "What do you think?"

Aren scratched his head. "I think it might work."

Perry grinned. "You still think they are something only females might wear?"

"No, not if Tarvos is wearing them." Aren laughed.

Tarvos finished putting on the shirt and belt. "Good functional clothes are not bound to the person's sex. Those who want to wear them, wear them at my father's forge, males, females, novices. We even got our father to wear one." Tarvos laughed. "He likes it, and mother likes him in it. So, wear what works for you."

Aren considered what Tarvos said. It was true. It was also meant he would have to wear one of the garments if he wanted his den to wear them. He couldn't very well order them to do what he did not or would not do. He looked at Vance. "You have one that will fit me?"

"I'm sure we do. Perry, take care of Tarvos, please, while I help Aren." They went back inside, and Vance pulled out two breacans and gave them to Aren. "You can change in the side room. Come back out, so I can see how it fits. If you want to try out the poppers, you can go outside as Trarvos did; you will have plenty of room there for a shift." Vance handed him the garments and went back to the worktable.

Aren tried both. While both were very adjustable for waist size, he decided on the second one. It was a heavier weight, dark green breacan. He nodded to Vance on his way outside to the side lot. There he shifted, and the breacan flew off his body. He shifted back and looked at the garment. The breacan was fine. The poppers had separated. He pressed the poppers back together, put it back on then headed back inside.

Tyr shook out his fur. *"**The little pelt is nice. It is very breezy. I would like larger nut sacks on our pelt. We are the alpha. We should have the biggest nut sacks on our pelt.**"*

Aren chuckled and shook his head. If big pockets were all it took to get Tyr on board with wearing it, it was fine by him. *"Ok, Brother."* He changed back into his clothes and took the beacans back to Vance. "I would like the green one for me with larger pockets and two for my den males. They will need them made with a durable cloth."

"We have a sturdy brown fabric that is very strong. If you want them now, we can do it for you. We are at a lull due to the war, but business will pick up quickly." Vance replied.

Sizes, prices, and a completion date of two days were negotiated. Aren left the tailor's shop and wandered towards the armory section of Irondenn. Crossing Gilded Way, a glint caught his eye in the window of the Brilliant World jeweler shop. There resting on a cushion of scarlet velvet was a gold, tree shaped pendant. Its roots intertwined to hold a black stone and reached around to form a frame around the tree. The tree looked exactly like the killing trees on the border of the magic lands. He immediately thought about the Fae female he saw in the forest.

"I think she would like the sparkly thing." Tyr nudged him while eyeing the necklace.

"Why do you think that?"

"She's a female, and many females like shiny things. She wears a red hat with a feather. That means she likes things that sparkle."

Honestly, when Aren thought back to the females he knew, he could not argue with Tyr's logic. The shop's sign indicated it was closed for the day. He made a mental note to come back. Making his way towards Hunter's Rest, he ran over the list of things he had promised to purchase for his den on his return trip. Each of the males had given him a list. He had shaken his head when he read off Laith and Hearne's list. Hearne had written "a hot guy and a barrel of ale," Laith penned a note on Hearne's list, "me too, but my guy needs a bigger dick than Hearne's guy." He had thought many a day that it would be simpler if Hearne and Laith were mates. They were best friends and a little like brothers with a love-to-fight-each-other relationship, but mates, they were not.

The lists from Sami and Bren were attainable. Aren reasoned he would have to purchase space on the teamster wagon that made regular trips from Irondenn to Cederton for some of the items. His two pack horses that carried his bear armor were fully loaded. By the time he had planned out his next two days, he was at Hunter's Rest. Tyr had advised him they were close when the wafting scent of cooking trout greeted them about four blocks away from the tavern.

Chapter 8

Late supper was being served, and the tavern was busy. Aren saw Tarvos and a similar-looking male at a table in the side yard. He walked over to greet them. Tarvos introduced his brother, Wheeler Kardos, to Aren. Tarvos poured Aren a large mug of ale from a pitcher on the table. They spent the rest of the evening sharing stories from the Warrior Camp. Tarvos had worked to advance his weapon-making skills with the forge masters at the camp, while Aren was fine honing his warrior skills. Wheeler looked like the rest of the Kardos males. He was tall and broad, with black hair shot with streaks of silver. Aren had only met Wheeler briefly at the Warrior Camp. He was leaving when Wheeler arrived a few days before he left. The three of them ate, drank, and retold stories of their time at the camp.

Tarvos shared some stories about his two children, both females nearing the age of majority. Tarvos shook his head. "I thank the goddess every day I forge weapons, Aren. You would not believe the males who think they might win my daughters' hearts. This must be payment for what I put my mate's father through when I pursued her."

Aren laughed as he slapped Tarvos on his back. "I do not think your holding a weapon could be more imposing than you just glaring at them."

Tarvos set his mug down and laughingly shook his head. "They would be better off dealing with me instead of my mate, Kylana. She is feisty and excellent with a knife. She has already threatened to cut the mating hammer off one of them already."

Wheeler nodded as he poured more ale in their cups. "Kylana's family are butchers. She well knows how to cut. Staying to her good side is wise; you keep all your parts."

Aren told them about his den north of Cederton and the beauty of the Kybor forest. Wheeler agreed. "I have thought about living in such a place." He said, staring into his ale cup. "Irondenn is fine, but my bear might be happier living in the wilds." He sighed. "Brother, I'm heading home." He clasped arms with Aren, wished him a safe journey, and left walking down Forge Road. They watched him go.

Tarvos sighed, "My youngest brother has never been happy in Irondenn. The last couple of years, it has gotten worse. I have three brothers. Me and Ryken run the family forge now. Our father has just retired from the business, but he comes in whenever he feels like it. Mostly he talks and visits with customers." Tarvos laughed, "That's fine with us. We can get more work done. Ba'khair makes locks. It's a lot of bear male in a shop." He took a long drink of ale. "Wheeler is a very talented blade and locksmith. He would probably be happier with his own forge in the outlands where his bear would be content."

Aren replied. "Some bears prefer the woodlands to towns. There are a couple of villages outside Irondenn among the forest that would benefit from his talent."

"We have discussed this with him. He was staying until our father retired, and the transition of the shop was handed over. Sometimes those do not go smoothly with egos getting in the way. We had no such problem. We each have a specialty, so there is no competition between us. We will now encourage him to follow his heart."

"I hope he finds what he seeks," Aren stated.

"As do we. Wheeler is a worthy and talented male."

They stayed a little longer before going in separate directions. When Aren made it back to Cooper's Inn, he went directly to bed. He was asleep almost as soon as his head hit the pillow.

Over the next couple of days, Aren busied himself with purchasing the items his den mates had requested on their list. He made arrangements with the teamster who drove his wagons between Irondenn and the outlying villages to the east to have most of the supplies shipped home. The smaller ones he could take back. He stopped by Sew Right to make sure the breacans would be ready for pick up the following evening. Perry handed him the green one created for him and assured Aren the other two would be ready the next evening. Aren decided he might as well wear it to get used to it. A quick change and he was done and striding towards Gilded Way Lane to Brilliant World Jewelers. He had to admit the breacan kicked up a nice breeze around his member as he walked.

Tyr seemed pleased as well. ***"A couple of the females have watched us. They seem to like what they see."*** Tyr boasted as he strutted in Aren's mind. ***"It's the big nut sacks,"*** Tyr stated smugly.

Aren had noticed more than one female had turned her head to watch him pass. *"Something has them looking, Brother,"* he thought back to him.

Turning on Gilded Way, he was pleased to see Brilliant World was open. A short time later, with a little bit of haggling, Aren was the owner of the necklace from the window. It now rested in a large pocket, securely buttoned shut. The remainder of the day and the next in Irondenn, he shifted and let Tyr enjoy the city. To Tyr, that meant snuffling around the parks and napping in the shade.

The next afternoon, with items from all the lists secured, except for the hot guys and barrels of ale, Aren went by Sew Right and picked up his nudist den members' garments. The beacans were exactly as promised. Perry had included extra poppers should any of them break. The following morning Aren headed home. Aren quickly discovered breacans were comfortable garments except for horse riding. He had not left the stable yard at the inn before the stirrup leathers had pinched him and pulled out a goodly number of leg hairs. He stopped and changed into a pair of pants. He shrugged his shoulders; nothing in life was perfect.

His journey home was uneventful. In the late evenings, he would make camp, eat and shift into bear form to sleep in the woods for the night. He made it home midafternoon on Gather Day. His den's tradition was to work on a project for their den, or they took wood or food items to Cederton for the village to disperse to those who might need it. Every Gather Day, they had a big communal meal for late supper.

Tyr rumbled in his head. ***"Maybe Laith and Hearne caught trout for late meal. That would be good."***

"Brother, I am going to have to take you trout fishing soon."

91

"Yes! Fresh trout is the best. We should fish here." Tyr sent him a picture of one of their favorite fishing spots. It was close to the border of the magic lands.

"Usually, the trout are not many in that part of the river this time of year. It wouldn't have anything to do with the Fae female, would it?"

Tyr rolled his eyes and huffed, **"Of course, it would, Brother! You should wear the small hairless pelt with the large nut sacks. She will be impressed."**

Aren shook his head. *"Who knows?"* he thought. Maybe she would be. Goddess knows she probably had not seen one before. *"We will catch her eye,"* he thought back. Aren turned his attention to his den, which was now in view. He had decided he would probably have to alpha order Laith and Hearne into wearing the breacans. He would change into his before late supper and spring it on everyone then. It was going to be a memorable meal.

Chapter 9

Fallon, Spring 2979: After the Battle of the Thorn, River Rest, Boar Clan territory

Fallon adjusted the load on her packhorse and firmly lashed it down in a diamond hitch while answering random questions thrown at her by her mother and father. Theron and Feron were doing the same. Bodhran was sitting on Badger and watching the barrage of questions Ambriel was lobbing at them with a smirk on his face. "Theron, Feron, did you pack soap and a drying cloth? Fallon, do you need an extra blanket? What about healing salve? Bodhran, did you fill your extra sack with the dried meat and fruit I gave you? Feron, did you have that loose shoe looked at on your horse? Ambriel asked in rapid-fire as she walked around them with a determined look.

Each question was answered with a "Yes."

Goron glanced up from his large cup of tea. "Do you have coin and your weapons?"

Fallon replied for the group, "Yes, Father."

"All of you stay out of trouble, look after each other, write often, and have fun." He hugged each of

93

them, then grasped Bodhran by the forearm. When he hugged Feron and Theron, he whispered. "Don't piss off the bears and stay out of trouble."

Bodhran turned his head to hide a smile. Goron handed a letter to Fallon. "Give this to Ranier when you pass through Oak Meadow."

Fallon wrapped the letter in oil skin before she secured it in her saddle bag. "I'll take care of it, Father."

Soon they were mounted and leaving River Rest. When they reached Oak Meadow, Fallon took the letter to Ranier at Lady Shael's shop, The Unicorn's Horn. She had tea with Shael. While they sat and talked after finishing the tea, Shael's gaze became unfocused for a few moments.

"Are you alright?" Fallon asked.

Ranier looked up from where he was helping a customer with a cooking pot. Lady Shael glanced around and smiled at her. "I just remembered what Ranier had told me about Theron and Feron. He mentioned their love for mischief, and I believe he said they were at the Warrior Camp for stealth training as well as combat training."

Fallon laughed. "Yes, it is true. They were also on the Shadow team to harry the Thorn's army."

Lady Shael's eyes brightened. "Then I think they may be the perfect solution to my problem. I have a couple of aerial illuminators I can't sell. They are very loud, and the sparkles are far too bright for a children's party. They are three samples. I think Feron and Theron might have a use for them, should the Shadow team ever need to be called for a task." Shael got up and rummaged around behind the desk, then gave Fallon three pouches. "There is one per bag. These are very durable and will not break down over time. They must be thrown with force into the ground to activate. They are loud and bright. I'm not sure what the magic-user was thinking. They simply will not work for a child's party unless you want all the children crying. I would be very pleased if you were to take them off my hands."

Fallon looked a little puzzled. She had seen a couple of aerial illuminators in the past at a tavern. They were harmless, and the sparkling blue birds fluttered cheerfully overhead for several minutes before they dissipated. "Thank you, Lady Shael. I'm sure Theron and Feron will find the perfect use for them."

When Fallon and the customer left, Ranier caught up Shael's hand and kissed it. "Is there a problem, beloved?"

Shael stroked his chest. "No, everything is fine now."

Fallon left the Unicorn's Horn heading for Lamp Lighter Inn, where they were staying. A hunter-green tunic caught her eye in the window of a shop. It had a riding split and gold thread embroidery decorating the neckline, sleeves, and hem edge. Fallon pondered purchasing the tunic. It had been a while since she bought any new clothing. As a Long Rider, her garments consisted mainly of durable tunics and breeches. Her fanciest tunic was getting old and needed to be replaced. With trade and more business for her unit when she returned, a lovely new tunic for meetings with merchants would be a prudent purchase. She walked into the shop and soon had the seamstress altering the tunic to fit her.

She found Bodhran, Theron, and Feran drinking at the Lamp Lighter when she came back. "You have got to try some of the Cave Bear summer ale that came in on the wagon from Ursa Minor. Wenna and Artos have a winner here." Feron announced as he downed the contents of his mug.

Violet came by the table and rested her tray on it. "Gimme a cold Cave Bear any day when it's hot outside!" She said with a grin as she left another mug for Fallon and a pitcher full of summer ale.

Fallon took a sip. It was divine! It was light and refreshing with a clean tang. "Feron, you are right. This is excellent! We will have to stop on the way back home and pick up some for mom and dad."

The following day, Fallon and Bodhran bought some Cave Bear summer ale and mead to take to the Gideon den. She picked up her newly altered tunic before they continued north on the Wheel Road.

The summer weather held for the most part while they traveled to Cederton. Merchants, Long Riders, and traders were seen at regular intervals along the Wheel Road. Business was picking up quickly after the Thorn's fall. Fallon greeted the Long Rider units when they passed. She knew each by name. They told her the roads were clear, and no problems were reported. They stayed some nights in inns, but most nights, they camped. Theron and Feron were on their best behavior. Fallon suspected they were still trying to make up for the fiasco in camp with the two males they brought for her. They rode ahead of her some days, like today, talking and laughing. Fallon could only wonder what they were planning. She examined her bedroll every evening before climbing in and checked her horse equipment before she mounted. There were never any pranks when they worked, but Fallon had no doubt they would try something on their off time. She loved them as they did her, but mischievous brothers were always a handful.

Feron glanced behind to see if they were far enough ahead of Bodhran and Fallon. He did not want to be overheard. "The new temporary cook at the Lamp Lighter would be perfect!" Feron started.

"Possibly. Did you talk to her?" Theron asked as he slyly reached back to adjust his saddle bags to gauge the distance between them and his sister. Bodhran, he was not worried about. Fallon, however, might try to rein in their plans. He could not blame her. When they brought the males to camp, it had been a disaster. That did not mean all their matchmaking was awful. Just look at Ken and Gael. It was working out fine.

"I did. Her name is Tatani Wesson, a shifter, in the Bison clan," Feron replied, keeping his voice low.

"What makes you think she might be a good mate for Evrard Hardy?" Theron asked.

"Tatani's a great cook. She wants a mate, family and has almost no interests outside cooking. You know, she's kinda boring like Evrard. I get the feeling they will be perfect."

"I don't know, Feron, it's not a lot to go on, boring, cooking and wants a family," Theron added.

"I didn't get to the best part," Feron grinned.

"The best part?" Theron asked, intrigued, "What's the best part?"

"When she shifts into her bison form, she will have more nipples than Evrard!" Feron finished looking quite pleased with himself.

"Brother, you are right!" Theron smacked his hand down on his thigh. He looked at Feron and nodded his head. "Yea, he seemed a little touchy about his third nip." They congratulated each other as they rode northeast on the River Road.

Fallon had been watching Bodhran for the last couple of days. He faithfully did his evening meditation with Fast Strike across his lap. What concerned her was sometimes during the day, he looked unfocused. It had happened again just a few minutes ago. His gaze went blank. "Bodhran, how are you faring? Are you tired, or do you need to meditate?" She asked, staying out of Badger's biting range.

Bodhran snapped out of it and looked her way. "We...I am fine."

"I'm worried about you, Bodhran. We can stop for as long as you need, a day a week, whatever you need. We are on no schedule. Besides, what will I tell your father if you are in a daze and Badger throws you, causing you to injure yourself?" She finished looking at him thoughtfully.

Bodhran grinned. "Do not worry, Fallon. I am well. I can move very fast, and I have a thick skull."

"Sometimes, you look like you are somewhere else when you gaze away. I was concerned."

"Fast Strike speaks to me. It may look like I am not here, but I know what is going on and what tricks Badger is up to. It is the bonding. This is why a time of peace is best. All is well."

"Alright, but let us know if you need anything."

Bodhran smiled. "I'll let you know."

Chapter 10

It was noon as they neared the Gideon den when Bodhran noticed a familiar scent on the breeze. He glanced in the direction and caught a glimpse of two bears, one black and the other brown. *"Laith and Hearne,"* he thought to himself. The two bears turned off onto a game trail which Bodhran knew headed home. He sighed. It was good to be home. The journey had taken almost three weeks. They arrived at the Gideon den midafternoon.

Nestled among a grove of trees that bordered a meadow, the Gideon den was comprised of four thick timber and stone cabins. There was a big barn and several sheds behind the homes. Pastures that extended part of the way into a vast meadow could be seen beyond the cottages. A couple of barking dogs and the baying of a mule near the barn heralded their arrival. Wearing a breacan, Aren walked off the porch of the largest of the cabins. He came up to Bodhran and dragged him from an arm grasp into a hug. As Aren welcomed Fallon, Theron, and Feron, the rest of the Gideon den members made their appearance.

Feron saw two males walking out of a cabin towards them, wearing a short skirt like Aren. He nudged Theron and whispered. "Brother, I did not know that Bear Clan dens wore skirts at home. Were we supposed to have brought one to wear?"

Theron caught sight of another big male coming from the direction of the barn wearing a shirt with short sleeves and breeches. He had a thick leather apron with a couple of tools stuck in pockets on it. "Um, no. I think it's just them."

Laith and Hearne were busy hugging Bodhran and missed the whispers between Theron and Feron. Aren introduced Laith and Hearne to Feron and Theron. After the traditional arm grasp, Laith stood back and gave both Theron and Feron a lengthy, apprising gaze. Hearne sighed and shook his head. Laith turned to Aren. "You did get everything on everyone's list." He smirked.

Feron shook his head. "No, we are not on that list. But those" as he waved his hand between Artos, Laith, and Hearne "are very fancy short skirts."

Fallon smacked her head with her hand. Leave it up to her brothers to make a great first impression. The male who wore the leather apron burst out in a deep barking laugh. "My words exactly! I'm Bren." He clasped their arms. "It's a new type of garment. Aren says they are called breacans. They are designed for shifters and won't be destroyed when we shift."

Feron rubbed his jaw. "Hum. That would save on sewing repairs."

"Yes, it does," Aren replied. He introduced everyone to Bren. "How about we get you settled in. Fallon, you are in my spare room, and your brothers will stay with Sami in his spare room. Right now, Sami is hunting. He will probably be back before late meal."

They pulled the gear off their horses. Laith and Hearne were insistent in helping Theron and Feron carry their bags into Sami's home. Laith's eyes stayed glued to Feron's butt when he walked behind him carrying some of Feron's things. Hearne made a concerted effort to be discrete when ogling Theron.

Sami's home was a stone and thick timber cabin with large windows. Their room was opposite Sami's. There were two rope beds, each with a thick mattress. The headboard and footboard were carved with a forest scene of bears playing. At the foot of the bed were two chests. A small table rested against the wall, and a short line of wooden pegs set in the wall finished the room. It was neat and clean. The window faced the area where they had arrived. Theron ran his hand over the carved footboard. "This is beautiful woodwork."

Hearne spoke up, "That is Bren's carving. He and I make furniture. I make the pieces; then he embellishes them with his carving."

Laith patted Hearne's shoulder. "Our den is lucky to have you two. Your work is strong and beautiful."

Feron watched the exchange between Laith and Hearne. He scratched his head and cleared his throat. "So, are you two together?"

Hearne's eyebrows shot up, and Laith laughed before he spoke. "No, we are not together, but we are both seeking male mates."

Hearne sighed. "By the goddess, no. Laith and I together, it would not work out."

"About that," Theron replied. "you should know when the time comes; my brother and I will be seeking female mates. We are not looking for males."

Feron nodded his head. "True, but we do a little matchmaking....."

For the next hour, after they stowed their gear and unsaddled their horses, Laith, Hearne, Feron, and Theron sat on the porch of Sami's home drinking mead and finding out what type of male Laith and Hearne were interested in finding. Who knew? Maybe they would run into the perfect one when they started back with the Long Riders. They certainly saw more people in a day than the Aren den probably saw in a month.

Fallon followed Bodhran up the stairs into Aren's home. The gathering room had exposed wood beams of heavy, gold-colored wood that crossed the large room near the ceiling. The front of the room where they entered held tables and chairs. Fallon could see the food preparation area and a large hearth in the far back of the room. Bodhran motioned to a door on his left. He opened it to reveal the bedroom where Fallon would stay. A rope bed was against the wall on the right. There was a dresser against the far wall. An oversized chair with a carved back occupied the left corner of the room. Close to the chair was another door leading out of the home. Fallon deposited her gear on the bed.

Aren came behind her with her other items. He placed them on the dresser. "You may want to enjoy the hot spring before our late meal. Bodhran can show you where it is and how to use the rain bucket. You don't have to worry about being seen as you bathe. There are a couple of fir trees blocking the hot spring. Cub, there is a white sign with an "X" on it. She can put it on the flat rock before the turn to the spring. That way, we will know if someone is bathing."

"Yes, Father."

"A bath would be most welcome. Thank you for your invitation and extending to us the hospitality of your den," Fallon replied.

"We are glad you came." He turned to Bodhran. "Cub, after you bring your gear in, I'll show you what Sami rigged up at the spring. We'll leave you to get settled in, Fallon."

After they left, Fallon unloaded the food and other items on her pack horse. She untacked her horses and turned them out in the grassy lot with the rest of their stock. Badger was in his private lot, complete with a heavy, wood fence. He was contentedly munching grass as Fallon passed. By the time she had finished putting away her things, Bodhran had knocked at her door and called her name. "Call me when you are ready to go to the spring."

"I'm ready now." Fallon grabbed up some clean clothes and headed out the back of the house with Bodhran. A path ran behind the home past the privy where a patch of wooly lambs ear and thimbleberry grew. The trail continued onward past the barn and outbuildings and hooked to the right, away from the pasture. Trees and shrubs had been trimmed back from the footpath, and white rocks along one side made it very easy to follow. A big, wide, flat stone with a white sign with a black "X" came into view up the trail. After the rock, the route took a sharp right. On either side of the path behind the stone, thick fir trees and lower growing juniper shrubs created a curtain.

Bodhran stopped by the flat rock. "That's the sign. Just sit it on top of the stone when you are bathing and put it down when you finish." Fallon set the sign on the rock and followed Bodhran down the trail. Past the trees, the course gently sloped down. The sound of water splashing met her as she neared the bottom. The path ended on a flat, sandy area where the water from a small pond lapped against the bank. Water was coming out of the rock outcropping in the hillside and into the pond to her right. A small part of the water flow was diverted into a suspended wooden bucket.

Bodhran pointed to the bucket. "This is the hot spring. Well, it is not hot as it is very warm when it comes out of the hill. That pipe leads to the rain bucket Sami rigged up. You just push this lever in, like this, and it shifts the pipe over to the water flow. The pipe fills up the bucket. When you pull on the chain, it opens the valve to the rain shower fitting. When you are finished with your rain shower, just pull the leaver to move the pipe away from the outcropping and empty the bucket. The pond's water is warmer towards the end, where the water comes out of the rock. In the jar, there is some soap if you ever need it." By the time he had finished talking, the bucket was beginning to overflow. Bodhran pulled the lever, and the pipe moved out of the flow of the water.

"It's a very clever design," Fallon remarked.

"It is. Father said Sami saw something like it in Irondenn a couple of years ago and brought the idea home. I'll leave you to it." He turned to leave and stopped. "I almost forgot. You may see a whisp, do not follow it. You will never catch it, and you will just end up lost like I did when I was young." He chuckled. "The den tore up half the countryside looking for me. I was grounded for a month afterward. It was a well-learned lesson."

Fallon laughed, "I imagine so. Don't worry; I won't go chasing any whisps, sprites, or anything else magical."

Bodhran chuckled, "Good plan. Enjoy."

The rain shower was amazing and felt as good as Fallon had imagined. The water was comfortably warm. Nothing beat having the chance to bathe in warm water after a long ride. She toyed with taking a swim but decided against it if others wanted to wash before late supper. She dried off, and after resetting the shower bucket, she made the ten-minute hike back to Aren's home. Another male she did not recognize was unloading an enormous basket of fish with Aren's help by one of the outbuildings. She put her things away and headed in their direction. Walking towards the outbuilding where Fallon had seen Aren, she caught sight of Theron and Feron as they disappeared down the hot spring trail.

Aren waived to her as she approached. "Boar Clan Long Rider Captain, Fallon Tulun, this is Bear Clan Archer, Sami West, who is the best gardener and fishing bear of our den. If you want to eat well, Sami is your bear."

Tyr raised his head from where he had been eyeing the fish on the table. ***"He is a good fishing bear, but I think we can out-fish our den mate."***

Aren thought back, *"The Boar Clan female, Fallon, is single. Sami is single......."*

Tyr scrunched up his face. ***"Yes, they are both not mated."***

"Maybe she will like him if she knows some good things about him. She might be his mate. Who knows?"

Tyr nodded his head. ***"Tell her about his honey boxes then. Those are great!"***

Aren sighed, leave it to Tyr to bring up Sami's beekeeping. Then again. He did have an impressive number of beehives. ***"See!"*** huffed Tyr.

"You should also know Sami probably has the largest number of beehives in the area. He and Laith harvest the honey and make several different products to sell in Cederton and Irondenn. You will have to get him to show them to you."

"I'd like that. One of my long rider friends, Wenna Pallin lives in Ursa Minor. She is mated to Artos Pernel; they make some delicious mead and honey ale. Do you make mead or ale from your honey, Bear Clan Archer, Sami West?" Fallon asked.

Tyr looked smugly at Aren and gave him his version of a bear smile. Sami grinned as he pulled another fish out of the basket to clean. "Call me Sami. I do make some mead and honey ale, just small batches for the den. Laith makes healing creams and salves with honey, herbs, and beeswax. He also makes candles. I would be happy to show you. I'll be checking the hives in a couple of days if you would like to go then."

"Sure," Fallon replied.

They talked for a while about the different products Sami and Laith made. Fallon looked at the meal preparation table. "What can I do to help?"

Aren nodded his head in the direction of some vegetables at the other end of the table. "If you want to chop those vegetables, they will be going in a pan over the fire. We are about halfway done cleaning the fish."

Fallon grabbed the vegetables and prepped them while talking about Sami's bees and the den's garden. When she finished cleaning and chopping the vegetables, she took the bowl to the fire. The brick fire pit was key-shaped with a long, cooking trough that ran off the round fire pit. Numerous brackets, hooks, and two grills could be swung over the fire. She grabbed a large shallow pan to place it on the grate over the trough. She added butter and herbs to the vegetables and started searing them. Aren brought the fish over to the fire and put a rack over the trough section on the other side of Fallon. "Do I need to send Bodhran for your brothers? I saw them headed for the spring."

"No, it won't be necessary. My brothers will be here when the food is nearly done," Fallon replied.

Sami swung a cookpot over the coals. "They have some shifter in them? I didn't think I smelled any."

Fallon laughed, "Our mother is Ambriel Tulun from the Wolf Clan, but she is not a shifter. Ever since the twins were little, they show up when a meal is ready. Our father swears there is a lot of wolf in them."

Sami chuckled. "Aye, that's probably where they got it. A good meal can call those with shifter blood from a distance."

True to form, as the meal cooked, the rest of the den showed up. The twins arrived still slightly damp, just before it came off the fire. Fallon looked at Sami and pointed to her brothers, grinning. Sami looked at the ground, shaking his head laughing.

Bren and Hearne set chairs around a couple of large sawhorse tables while Bodhran placed a couple of large pitchers of ale on the table. Fallon had taken the cooked vegetables off the fire when Aren announced that the fish was ready to eat. Plates were filled, and one by one, they found a seat at the tables. At Aren's request, Theron and Feron entertained them with their missions to harry Pax's army. Soon they were all talking, laughing, and sharing stories of past missions. The crescent moon had risen when Aren changed the topic of conversation to dragon watching. Theron and Feron recounted their dragon sighting eight years ago in the Bear Clan lands as novice warriors.

"After breakfast, I'll take you out to a spot where you can dragon-watch for the day. It's the area where I saw the silver one take a doe from the meadow. Who knows, maybe it is the same one your brothers saw."

"Thank you so much for doing this. While they have seen one before, I'm excited to get the opportunity to look for one," Fallon exclaimed.

Feron piped up, "Sister, it was an impressive sight!"

"Definitely impressive. Dragons are much larger than I thought they would be," Theron added.

Fallon flashed Aren a big smile. "I can't wait." She turned to Sami. "Sami, Aren, the fish was wonderful, and the company is enjoyable, but I'm headed to bed. I would hate to miss a sighting because I nodded off in the woods."

Aren replied. "Glad you liked it. See you in the morning." Fallon turned and headed for her bed.

Chapter 11

Just before dawn, Bodhran tapped lightly at her bedroom door.

"I'm up," Fallon called out groggily as she rubbed her eyes.

She rolled over to sit on the edge of the bed. She had a very odd dream; she was flying. She was high in the sky over a forest with a winding river cutting through it. In her dream, the area was as familiar to her as the back of her hand. In reality, she had never seen this place before. She shook her head and chuckled. Her dragon-watching trip was starting to affect her dreams. It was fun, though, high in the sky flying over the land below. She could still feel the brisk wind rushing over her body. When she thought back to it, Fallon could not remember if she was doing the flying or if she was on something moving through the air. Maybe she was a cloud? She scrunched up her forehead in thought. That part seemed vague. She shrugged her shoulders and stretched. Maybe her strange dream was just the ale she drank last night. She pushed off the bed and readied herself for the day.

After breakfast, they saddled their horses and followed Aren as he led them northeast away from his den on a well-worn game trail. Aren would often stop by a tree and take his hatchet and cut a "V" shaped notch into it. About an hour into the ride, Aren stopped and cut two marks into a tree. He pointed to a smaller path leading due east through some thick cedar trees. "That route leads to a big meadow we call "Blue Flower" when you see it, you will know why. The blue flowers bloom most of the summer and sometimes into the fall. Sami has some of his beehives here. I can put all three of you here, or I can split you up. Either way, you will be fine. Our bears keep the large predators away, so you are safe."

Theron spoke up. "Not that we don't love you, Sis, but we might be able to view more of the area if we split up."

Fallon inwardly groaned when Aren suggested they could be together. If she could keep them busy, they were fine, but just sitting and waiting all day. No. She was elated when Theron suggested they split up. "Great idea, Theron!" She ecstatically replied.

Aren pointed down the small path between the cedar trees. "Alright, then I'll take Feron and Theron farther north towards the river. If you see a big bear, don't worry. It's me. I'm going to shift and do some fishing. I'll probably come by to check on you three. I'll leave my horse with Theron and Feron." He

116

pointed at the Fallon. "Fallon, just head down the path, and it will end at the meadow. You can't miss it. The path is almost as straight as an arrow heading east. Stay close to the tree line on this side of the meadow. That will give you good coverage under the cedars. Across the meadow and farther east is the line of killing trees marking the lands of Valair. Don't go there. The Blue Flower meadow is where I saw the silver dragon pluck up doe. No one from my den has seen anything since, but then we are not watching for one. It knows there is food here; it may come back. I'll come back late this afternoon and get you unless you want to leave early, then take the trail back. Take the big, forked branch there and put it upside down on the marked cedar, and I'll know you went back to the den. I marked it pretty clear with the hatchet coming in. You should be fine finding your way back home."

"Will do," Fallon said before she headed her horse east on the path. She heard the others riding towards the north and Feron asking Aren where a good fishing hole might be found. Fallon smiled to herself. A blissful, peaceful day was just a short ride ahead. If she got tired of sitting in the woods, she could go back and swim in the spring. Aren had marked the trail going out so clearly, a child could follow back to the den.

She focused on the track before her. Summer was past midpoint, and the woods were filled with the sounds of birds and insects. A squirrel barked a warning she was trespassing in his territory. She looked up to see him angrily whipping his tail around as he watched her passing from the safety of a tree branch high above the forest floor. A few more minutes of riding and the path entered the Blue Meadow. Vibrant patches of bright blue flowers dotted the massive meadow. Across the carpet of flowers and grass, trees spang up. Past the trees, she could see the Calterra Mountains in the magic lands. To her left, there were several cedar trees right off the trail. Behind the trees, she could see a small grassy glade.

Fallon dismounted and unsaddled her horse. She hobbled the gelding so he could graze in the glade. Picking up her pack, Fallon headed for the thick cedar trees. She pushed aside some branches and found an excellent place to sit and view the meadow. Both her father and Aren mentioned they were alerted to the dragon by its shadow racing along the ground. She looked up. The sky was clear except for a few high, thin clouds. She set out her gear, got comfortable leaning against the tree, and started dragon-watching.

Aren deposited the twins a mile north of Fallon; then, he continued to the river in bear form carrying a sack.

"That was a good idea throwing the nut sack pelt in the fishing bag. The Fae female might be hungry from pulling up trees. We will catch some fish and cook them for her. We will wear the nut sack pelt.

The Fae female will be impressed. She will come close enough for me to smell her and tell if she is our mate." Tyr finished looking quite pleased with himself.

Aren scratched his head; apparently, Tyr had been putting a lot of thought into how to charm this female. He considered Tyr's plan. As far as plans go, it was not a bad one. Besides, quite frankly, he did not have a plan at all except "find her." Step two was a vast, blank space labeled "?" in his brain. *"Sounds like a solid plan, Brother."*

When they made it to the river Aren, let Tyr take over. Tyr waded into the river and found a spot teeming with fish. He caught several and dumped them into a catch basin they had built at an earlier visit. He frequently turned his attention to the magic lands, but he heard nothing. Close to noon, he clambered out of the river with a fish. He snacked on it and a couple of others out of the catch basin. When he finished, Tyr looked longingly at the cool shady woods considering the best place for a nap. *"Tyr, we should go check on the dragon watchers. When we get back, we can fish some more, collect everyone, and take them back to the den."* Tyr nodded his head in agreement, and they walked back along the edge of the meadow.

He found Theron and Feron fast asleep in the grass under a big oak with low branches. ***"They have the right idea,"*** Tyr chuffed.

Further south, Tyr heard a scrabbling sound. He picked up his ears. As he approached the tree where Fallon should be, he noticed a branch wiggling midway up the tree. He looked harder and saw Fallon looking back at him. "It's me. Just checking on you," He called.

"Thanks," replied Fallon as she climbed back down the tree.

Tyr turned and headed back to the river. ***"The Boar clan female is a good climber,"*** Tyr thought to Aren.

"S*he is,*" returned Aren.

When he went by Theron and Feron, they had finished with their nap and were playing dice under the oak. He called to them and kept going. Back at the river, he caught a few more fish before he shifted and dressed. He saddled his horse, collected the fish from the catch basin, and headed back to gather up his guests.

After Fallon had climbed back down out of the cedar tree, she sat and watched the meadow. The blue flowers waved in the breeze that blew from the west while butterflies flitted across the grassland. She looked skyward. No dragons. She continued to scan the meadow for fast-moving shadows. None appeared. After a while, her thoughts turned towards finding a mate.

When she left River Rest to come to the Bear lands, she realized she felt less restless. *"Hum,"* she thought, *"Lonan was right. My mate was not there."* This place felt peaceful, but it did not feel exactly right either. Sami and Bren were attractive males, but they were like every other male she had met. She felt nothing special towards them.

"Ok. Lonan was different," she pondered. "There was something there. By the goddess, he was captivatingly.....sexy. Hum....maybe it's a wolf shifter?" She mulled over the times she had visited her grandmother in the Wolf Clan lands when she was younger. She loved staying with her and playing with her cousins and their friends. Fallon visited with her grandmother for several weeks each year before becoming an apprentice Long Rider. She had many fond memories of hunting with them and swimming in the pond.

Fallon had met many males there when she delivered merchants or their stock to the Wolf Clan lands. Fallon realized no one especially stood out as she pondered this, but it did feel like a second home to her. *"The Frost Run! It's in a few months. I could visit my grandmother to see if there is a male there who interests me. Yes! That will work. Almost all the available males take part in it."* She pulled out a piece of paper from her saddlebag and made a note about the Frost Run under her list titled "Mate Search."

The Frost Run was the yearly Wolf Clan gathering. The gathering included competitions, trade, those looking for mates, and pack business. It was held for four days during the first full moon after the crops were harvested. Family packs camped together in the High Brook Forest north of Evenridge. Though it had been a couple of years since Fallon had been, she had always enjoyed attending.

The sound of horses approaching signaled the return of Aren and her brothers. She gathered up her gear and caught her horse to head back to the Aren den. The following days saw the same pattern. Fallon got up just before dawn and followed Aren out to a spot along the Blue Flower or the Little Creek meadow, where she spent her day watching for dragons while fine honing a plan to find a life mate. By the second week, she knew the area well enough she didn't need a guide. She told Aren where she was going to be and left. Aren had also marked the trails sufficiently so anyone could follow them. Aren or one of the other males always insisted on checking on her during the day if she went out by herself. Sometimes Aren took her to a new place. The males at the den seemed to be protective of her. At least one of them always came by, most of the time in bear form, to see how she was doing.

When she mentioned this to Bodhran, he shrugged his shoulders. "Males of the shifter clans tend to be a little more protective of females. You and your brothers are guests at the den, and they want to make sure all of you are safe. If you are wondering, yes, I checked on you too. You just didn't hear me."

Fallon was enjoying the solitude and reflection. Both had been missing from her life in the last few years. Her quiet time and musing had made for a lengthy strategy to find a life mate by the end of the second week. At the end of the third week, she had listed the criteria she thought would be necessary for a life mate. Fallon considered faithfulness, honesty, courage, compassion, humor, dependability, intelligence, and work ethic were all high priorities for her. She was pleased with her plan and her decision about what she wanted in a life mate, even if the number of dragons she had seen was still zero. *"Oh well,"* she thought. *"I still have a few more weeks before we have to leave. I might get lucky and see one."*

Theron and Feron had given up on looking for dragons on day four, which was two days longer than Fallon had thought they would stay still under a tree all day. They now spent their days in warrior practice with the den, fine honing their tracking skills with

123

Laith and Hearne, and woodworking with Bren and Hearne. Fallon sent a letter to her parents with Bren on one of his trips into Cederton. She also saw a couple of parcels Theron had wrapped to be sent out with hers in the bundle. One was addressed to their parents. The other two were addressed to a Tatani Wesson at the Lamp Lighter in Oak Meadow and Marjorie Bierdon at the Bronze Tusk at home in River Rest. She thought it was curious, but if it did not affect her or the Long Riders, well, Theron was an adult and entitled to his own life.

Chapter 12

Fallon was surprised her brothers seemed to have settled into a comfortable routine. It was a very different pace than what they had been accustomed. Aren's den was remote. The journey to the small village of Cederton took three hours. There was the work that went into maintaining a den on the edge of the border, and that was about it. They did tell stories of their past exploits, Bear and Boar Clan history, retold legends, did weapon competitions, and played games. This was what was in store for them today as it was raining. Everyone was gathered under the sizeable overhang off Bren's house swapping stories and watching the water fall off the roof.

Fallon took the opportunity to use the fresh rainwater to wash most of her clothes before pulling an oilskin over her head and heading over to Bren's. As she walked under the shed, she heard Feron talking. "No, we don't know exactly what they do. They are aerial illuminators Lady Shael could not sell. Fallon, why did Shael say she couldn't sell them?"

Fallon shook off her oilskin. "She told me they were too loud, and the sparkles were too bright for a children's party. She said you and Theron might find a use for them since you both had been on the Shadow Team." She drew up a chair to the loose circle of men

125

and sat down. "Oh, she also indicated you have to throw them with great force to get them to activate."

Aren rubbed his jaw. "I've seen a couple of those illuminators. They were harmless. They formed glowing rabbits that hopped around. If the ones you possess have extremely bright sparkles, it could cause a fire."

Feron nodded his head. "I thought so too. That's why we wanted to try one in the middle of a break in the rain today."

"Should work. The grass is soaked since it has been raining most of the morning. Hearne, Sami, what do you think the weather is going to do?"

Hearne looked up from the wood carving he was working on. He stared at the rain with his head canted to the side. "Bear says it will stop maybe by noon. It's mostly over."

Sami walked to the edge of the shed and took a deep breath. "Yep, he's right. This will slack off in about an hour. We could do it then. It shouldn't rain after it stops today."

Aren looked at Feron. "We will go when the rain breaks. We will take a couple of buckets of water just in case, although I don't think we will need them, as wet as it is."

"Yes!" Laith jumped up, high and fast enough his breacan flipped up, flashing everyone except Hearne and Bren, who had resumed their wood carving. "This calls for some of the summer ale Sami, and I finished putting up yesterday."

"By the goddess, Laith, we are going to have to put some weights in the hem of your skirt," Sami muttered as he turned back to watch the rain fall.

Laith laughed. "It's a breacan, and don't be angry you didn't get one." He sauntered off into the rain to fetch the ale. Sami shook his head and resumed watching the rain as the group fell silent for a few minutes.

"Pass me the aerial illuminator," Aren said to Feron.

Feron handed him the bag with the illuminator. Aren took it out and looked at it. The illuminator was twice the size of the ones he had seen at the tavern. It was a shiny silver ball with the words "Villr Piccare Detionair" written on it. He repeated the words out loud. "Anyone know what it means?" he asked.

"It must be in the language of Valair," Bren piped up. "I've never heard of those words before."

"Hum," Muttered Theron, "it almost sounds like 'vile pictures in the air.' Maybe that's why she could not sell them. It looks like big sparkling cocks flying around."

"Or female parts," Hearne supplied.

A few moments of quiet introspection on what "vile pictures in the air" might be, was interrupted by Theron and Feron exclaiming in unison. "What if it's both?"

Surprised looks gave way to bawdy laughter. "We are doing this when the rain breaks," Laith replied as he set a small keg and a tray of mugs down on the table. They spent the rest of the wait drinking ale, laughing, and impatiently waiting on the rain to stop. Fallon drank the ale and reasoned she would never be bored with her brothers around.

The rain stopped as they were nearing the bottom of the small keg of ale. Sami and Bren both concurred this was the break in the rain for the day. The rest of the day, they advised, would mostly be cloudy. They grabbed up some buckets and headed for the stream in the meadow, south of the pasture. While Feron unwrapped the aerial illuminator, the rest of the crew filled up the buckets. Aren walked the area before he decided the clearing was sufficiently wet. The chance of fire would be low. The space was primarily rocky, with a few trees and a log that had washed down from spring snow runoff.

They stood in a loose semi-circle facing the stream. Aren nodded his head at Feron. "Alright, throw it on the ground towards the stream."

Feron lobbed it with moderate effort, and it hit the sandy ground with a thud. Nothing happened. He waited a few moments. Still, nothing happened. He looked at Fallon. Fallon shrugged her shoulders. "Lady Shael did say that it had to be thrown with force."

Feron grunted an acknowledgment. He picked up the silver sphere, reared back, then threw it hard. It hit the ground with a thud and rolled a few inches. Nothing happened. Aren approached Feron and tapped him on the shoulder. "Do you mind if I try?"

"Sure, go ahead. The only thing else I could do would be to hit it with a rock." Feron replied as he studied the sphere. There was a small dent on one side where it hit the ground from the last throw, but it was otherwise undamaged.

"Hey, alpha." Bren called, "Maybe try hitting that rock lying next to the log by the creek. That might break it."

"Good idea, Bren." Aren drew back his arm. *"Tyr, give me a little extra boost with this."*

"You got it, Brother," Tyr sent back.

Aren hurled the illuminator towards the rock with such force it was almost impossible to follow it with the eye. It hit the rock next to the log to explode with a roaring boom and a flash of light. The explosion sent the log sailing straight up into the sky. A sparkling column of light followed the log up into the air. Rolling and twisting, the tree trunk reached a peak height of about three hundred feet. It seemed to hang motionless for a couple of seconds before it plummeted back to the ground.

"Take cover!" Aren barked. He grabbed Feron and sprinted back to the group, who were hastily moving away from the stream. When he reached them, he turned to see the wood land top-down in water with a splash. The root end was sticking up about four feet out of the stream. He glanced skyward. The sparkling column slowed. If Aren had to guess, he thought it was as tall as the mountains in the Calterra.

Tyr popped into his head. **"This is bad. Shift. Now!"**

"Shift!" Thundered Aren in a voice more animal than man when he bellowed the command. Clothes ripped, and breacans flew apart as the five Bear Clan shifters went from man to massive bears in the blink of an eye.

Fallon glanced around her. The Aren den were all now in their bear forms, looking warily at the column of light. Bodhran was at her side with Fast Strike in his hand. The blazing pillar had stopped going up. She breathed a sigh of relief before a colossal silver ball of light that looked like thousands of stars shot out like a dandelion puffball. An enormous blast sounding like a near miss from a lightning strike roared powerful enough she could feel it reverberate in her sternum. The stars merged as they fell into red spikes of fire that circled, twisted, and spun their way back down towards them.

"Arrows," bellowed Aren as he grabbed up Feron in his mouth before he lunged towards the tree line. Bodhran shoved Fallon underneath a cedar tree. Fallon caught sight of one of the bears with Theron in his mouth headed towards her. He threw Theron at her just before he dove to cover them with his body.

Bodhran stood with Fast Strike in front of the tree where Hearne had thrown Theron on top of Fallon. Fast Strike spoke in his mind, ***"Ah!.......an imitation daith blost. Perchance it will be fine."***

In that second, Bodhran knew the unfamiliar words meant "death bloom." "Perchance? What do you mean, perchance?" Bodhran thought back as he watched the red spikes twist and writhe.

"Bodhran?" Fast Strike sent back very patiently, *"Perchance means probably."*

"Yes! I know perchance means probably. You can't use 'death blossom' and 'perchance things will be fine' in the next sentence. It would have been helpful if you had mentioned this when we were talking about what the words meant before we activated the orb!" Bodhran shifted into a defensive position and took a glance to assess his den mate's location relative to his.

"You didn't ask me. I also said imitation daith blost." Fast Strike muttered to itself about the unmajous and their penchant for curiosity, which would undoubtedly get them into trouble.

"How do you know it's an imitation, and what does it do?" Bodhran also now knew "unmajos" meant "the non-magical ones."

"The blood petals have not aligned to target anyone. They also don't feel lethal. Best to avoid being hit with one, though." Fast Strike advised.

Bodhran grunted and watched a handful of petals that looked more like spears head their way. The first hit the stream in a cloud of sparkling red dust. The rest fell on the trees bursting into a shower of glittering red and gold particles covering everything in a layer of glowing dust. One careened towards him. Bodhran sliced at it with Fast Strike, only to have it burst into a glimmering cloud as soon as the sword touched it. The twinkling, crimson dust coated him. From the corner of his eye, he saw the last petal hit Sami squarely on his back. Sami roared as the petal shattered to shower him in a billowing wave of gold sparkles. Bodhran looked skyward. The rest of the projectiles were landing across the creek with soft pops and puffs of glittering mist. No more were heading towards them. Aren stalked out of the tree line as the sparkling dust rained down from the branches above him. A dazed-looking Feron trailed after him.

"Everyone ok?" Aren yelled.

One by one, the rest of the den sounded off. Hearne hauled himself off Theron and Fallon. They wandered out from under the cedar tree to where the rest of the den was assembling. Thankfully, no one was injured. Fallon stared at the landscape around her. The entire stream bed and the bank around it was covered in a thin coating of glittering red powder. Splotches of gold dust broke up the frosty, scarlet scenery. The glowing particles clung to the wet trees and grass. She touched the sparkling dust and examined it. What looked like shiny dust was incredibly tiny square pieces of glittering material. It felt a little gritty like fine sand when she rolled it between her fingers.

"By the goddess, that was amazing! We have two more......" Feron exclaimed excitedly. A chorus of snarling "no's" cut him off before he could finish.

"Oh.....shite," Theron murmured next to her. "Would you look at that." He pointed to where Sami was lumbering over to join them.

Fallon's eyes were wide as she took in the sight. Sami was coated in sparkling gold from his nose to his tail. The dust fell off him by handfuls as he moved towards them. Hearing Theron, Sami stopped and glanced down at his paws. He sniffed them and inhaled some of the powder, making him sneeze. He turned his head from side to side to find that his whole body was glowing. No one spoke for the longest before the bear that was Laith pointed his paw at Sami and broke out laughing. Sami growled and made a swipe at Laith, who nimbly dodged out of the way and kept laughing. Sami growled again and shook himself, sending a thick cloud of gold glitter to settle on everyone near him.

Fallon fanned her face and tried to step back, but it was too late. She and Theron, like the rest of the den, were covered in glowing, sparkling glitter. Sami tried rolling on the ground to get rid of it but ended up making things worse. He picked up a good deal of the red glitter in the process and now shone with a rose-gold brilliance to rival a sunset. He snarled and thrashed as Laith laughed unabashedly at Sami's struggle to get rid of the sparkling dust that hung with grim tenacity to his fur. Theron had his hand over his mouth, trying not to laugh. When he saw Bodhran, he broke out in guffaws. Fallon turned to see Bodhran was solidly covered in gleaming red glitter. His stoic stance and feigned detachment from his condition sent Fallon to her knees, howling. One by one, the rest of the den broke out in fits of laughter. Well, all but Sami, who was doing his best to rid himself of the stuff and getting angrier by the second. It did not help matters when Laith started calling Sami Sparkle Butt Bear.

Aren sighed, "No one was hurt. Thank the goddess."

Tyr looked cautiously around. ***"Ooh, that's a lot of sparkles."*** He turned his head to look at himself. ***"We should get this off."***

"Don't roll. Sami and Donn are just picking up more of the stuff," Aren commented as he watched Sami's bear, Donn, rolling around on the ground unproductively trying to get rid of the glitter.

"Wash it off?" Tyr replied. He plodded into the water chest deep and plunged under, shaking his body as he submerged. He repeated that a few times before wading out on the bank to shake again. The rest of the den followed his lead and vigorously tried to wash off the dust. They headed back to the den, leaving a trail behind them as they passed through the glitter that covered the range of the illuminator's blast.

Back at Aren's, Fallon brushed her hair outside, attempting to remove the glowing flakes. She gave up as it seemed most of them refused to budge. She was able to wash the majority of it off her skin. After washing her sparkly and muddy tunic, she was relegated to wearing her new green one. Her laundry from the morning was still wet. After she dressed, she considered her options for the rest of the day. The cool breeze after the rain and sunshine was too tempting to pass up. She grabbed up her saddlebag and headed for the barn.

"That's a fancy tunic for dragon-watching, Fallon," Laith called.

"Thanks," Fallon replied. "I'm going to the Blue Flower meadow to collect some purple yarrow seed. I saw some when I was coming back last week. This is a different type than what we grow at home. We have the tall yellow yarrow. Our healers might have use for it. I'm not staying to watch for dragons today."

"It's Gatherday, and Hearne is cooking chicken. You don't want to miss that. It's delicious, and there won't be any leftovers." Laith pulled along beside her as she walked to the barn.

"I remember his delicious chicken. Don't worry; I won't miss it. I'm just going there and back. It should only take three hours at most. I'll be back before late supper."

"Ok, if you are late, I'll try to save you some, but no promises." Laith grinned.

"Fair enough," Fallon laughed. She imagined tasty food being saved in a den of bears was as unlikely as spotting a dragon. She saddled her horse and headed out towards the Blue Flower meadow.

Chapter 13

Keegan Varin, Fall 2974: Valair, Dragon Dynasty

Keegan's parents had found out a week after the enforcers had dragged off Basia. He had held out a minute bit of hope they might not find out. He had no desire to bother them with something he perceived as this trivial. It's what he told himself. Truthfully, he was reluctant to tell them. He was a mature, royal, gold dragon male; he should handle his affairs without asking his parents for assistance. As a diplomat, his mother, Kalasa Tanit, had sources all over Valair. When she learned what happened, she formally petitioned her distant cousin, King Palorin Alvorith, to consider a law to protect those from this type of unwanted behavior.

The king had responded swiftly and favorably to her petition. Keegan was called before the king to be questioned, and the incident report from the Enforcers was read. The longer the Enforcers read the documents about their findings of her past behavior, the more smoke seeped out of the king's nose. It swirled to create a twisting ribbon in the air around his head. His reaction had been swift and decisive. There was now a law on the steel scrolls forbidding stalking, including a stiff penalty, should the perpetrator continue to harass the individual after a warning by the Enforcers to desist immediately. Keegan was surprised at the short time it took for the king to make the decree and the Enforcers to officially warn Basia Embyr.

He even mentioned it to Kalasa, to which she had responded. "You are the second gold dragon she has gone after. One of your cousins paid off Mrithum because Basia Embyr was stalking him. King Alvorith was not in a mood to be lenient again."

His father, Laidon Varin, had offered words of wisdom. "Family is there for you. All of us, the whole Tanit-Varin wing. No one has to go it alone."

Helios had been sulky for a few days following the king's decree. Keegan finally managed to get the reason out of his grumpy dragon when Helios huffed, *"We will be forever known in the Law Scrolls as DDC (Dragon Domestic Code) Royal Legal Decree 34 Section 12: Anti-Stalking Law also known as "Helping Helios to Keep Keegan Safe" or the "HK2" I do not need any help to keep us safe. It's insulting. I should have bitten her head off when I had my claws around her noxious neck."*

"I know you are angry. We could have easily killed Basia. Now there is a law to help someone who is not as good of a fighter. If it helps someone, think of how favorably we will be remembered." Keegan reasoned, playing to Helios' vanity.

140

"Humph!" Snorted Helios, **"I hoped we would have our names written in the Eternal Scrolls for something heroic."**

"What did you envision?" Asked Keegan with some trepidation.

"Defending Valair against invaders," Helios answered decisively. **"Our grandsire, Orind Varin, fought in the war. The Fighting Fifth flew in formation, flaming all those who would attack our lands, emerging victorious. This would be a very gallant and noble way to be recorded in the Eternal Scrolls."**

"Er....yes...it would be. But no one is at war. Protecting Valair at war is sort of like the law named after us, which protects others."

Helios harrumphed as he flopped down, *"It is a feeble comparison."*

"It's done. Being sullen and disappointed is not going to change anything. We need to move forward."

Helios sighed, **"The fusty female will not stop. I asked Velli to get her to cease because we would never accept Basia. Velli said she would try, but she does not have much hope for that. Velli thinks if**

141

Basia cannot have us, then she would attack anyone who is our mate."

"What do you want to do?" Keegan asked.

"We need a more secure dwelling if we want a life mate." Helios thought for a while. **"We should set up a home at Aurium."**

Keegan pondered Helios' suggestion. Aurium was their mine where they extracted precious minerals and gemstones. They stayed there when they were working. The accommodations were modest. It was located across the Calterra mountains near the border. The cave entrance was high and provided an excellent view of the surrounding lands, including part of Therus inhabited by a bear shifting tribe. A concealment charm hid the opening, and a boundary spell alerted him to those who crossed the mountain's border. *"It will take some work,"* Keegan thought. *"Clearing out for a little while until things settle might not be a bad idea."*

"Yes. We will use the concealment spell before we fly anywhere. I don't trust Basia not to watch or follow us."

Keegan left the same day. Over the next three seasons, he and Helios built a handsomely comfortable second residence at Aurium. The entrance chamber was big enough for Helios to stretch his wings if

142

needed. They discovered a second chamber hidden with warding glyphs so old they dissipated when Helios accidentally ran his talon across them while cleaning. The wall disappeared to reveal a thermal pool with warm sand around the perimeter.

Helios was delighted as he walked around the cavern. ***"This is marvelous! Oh, look, another entrance. We could lounge in the warm water, watch the sunset, or take a nap on the warm sand. How glorious!"*** He poked his toe in the water. ***"It's perfect! I can't wait to soak."*** Helios made to wade into the warm water.

"Hold up, Helios. We need to explore this before we go jumping in headfirst." Keegan looked at the luminary fixtures bracketed against the walls. They did not glow when they came in.

"I thought I'd wade in and roll around." The dragon eyed the colossal pool. ***"Maybe it's deep enough we can float. Jumping in headfirst is probably a bad idea. I don't think it's that deep."***

"Not what I meant. We should examine this place more closely. We never noticed those glyphs of cloaking until our claws ran over them. There could be protection or entrapment charms. Who knows? We need to do a thorough search first."

143

"That might be wise." Helios retreated, giving Keegan his body back. Keegan retrieved the unveiling powder and poured some into a small pouch. He went back to the thermal pool and shifted into his dragon. Helios tossed the bag into the ceiling, causing it to rupture. He then used his wings to fan the dust around the cave. After sneezing a couple of times, he looked around. After a lengthy search of the area, the only thing glowing was him.

Helios looked closer at the sconces in the wall. Dust and cobwebs covered the fixtures. While simple in design, they were gracefully curved with a scroll pattern holding the globes in place. *"Looks Fae to me. Maybe a short burst of fire will charge anything that might be left in it."*

"Couldn't hurt, and it will save cleaning the dirt and cobwebs off. There is not much unveiling powder in here. There shouldn't be much flashback."

Helios pulled in a deep breath and sent a wide cone of flame around the cavern. It licked up the walls burning off the dust and webs. A few patches of fire flared up when the dragon's breath encountered a dense pocket of magic powder, but most of the charm had already dissipated. The lights remained dark.

"Huh. They must be ancient." Helios mused as he scrutinized the now clean and shiny fixtures. *"I guess we can add that to the list of things to bring back. It*

will be a small price to pay to have the cavern lit. I think if our cousin knew the thermal pool was here, we would have paid much more for it.*

"True. She did not want to be on the border, and she wanted to expand her horde. It came along at the right time for us," Keegan replied.

"No one wants to live on the border next to the primitives. Besides the watch who monitor the border, there is no one around here for miles except us."

Keegan wrinkled his forehead. *"About that. What if our mate is one of the 'primitives' as you just called them?"*

"That's different. She's our mate. She will be perfect," Helios resolutely returned.

"Uh-huh, well, what if our mate is a Badger female? What then?"

Helios shook his head and breathed out a heavy sigh. **"It a good thing we have a massive, heated pool with plenty of sand to scrub her down. Add 'buy a sack of soap' to the list. I'll send up a prayer to the goddess asking for guidance if she is from the toxic tribe."**

Chapter 14

Basia Embyr: 2979 Summer, Valair, Fae Realm, Valley of the Mists

Basia Embyr held the wizard in her talons, glaring at him. "I'm not interested in your excuses Igreth. I need the concealment and suppression spell to last longer."

"Lady Basia….." His words were cut off as Basia barely tightened her grip on him. "Forgive me…. Marquesa Basia." Basia loosened her grip slightly. A thin whip of smoke curled out of her nostrils as she sneered. Igreth pulled in a few deep breaths. She was no more a marquesa than he was king of the Drow. She liked the false sense of power the title suggested. If he wanted to breathe, he needed to consider his words carefully. "Marquesa Basia if you continue to use the suppression spell, you are risking destroying the dragon anima who inhabits the body with you. It would be murder."

"Not your concern."

"It is my concern when I am the wizard casting it. It makes me complicit," Igreth replied.

"You should be more concerned about the Council finding out about your sale of ancient magic weapons to the lands of the savage horde. They will sign a warrant for Mythrum "The Death" Drow, who will neatly lop off your head with Soul Taker." She looked at him with feigned concern. "Who will take care of your poor bond-mate?"

Igreth dropped his head. He silently cursed the day he had gotten so drunk at the winter festival. He had been exhausted from taking care of his life mate and working to buy ingredients from the Drow to restore his health. He had gotten very drunk. Basia had heard his ramblings and figured out he had sold the ancient weapon aerial illuminators, which had ended up in the hands of the Therus. He fervently wished he had never found the old relics under the floorboards of his home. Now because of it and his drunken stupidity, Basia was blackmailing him. She was milking him for everything he was worth, and he was heartedly tired of it.

From the threats to reveal him to the Council to vowing to harm his bond mate, he was drained to the point he no longer cared. Death at the hands of the Drow elf would be kinder than dealing with this loathsome female and her fixation with the gold dragon male. A dragon who he heartedly felt great pity for because he was squarely in Basia's deranged sights. Igreth had passed weariness and felt coldly hollow inside now. She no longer scared him because he no longer cared. He was done. He was through with Basia and her unhinged plans to entrap and force a royal, dragon line male into being her mate and having offspring with her. She was utterly plagued with having a family with this unwilling male. A gold dragon male, Basia could no longer find.

He would have laughed if he had enough lung space to draw in breath. Basia's conniving was going to end because he no longer minded who found out or what happened to him. He told his bond mate and sent him away with a letter and a box to the Council advising them what happened. A spell he cast on his home made it seem as though his life mate was still there. With Basia's limited magic ability, she could not detect the difference. He was through with Basia and her madness. He had a strategy to defeat her. "I have the spell components." He said wearily. He just needed to keep up the facade of compliance for a little longer.

"Good. Things go better when you do as you are told. And the longer concealment charm? I require it," she purred.

"The charm is more complex; it will last a few days longer."

"A few days!" Basia shrieked. "I need weeks longer." She clicked her fire starter in anger at being denied what she wanted. "I've almost found where my beloved has our new home. He is playing coy with me. He wants me to prove that I am a worthy mate by finding our home where we will raise our nine beautiful royal dragonettes. I'll find it and prove to him how much I love him. You will help, or I'll kill your mate!"

It was the exact same tirade Igreth had heard the last time Basia was here. Her dragon, Velli, had grown tired of her mechanizations. Velli had tried to stop her when it became clear the gold male did not want her, just like the long line of males before him did not want to saddle themselves with a baby-obsessed lunatic. Basia responded by shutting Velli behind a wall of magical suppressants he had crafted. Now Basia was in control in both forms. The balance between the life force of Basia and her dragon, Velli, was broken. Igreth inwardly groaned. It had gotten much worse. She was repeating herself. Her break with reality was a chasm that had passed the point of mending. The split in the two souls made her more dangerous than ever. The dragon tempered the power; now, the breaks were entirely off.

"My dear Marquesa Basia, that is why I have a special gift to help you in your quest to find him faster," Igreth smoothly lied.

"A gift. I love gifts! Is it a gift for our first newborn? My dearest Keegan will love it." Basa purred while eyeing him with rapt attention.

Igreth froze. She had never mentioned his name until now. He had gathered he was a gold dragon because all gold dragons were royal. Where else would she get "royal dragonettes"? He guessed she could have kidnapped one; she was that disturbed. Now he had a name she had been careful not to give before.

"It is a strength talisman. It will make a powerful dragon such as yourself even stronger. It will help you find the one you seek quicker."

"Brilliant!" Basia exclaimed. She lowered her head towards him. "Why haven't you given me this before?" She warily questioned.

"Marquesa, the components of the talisman are hard to find and make. I can assure you no one in the Realm or Dynasty has one. It will be as unique as you are," he finished.

"Yes, I am special. That is why he loves me so."

"Indeed, Marquesa, indeed. Tilt your head so I can attach the concealment and strength charms. Like the last time, they will size down or up as you shift." Igreth fastened the clasp linking the chain around her neck. "You must put me down so I can say the suppression spell."

Basia released him. Igreth stood back and recited the spell. He held back the inflection on the word of holding. Hopefully, it would be enough for Velli to fight through soon if she had not given up. Once he finished speaking the words, Basia launched herself into the air heading north.

Chapter 15

Keegan, 2979, Summer, Valair, Dragon Dynasty, North Calterra Mountains

Keegan was heading home to Aurium, his mountain retreat. He had spent as much time home visiting with his family as he deemed prudent. It had been five years since the fateful day in 2974 when the enforcers had to drag Basia Embyr away from his house. Even though there was an order in place for her to have no contact with him or anyone in the Varin Tanit wing, Helios sensed she still looked for him. It was not enough to take to the Enforcers; he had no proof. Her death at Helios' teeth was still one of his dragon's top three wishes. The other two were "find our mate" and "please by the goddess, don't let her be a Badger."

As to the last wish, he was a favorite at several herbalist shops in Valair due to Helios' newfound soap and fragrance fetish. His horde included what he conservatively estimated to be a hundred and fifty-year supply of almost every imaginable fragrance of soap, bath mineral, body scrub, powder, lotion, and perfume. He also had at least a barrel each of shampoo and mouth wash. Helios had been studying herbology scrolls, books, and archive crystals. His dragon was now an expert on anything fragrant for personal use and considered making his own products. *"Why do you want to do that? How about we just buy them?"*

"Do we truly know what is in them when we buy them? We can also make our own signature fragrance." Helios thought back as they flew over the woodlands. The Calterra mountains rose to meet them directly ahead.

"Have you considered scents may affect her like you, and she might prefer no fragrance? What if it makes her sneeze or irritates her skin?"

Helios was surprised enough he missed a wing flap. **"By the Tooth! You are right. Why did I not consider that?"** He made to bank to turn around and head back.

"No. Head home to Aurium. We can get some scent-free soaps when we go to visit."

Keegan mentally shook his head. It was a good thing gold dragon hordes were not limited by space. He could hear Helios' thoughts about how much and what type of fragrance-free things would need to be purchased. Keegan chuckled to himself. If buying soap made Helios happy, it was just fine with him. Helios was even considering going back to the clan Althing. Keegan reasoned his dragon half must be desperate to find a mate if he was willing to go back to what his dragon called "The Fetid Festival: A Tribute to Deplorable Hygiene." Hum....maybe he could sell some of the grooming products? Goddess knows they had a shite ton of it. Possibly literally, they had a ton of it.

Helios' hoard of hygiene products came in handy last year when his aunt, Linnea Tanit, stopped in to visit. Besides his cousin, who sold it to him, only his parents and grandparents knew the exact location of Aurium. Linnea knew because she had also considered purchasing the mine. Its location on the border with the clans would have made it a good base for her while she and the rest of her guild tended the border. They cared for the Obsidian Oaks and cleared the borderline of trees and brush between the two countries.

She had been clearing the boundary near Aurium and came by to visit. She had been very impressed with the thermal pool sizeable enough for her to float around in her dragon form. Each evening after working in the forest, Linnea could be found lounging in the warm water. Keegan had chuckled at the sight of her in dragon form floating, eyes half-closed in the cave's pond. Helios seemed pleased their company was happy.

"If I had known this wonderous thermal pool was in the property our cousin wanted to sell, I would have offered to pay double." She announced to Keegan as he walked into the cavern.

"It was a most pleasing discovery, Aunt Linnea. I have used it many times." He picked up a thick towel to lay it on a carved marble pedestal by the water's edge. "I'm glad you were able to drop by. The borderlands do not lend themselves to entertaining."

Linnea laughed, "No, they do not. Your closest neighbor would probably be one of the bear shifter hordes or the guard at the watch station to the north."

"Will your duties to Valair allow for a long visit?" Keegan asked.

"Perhaps a day or two longer. I am nearly finished in the sector," Linnea returned.

"Which gives us plenty of time to catch up. The evening meal is almost done. We are having aurochs stew with root vegetables and a berry compote for dessert."

"Sounds delicious! You are going to make your future mate very happy with your cooking skills. I'll be right there."

"I have you to thank for the fine aurochs. The young bull was very tender," Keegan replied.

She waved him off with a flick of her hand. "It was the least I could do since you were letting me stay here and treating me to luxury accommodations with the splendid soaking pool." She waded to the water's edge when Keegan left to finish preparing their meal.

They enjoyed their meal by the cave entrance watching the sunset. The evening breeze cooled them and rustled the glossy black feather in her red cap. Linnea told him about her day working along the border.

"Aunt Linnea, you were never interested in being a diplomat?" Keegan asked while pouring her another glass of wine.

Linnea laughed, "My sister, your mother, is the diplomat of the family. Kalasa is very accomplished and well respected. I think she wanted that job ever since she hatched. I do not have the patience for it, and my dragon is most content in the forest. I serve Valair by helping to keep her safe from the tribes of savages to the west. There were times I thought all the primitives should have been flamed in the Great Fae War. We showed restraint when we did not exterminate them all." She studied the wine in the glass and fell silent.

"There have been those in Valair who have found life mates in the lands of Therus." Keegan replied, gazing at her to study her reaction.

Linnea didn't answer him right away. She raised her glass and drained its contents before she replied.

Keegan could detect her heart had rate sped up. She didn't look at him when she answered. "It's true. On the rare occasion, one in Valair finds their life mate among the barbarians."

"What do you think about that?" Keegan asked.

"I guess it's the goddess' will. None can gainsay her divine scheme. As a practical matter, the high Council speaks an enchantment on them so they cannot betray or reveal anything about our lands to others."

"Yes, all true, but what do you think of it?" He pressed, refilling her glass.

She sighed, "I used to disagree with it. Now, I don't know. If they are a shifter, the bonding causes them to have the same life span as we have. If they are not a shifter, you have two choices. Watch them grow old and die in their normal life length or give them half of your life span. To me, it seemed they were throwing away half of their life if their mate was a simple mortal." She whipped her head around. "Why? Are you still on shyn esari? Is your mate in the savage lands?"

"Perhaps. She is not in Valair. If she is of magic or mortal, so be it. I would rather live a shorter, happy life than a long, lonely one."

"Exactly!" thought Helios.

"There is wisdom in your words, Keegan." She put her glass down. 'I'm going to take a quick flight to look at the section I'm clearing."

"Would you like some company?" Keegan asked.

Linnea replied quickly. "Oh no, no, don't bother yourself. Um…this will be a quick look." Her red tunic whipped around her as she turned and disappeared. Keegan could feel the wind from her wings as she flew concealed to the southwest.

"That.....that was odd. This is the second day she has gone back to check her work." He thought to Helios.

"Our aunt is a rare jewel. She is the strongest female gold dragon. She prefers the forest. She is independent and self-reliant. With her love of maintaining the border, I did not think she would feel the need to find a life mate. I had considered her life's work to be her life mate if such can be." Helios paced in Keegan's mind and considered his following words. **"Something happened yesterday while she was on the border to cause her to think about a life mate. Her dragon will not say, and in truth, it is not our concern."**

"True. We will help her, if she asks," Keegan replied.

"If it's her life mate....perhaps even if she does not," Helios answered.

**

The previous day:
Linnea flew over the border where she had been clearing the saplings and brush around the obsidian oaks. Everything was as she left it. That is not why she came. Her dragon, Nyret, had told her someone was watching them as they worked. Linnea wanted to find out if the tribes had posted a watch as Valair had. She glided silently high over the meadow that separated the kingdoms. She was careful to make sure her shadow did not trail along the ground, alerting anyone to her presence. The concealment spell made them invisible and their wings silent, but it did not hide their shadow. Nyret found him quickly. He was warmer than the surrounding trees and bushes.

"A bear was watching us?" Linnea thought to Nyret.

"It is a bear shifter of the savage lands. There is only one." Nyred sent back.

"It's better camouflage than just sitting in the trees as a person. I'll give him or her that," Linnea replied.

"It's a male. I will fly past him and dip down into the meadow on the other side of the thicket he is hiding in. The north wind will bring me his scent there. Then we will know him anywhere in any form." Nyret glided behind him. She banked into the sun and circled. Nyret flew down to make a pass low to the ground. She caught his scent in between the smell of birch and flowers from the meadow. Her eyes flew wide with surprise. Linnea felt Nyret's reaction.

"What's wrong?" Linnea sent through their telepathic link.

"Nothing is …...wrong…per se," Nyret replied. *"I will speak of it when we are safely out of the tribe's lands."* Nyret pulled up and angled back to the west. Her shadow from the setting sun stayed in the trees and far behind the bear hiding in the copse of trees and underbrush, watching the territory line. When they crossed back into Valair, Nyret sighed, *"The bear shifter is our mate."*

"What! What do you mean 'our mate'? I thought we would work to ensure the safety of Valair and be 'The Fun Aunt.' That's our title, and we are good at it, by the way. We are supposed to live mate-free. How can he be our mate?" Linnea finished sounding as dumbfounded as if she had been struck with a thunderbolt.

"I do not know why he came into our life at this point. He is our mate. Of that, there is no doubt." Nyret finished decisively.

"Do we even want a mate? We don't have to have one just because he is out there. We are content, right?" Linnea paused to think.

"We have been tending the Kybor territory line for a little over two hundred years. Really, Linnea, do you want to pull up trees and bushes for another thousand years?" Nyret rumbled seductively, **"Besides, his bear looks huge. I bet he is one big male."**

Nyret was right. They essentially had been pulling up trees, bushes and planting an extra row of Obsidian Oaks for over two hundred years. To be exact, they had been on the border project for two hundred and twenty-three years. Over the last forty years, it had gotten a little boring. She agreed with Nyret about that. A mate, however, was a considerable change. It was completely different from the life they were leading. *"We should think about why we would want to be in a relationship in the first place."*

Nyret replied sulkily, **"Fine, on two conditions. One, we hunt for an aurochs to take back. I'm hungry. And two, we do our thinking in the thermal pool."**

"I like beef. We can cut it in half and take back the rest to our nephew, who graciously lets us stay with him. And Nyret, my dear, we can soak until we are waterlogged."

"Done," returned Nyret as she headed towards a patch of grassland where she had seen a herd of aurochs grazing on their flight from Keegan's home.

One short and successful hunt finished, and they were floating in the thermal pool pondering why they wanted a relationship in the first place. They ultimately decided to consider it. They avoided the Bear Clan lands the next day and worked on a section farther north that bordered the White Fox Clan. By midafternoon they were flying back to Aurium.

"We should go see if the cute bear shifter is still there," Nyret spoke up.

"Cute, Nyret?" Linnea chuckled. *"I thought we were going to evaluate the positive and negatives of a life mate to make sure we were doing this for the right reasons, not just because we were horny."*

"He's so fluffy! I just want to squeeze him and rub his soft fur..." Nyret paused as she imagined cuddling with the bear in her dragon form, **"but.. not hard. He is probably delicate and breakable."**

163

"Compared to us, yes, he is fragile." She thought a moment and smiled to herself. *"We are not stopping, and it is just a flyover. Don't get your hopes up. He may have left. We will stop by Keegan's first, have the evening meal with him and then fly out to where we saw him."*

This time Nyret chuckled, **"I'm not the only one who wants to see him."**

"Yes, I kinda want to see him too," Linnea blushed, "but we are not rushing into this."

**

After eating the evening meal of aurochs stew with Keegan, she flew concealed to the southwest to catch another glance of the bear shifter male. *"We will have to be stealthier today. We don't know where he might be. Maybe he brought others with him?"* Linnea advised Nyret.

"Yes, I agree. We will stay high and to the west," Nyret replied.

They did not have to search long before they found him. He was walking in his bear form near the same position as the previous day when they worked on the border in the bear tribe land. He was just inside the tree line. He paused from time to time to look intently at the line of Obsidian Oaks.

"He is alone again today. He looks for us." Nyret sent Linnea.

"Do you think he knows we are his life mate?"

"I do not know. Let's watch him a bit longer. If we stay too long, he will sense he is being watched like we did yesterday."

They watched the bear roam the woods near the meadow. When he crossed into the grass between the trees, they caught a good view of him. *"By the Tooth! That is one big bear male!"* Nyret exclaimed. They glided down as close as they dared. Nyret pulled up and swung to the west. *"That is not all; he is a warrior of the tribes."*

Linnea's heart sank. Of all the things he could be, why a warrior? She had dedicated her life to making sure that Valair was protected from the warriors of the tribes. Now her supposed life mate was one. *"I've seen enough. Go back. It's too much to consider,"* Linnea sent.

"We will ponder it and consult the elders at the library," Nyret returned firmly.

"Truly, is it necessary? He's a warrior of the horde!" Linnea replied. Her intonation told Nyret she was slightly piqued.

A thin trail of smoke seeped out of Nyret's nostrils. She shot back. *"I know about life mates and dragon matters. You have vast knowledge...about.... trees. So yes, a lengthy visit to the library is happening tomorrow."* Linnea was an independent and tough female, but Nyret was nothing to be trifled with. In their strength and determination, they were equally yoked. The next day Linnea said goodbye to Keegan. She shifted and flew southeast back across the Calterra mountain range for the Athenaeum Contemplari in the city of Shal H'jarta.

Chapter 16

Keegan, Summer 2979, Valair, Calterra Mountains, Aurium

Keegan watched the summer rain fall a few moments before returning to his workbench to pick up where he left off on a gold piece. He had a couple more hours of work, and it would be done. He buffed the rough edges with practiced ease and put the finishing touches on the vine details before setting the final stone. *"Helios, call up the emerald to be used in this piece,"* Keegan asked.

"I certainly like the stone. Let us keep it. It will look wonderful as an addition to our horde when it's set in the vine pattern." Helios thought back as he admired the sparkling green stone.

"You like them all. I told you not to put it with our other gems in the private horde because you would get attached to it."

"I can't help it. It called to me and told me it wanted to live with us."

"Yes, we are a dragon, they all want to live with us, but they can't. Come on now, put it in the prongs."

Helios muttered a little before the emerald materialized in the prong setting. Keegan magically closed the prongs around the stone and spoke a spell to keep it in place. He sat back to admire his work. After seeing the design in a dream, the reality was better. He thought about selling the piece and just could not bring himself to put a price on it. He sighed, *"Ok, Helios, add this one to our collection."*

The ring vanished from sight into the very happy talons of Helios, who seemed particularly delighted with the piece as he stroked it and hummed to it. The ring trilled back, mirroring Helios' joyful tune.

"No more gemstones going in pieces designated to be sold will be stored in the horde vault." Keegan firmly stated.

Helios brushed up against his mind, still admiring the ring. **"Hum…yes..That must be why there are not many dragon jewelers."**

"Exactly," replied Keegan.

Helios broke away from doting on the ring to look at the steady rain falling outside the cave entrance. **"This gray, dreary weather will be out of here by high sun. We should soak in the thermal pool and then go on a flight. Perhaps we can visit our grandsire and get in some more training."**

"A good plan." Keegan walked to the bathing chamber and shifted.

Helios waded into the warm water and let out a contented sigh. *"A beautiful ring for our horde, a warm soak, and training to save Valair. Add a fat mountain goat, and this day is perfect!"* muttered Helios. As he submerged under the water, he added, *"On our way back from Grandsire Varin's, we need to pick up some scent-free soap, shampoo, lotion..........."*

Keegan ignored him and concentrated on the blissfully soothing water. They had been meeting their grandsire, his comrades who fought in the Great War, and a few of the royal guard for fighter practice. Helios wanted to be remembered in the Eternal Scrolls as a "Defender of Valair," and not as the originator of the "HK2" royal decree in the Steel Scrolls under the Dragon Domestic Code, so they went for regular fighter practice. It made Helios feel better, and Keegan liked the competition.

"Are you asleep?" Helios asked.

"Um...no..not yet. What is it?" Keegan replied, wondering what he had missed and hoping it was not another perceived soap supply emergency.

"We should invite some of the family to come and visit," Helios stated

"Do we have enough soap?" Keegan thought back, laughing.

"Ha Ha," Helios returned.

"Aunt Linnea was here last year; Father came in the fall, and Dane stayed with us this spring. We will invite them. Mother is busy with diplomat duties. We could invite grandfather Varin."

Helios hastily shook his head. **"Having Grandsire here is not wise. He truly wants to flame all the lands of Therus after fighting in the Great War. I think it will be too tempting for him to be this close to the border."**

"Yes, I suppose you are right."

Helios paddled over to the edge of the pool that provided a stunning view of the Kybor. The Obsidian Oak line was visible in the far distance. They watched the rain fall until the sun came out. Just as they were about to turn to leave the pool, they heard a massive explosion to the southwest. Helios whipped his head around. A couple of seconds later, they saw a column of light streaking up from the ground.

"Shitfire!" Helios exclaimed as they watched the flame rise higher and higher.

"*That's............*" Keegan's words were cut off as flashes of light shot out from the column in all directions. A few moments later, they heard the explosion.

"By all the old gods! We are under attack!" Helios shouted the concealment charm, grabbed the edge of the pool, and flung himself out. He ducked out the cave entrance, hurled himself into the air, and flew towards it.

"*Pull up and head towards the north watchtower. It's the closest,*" Keegan shouted to Helios.

"We are under attack! There is no time to fly to the watchtower for reinforcements!" Helios pulled hard to fly to the southwest.

"*We do not know if we are under attack. We do not know how many. We do not know if they possess more of those magic exploders. We do not know if it would kill us. If we are dead, a fat lot of good it will do Valair. We need to alert the watch. We can go and scout after that.*"

"Fine," huffed Helios. **"But we ARE going back to see what it was. This is what we have been training for!"** Helios turned and flew to the north watchtower.

An hour later, Keegan was arguing with the lone guard at the post. "What do you mean you are not going to check the explosion in the tribe lands?" He asked the brass dragon guard.

"I did not see or hear anything. I can only act on and report on things I see and hear. If we were being attacked, the alarm would have been sounded." The guard calmly replied to Keegan.

"I saw an explosion, and you don't want to investigate? Explain that to me." Keegan returned while Helios hopped around, scrambling in his mind trying to push for a shift. Keegan slammed down an iron wall between him and his dragon. Helios was not helping.

The guard looked up from the scroll he was writing on and blandly answered him. "I can't fly off. It would leave the post unguarded."

"Um-hum. So, what do you suggest then?" Keegan shot back as a thin wisp of smoke slipped out of his nose.

The brass dragon guard was decidedly unimpressed with an angry, royal dragon in his watchtower. He waived some paper at him. "I'll need you to fill out this form. I'll send it with my daily ledger report. The watch commanders will read it. They will determine what will be done from there."

Keegan grabbed up the paper and began to fill out the form. Smoke was now pouring out of him at a steady clip. "Sir." The brass dragon called. "I'll have to ask you not to smoke in the tower." Keegan took the paperwork and completed it outside. He brought it back in when he finished.   The watchtower guard took the paperwork and painstakingly reviewed it. "I do not advise you fly to check out the area in question for yourself. If you have any other concerns, let us know. Thank you for your report, citizen." When the brass dragon finished speaking, he returned to his paperwork.

Keegan shifted when he left the tower. Helios cloaked and flew south, muttering about bureaucracy and brass dragons. ***"By the time we get there, three hours will have passed. Whoever it was has probably invaded and is having a lovely cup of tea by now."*** Helios complained.

"The perimeter alarm has not sounded. At the most, this may have been some sort of test. We will scan the area of the blast and decide what to do then."

They flew for about two hours before Helios announced. ***"There is some sort of magical smoke in the air. It smells like aerial illuminators after they dissipate. We are getting close. The south wind is pushing the residue north to meet us."***

"This was no aerial illuminator. It was far too big," Keegan mused.

A short while later, they came upon a meadow of blue flowers. Close to the meadow's east side, he saw a horse, and just on the other side of the horse was someone bent over in the grass wearing a green tunic. He could not see exactly what they were doing because the horse was partially blocking his view, so he glided down to get a better look. He stretched his senses outward. There was no one else around. The woods to the west and east were alive with insects and birds. The southern breeze sent him the smells of the meadow, the blue flowers, the damp earth, the horse, ...and something else. There in the wind was the sweetest and spiciest fragrance he had ever smelled. It danced on the air, curling around his nostrils. He wanted to wrap himself in it. It was richer and sweeter than any perfume or soap in Helios' collection. Notes of basil, citrus, cinnamon, and vanilla toyed with him, tempting him to drink in more. Helios greedily gulped in another big breath of the delicious smelling air, angling to scoop up as much as possible. The next deep breath, he broke out of his stupor. Helios' eyes shot wide open. He uncloaked and roared, ***"Our mate!"***

**

Bramble had been peacefully cropping mouthfuls of grass as Fallon worked to collect the seed heads of

174

purple yarrow. The tall, rugged brown bay gelding had long ago figured out a grazing opportunity was one not to be wasted. He was making quick work of getting as much of the tasty grass as possible before they left. The reins were tied to the top of the bridle. It allowed him to eat and not step on or through them.

Fallon busied herself with collecting the dry flowers. She took only a few from each patch of yarrow to ensure there would be plenty for the next year in the meadow. Fallon had her saddlebags on the ground near her feet. She held a cloth bag with some of the seed heads in it she had already harvested. Fallon had just started and intended to pick half a bag of the dry flower heads. Reaching down to pluck off another dead bloom cluster, she heard a deafening roar and was slammed to the earth. She felt the impact of the ground before everything went black.

**

Helios landed next to the unconscious female who lay sprawled in the meadow grass. He reached down and nuzzled her with his snout. ***"Our mate is glorious, and she smells divine! Goddess be praised! She is not a Badger! My prayers have been answered."***

"Are you sure this is her, Helios?" Even as he asked this question, he knew she was, without a doubt, his life mate. She was beautiful and smelled sublime. There was also the metallic scent of blood in the air.

175

His instincts to protect soared. *"She might be injured."* He sent Helios.

Helios grabbed her up and teleported her saddlebags and cloth sack to his horde. He glanced around. ***"I thought I felt someone….."*** He sent telepathically to Keegan. He stretched his senses forward but detected nothing. He only sensed the woman and the horse running to the tree line on the west of the meadow. He hurriedly launched into the air holding the unconscious woman. He glanced back and magically erased his prints from his landing on the soft ground. He started traveling to the southeast before he cloaked and circled, heading swiftly north for home.

**

A few moments later, Basia Embyr landed where Keegan had just been. She scented the ground. It was a female he just picked up, claiming to be his mate. "How can that be? I'm his mate!" Basia's anger knew no bounds as she leaped into the air flying south following the path she had seen Helios take. "I'll kill her for taking my mate and future father of my royal dragonettes."

Chapter 17

Keegan glanced down to where they carried her. He could hear her heart beating at a steady, unhurried pace. Helios reached down to sniff her again. The blood he smelled was only a tiny amount. ***"Our mate! We so overcame her, she fainted when I greeted her! Just like I knew she would."*** Helios thought smugly.

"Or when you decloaked roaring, the horse spooked and plowed into her trying to flee us. Then she hit her head on something," Keegan replied.

"It is apparently a very excitable and temperamental beast. I'm not sure why she would want to ride something so unpredictable," Helios snorted. ***"She could have been hurt. If she wishes to ride, we will find her a suitable mount, one more tractable and sensible, not something half-wild. How she has not been injured before riding something that fractious is beyond me. Thank the goddess we arrived when we did!"***

Keegan mentally rubbed his forehead. *"Yes.....she must be fortunate."* There were bigger things to figure out. He had a mate! That was wonderful, with a dash of slightly intimidating. *"Now what?"* he mused.

"Now what? What do you mean 'now what'? You woo her, that's what," Helios said as he raced home.

"Hold up… Woo her? What do you mean woo her? She is our life mate. There is no wooing with life mates. They know their other half when they see or smell them."

"Our life mate is mortal and a non-shifter, so no, they do not feel the mate connection, from what I have been told. So yes, you must successfully woo her, or she will not like us and leave. So….. get to it."

He glanced down at the woman who was still unconscious. *"The wooing will have to wait until she is awake."*

"A fair point," Helios conceded.

Keegan decided a mortal waking up in the clutches of a dragon flying might make his wooing job more difficult. He sent a spell to Helios so she would sleep for a couple of hours. He reasoned that would give him enough time to get her home.

At Aurium, he seamlessly shifted from flying to holding her and walking. He laid her on the bed and pulled back the covers. *"Our broach looks very nice on her,"* Helios commented.

178

"I believe it is one of the two I traded for the trim for our sisters."

"It is. Curious how she ended up with it. It must be fate," Helios returned.

Keegan took her boots, socks, and belt off. He unpinned the broach and left it on top of her things he had folded and placed on a side table. Keegan looked at her scalp to see how bad the cut was. After determining it was minor. He cleaned off the dried blood and put a small amount of healing powder in the wound. **"Our glorious mate's hair sparkles!"** Helios announced after Keegan had finished.

"Yes, it does." His mate had put some sort of sparkling powder on her hair, and some of it had fallen off onto her tunic and the bed. Keegan noticed a few of the flakes were on his clothes. *"The stuff sure seems to get everywhere."*

Helios watched intently through Keegan's eyes. ***"I don't think we have any glittering hair products. Hum...our mate must be an herbalist! That's why she was collecting the yarrow in the small bag. She is trying out something new. It's gold-colored, and it glitters. I love it!"***

Keegan moved the sleeve of the tunic up Fallon's arm exposing her clan tattoos. *"Her markings say our mate is Boar Clan. She is a Long Rider leader."*

179

"Hum...yarrow can be used as a skin wash, for some digestive problems, or to help wounds stop bleeding. I wonder why she was collecting it if she is a Long Rider of the tribes?"

"I'm not sure. While she sleeps, we can see what is in her saddlebags. Maybe we can learn more about her."

He drew the door closed to the bedroom. In the sitting area, Helios materialized the saddlebags and cloth sack of yarrow on the low table in front of him. The saddlebags were made of brown leather with rugged straps and buckles. They were embossed with the Boar Clan and Long Rider emblem. Underneath carved in the leather was what he thought must be her name, "Fallon Tulun." The first one he opened held hobbles, a tinderbox, a length of rope, a curry comb, and a hoof pick. The second one had some paper wrapped in oilskin, a writing instrument, a pouch of dried fruit & meat, and a jar of ointment.

Helios nudged Keegan. *"Unwrap the oilskin. Let's see what is on the paper."*

Keegan untied the bindings and unfolded the cloth to uncover the paper. One sheet was labeled "Mate Search." It listed: "Plan Long Rider Commissions to be able to attend the Frost Run, Oakenvault Harvest Market, Bear Clan Snow Hunt, and Berry Moon Eagle

Clan Gathering." Underneath, she wrote, "If no luck, then attend Althing and regroup."

"Seems like a well-thought-out plan to search for a mate she won't be needing now."

"I agree. We will win her. We just need a little time." Keegan replied. He turned over the next sheet to see "Important to me: faithfulness, honesty, courage, compassion, humor, dependability, intelligence, and work ethic."

Helios purred, *"An excellent description of us!"*

Keegan chuckled as he carefully put back the items. He took the saddlebags and cloth sack and put them on the table in the bedroom. His mate was still sleeping peacefully. He quietly shut the door and went to the kitchen.

Chapter 18

Fallon woke up in a comfortable, plush bed. The sheets were soft and silky to the touch. A faint smell of clove, musk, and hint of smoke clung to the bedding. She rolled over and looked around. This was not her bed or her room. In the low light, she glanced down to see she was still wearing her tunic and breeches. The rest of her things were folded on a side table with her boots neatly placed next to the table. She rolled over to sit up. The lights in the room brightened. She could not remember how she got here. The last thing she remembered was a roar and the brown shoulder of her horse hitting her.

She thought she must be in one of Aren's den's homes. No, that was not right; she had not seen lights like these except those at the Lamp Lighter and one or two other places. The floor was stone with thick rugs in patterns of blue and gold. A hearth was on one side of the room with two chairs. The other side of the room held the table with her clothes and a large wardrobe. The back of her head was sore. She felt the area and discovered a tender place. She guessed it is where she hit her head. Now to figure out where she was and to get back to Aren's.

As Fallon got up to pull on her boots, there was a knock at the door. "Yes," she called before hastily putting them on. The door opened, and a handsome, tall, blonde male entered. He stopped just inside the room.

"I heard you moving around and came to check on you. I am Keegan Varin." His words purred seductively with a faint exotic accent that made Fallon's heart skip a beat. She stopped where she sat for a couple of seconds and gazed at him. If there were a description in the Panther library of "classically handsome," this would be the male who was the definition.

She drew in a deep breath to gather her thoughts. "I am Boar Clan Fallon Tulun, Long Rider Captain. Where am I?" She asked as she buckled her belt.

"You are in Aurium, my home. The evening meal will be ready soon. You have a few options until then. You can rest in here, bathe in the thermal pool, or sit and have some wine while I finish preparing the meal."

"How did I get here?" Fallon asked, standing. Her hand dropped automatically to the knife on her belt.

"I brought you here. You were lying in a meadow." He stepped back towards the door. "You could come and sit in the great room and ask your questions while you enjoy some Fae wine." He turned and walked out, shutting the door.

"Fae wine?" Fallon thought.

Walking back through the great room, Helios said, **"Our mate likes what she sees, but she is apprehensive."**

"Yes, it was best to leave and not make her feel cornered in there. She needs some space. She will probably come out shortly." Neither he nor Helios wanted to leave the bedchamber. Keegan had an almost overwhelming desire to stay with her, but he knew pressuring Fallon would not be well received. He suspected she would not hesitate to pull the knife her hand drifted down towards.

Keegan checked the bread and pulled it out of the stone oven. His sharp hearing caught the click of the door latch to the bedchambers as Fallon opened the door. He pulled the wine out and grabbed two silver goblets.

Fallon walked out of the bedroom into the great hall. Directly across the enormous chamber, she could see Keegan working in a food preparation area. Slightly to the left of the kitchen bed a massive opening wide enough for a dozen wagons to drive out side-by-side with ease. Outside, there was blue sky.

She was in a cave! She continued to gaze in amazement at the chamber. Between her and the kitchen was a sitting area with light blue and cream rugs on the smooth burnished rock floor. To her left, she saw an alcove with what looked like a worktable. To her right were two other doors, and closest to the kitchen area was another alcove she could not see into from where she stood. She walked towards the cave entrance and stopped near the opening. The view was breathtaking. The sun was near the horizon, and the sky blazed in color.

"How beautiful!" She thought. *"Wait....This can't be right...I'm on the wrong side of the killing trees. Goddess help me; I'm in the magic lands."* She whirled around to face Keegan, who was standing back watching her take in the view. "I'm in the magic lands. I mean Valair? That means…."

"Yes, I was born and live in Valair. Your wine. It's a Fae summer wine, a little fruity, but very refreshing." He handed her the goblet, and his fingers brushed hers. A warm tingling current shot up her arm straight to the center of her chest, making her feel flushed and slightly lightheaded. Fallon's mouth was still open. Keegan continued, "Would you like me to bring you a chair so you can enjoy the sunset? It looks like it will be quite spectacular this evening."

"I…..uh…well," Fallon stammered.

Keegan turned to get a chair to bring closer to the cavern entrance. He turned to find Fallon trailing behind him. "Or you can sit at the table while I finish our meal," he said with a dazzling smile. Fallon nodded her head and followed him to the kitchen. He pulled out a chair and motioned for her to take a seat.

"Helios, I think she injured her head worse than what we thought."

Helios chuckled, ***"No, she's fine. She is just a little surprised. It's probably a lot for our mortal mate to take in."*** He purred. ***"I'm off to look through our horde to find the perfect h'jarta kayzaire gift."***

Fallon sat in the chair he pulled out for her and took a sip of the wine. He was right; it was light, sparkling, and refreshing. She emptied the contents of the goblet. The wine hit her stomach and spread out, warming her. Keegan smiled and set another larger goblet in front of her; this one was filled with water. He brought the bottle of wine over and refilled her goblet. "The wine is stronger than what you may have had in the clan lands. You might want to partake of the water if you are thirsty. There is cider if you prefer."

"Er, no, this is fine, thanks," Fallon managed. She drank some of the water while she gathered her thoughts. Keegan had gone back to preparing the meal. If the smell was anything to judge it by, it was going to be incredible. Her stomach growled in anticipation.

Keegan eyed her and chuckled, "Someone is hungry. It will be ready soon. We are having roasted aurochs, peas, and baked honey apples for dessert."

"It smells marvelous," Fallon replied, toying with her water goblet. She studied the handsome male in front of her. She would have judged him to be six feet tall. He was wearing a fitted brown brocade jacket with gold thread accents that fell to his knees. There was a riding split that flashed his legs when he walked. It was open and held together by a wide tooled leather belt with decorative buckles. The shirt under the jacket opened to a deep "V" that went down to the belt giving Fallon an excellent view of his chest. Under the jacket, he wore dark, green, fitted breeches and tall, decorative boots. His eyes were the sparkling green of fresh dew glinting in the grass at dawn. He had thick and lustrous blonde hair pulled back with an embellished leather tie. His face was strong and defined; his features almost seemed to be molded from stone. The strength of his neck showed in the twining cords of muscle that shaped his entire body. He had broad shoulders that tapered down neatly in a "V" shape to his hips. His strong arms, sculpted thighs, and calves projected warrior and something more. Fallon could not immediately puzzle it out, but it called her and made her heart beat a little faster.

Keegan replied, "Thank you. The meal is simple. We should eat near the cavern entrance and enjoy the sunset." He pulled the roasted meat off the grill and set it on a platter.

"Sounds nice," Fallon replied.

"There is already a small table near the entrance. I enjoy the view." Keegan started filling the plates with food.

"Let me help. I'm sorry, I am not quite myself." She got up and took the plate Keegan offered her. She grabbed the water goblet and followed Keegan to the cave entrance. The sun was sitting just on the horizon, and it painted the sky with blazing colors.

"Don't worry. You hit your head and woke up someplace you did not expect. It would be startling."

"About that," Fallon replied. "You said found me in the blue flower meadow and brought me here?"

"Yes," Keegan replied.

Fallon forked some of the roast into her mouth; it was so tender and savory she almost groaned. She swallowed and continued, "I hit my head?"

"I assume so. There was a little bit of blood on the back of your scalp," Keegan casually replied and continued eating.

"The blue flower meadow must be a good distance from here. I do not see it from the cave entrance."

Keegan shrugged. "I do not know the name of the meadow. Now you mention it, there were blue flowers. It is about an hour away from here."

Fallon looked at the land to the west. Nothing seemed familiar. Keegan pointed. "The meadow where you were is to the south." Fallon gazed south. There were no landmarks she recognized.

Fallon thought about it. The time just did not add up. The meadow was so far away she could not see it. The journey to the meadow and back would have taken much, much longer than what she had been asleep for. "And you traveled with me here in that short of a time?"

"Yes," Keegan said simply.

"How is that possible? Magic?" Fallon smiled.

Keegan set his knife and fork down. *"Well, Helios, here we go."*

Excellent! We'll just shift and show her. This is great! I can't wait for her to see how big we are and far we can shoot flame!" Helios preened.

"No flaming right now. Let me handle this." He looked Fallon straight in the eyes. "I flew and carried you here."

"You flew?" Fallon asked, her forehead wrinkling.

"Yes, I flew, holding you." Keegan made himself relax in his chair.

"How is it possible? Are your wings hidden?" Fallon didn't remember any wings on his back. Maybe they were invisible, or he had a spell which could let him fly. Those were the only two options she could think of at the moment.

"In a manner of speaking, yes, I guess they are," Keegan replied smiling. His mate was going to be so surprised. He thought.

"Can you tell me, or is it rude of me to ask?"

"You can ask me anything. I'm a dragon, and I brought you here." He sat back and waited for her reaction.

Fallon inwardly sighed. The male she thought was handsome, and one she felt an interest in was touched

191

in the head, which explained why he lived by himself in a cave. Wonderful. In addition to being a consummate pain in the ass, this drive to find a life mate was interfering with her judgment. How did she miss the fact he was crazy? She steeled her expression. "Uh-hum, well, yes, it would make the journey much quicker." Fallon deadpanned and resumed eating.

Helios, who had been eagerly awaiting her response, was taken aback at her reply. *"What?...Hum....yea...this was not the reaction I was expecting."* Crossing his forearms, he watched her through Keegan's eyes. *"I am pretty sure she does not believe you. Try this. Tell her we breathe fire. See what she says."*

"Yes, her words and demeanor are curious considering what I said," Keegan sent back. Keegan laced his fingers together in his lap and smiled. "And, of course, since I'm a gold dragon, I do breathe fire."

"Certainly," replied Fallon. "Such would be expected." She set her fork down. "I appreciate all your help and the hospitality of your home, but I will need to return. I'm sure my family will be worried."

Keegan stood, walked to the edge of the cave entrance, then said, "Just know I would never hurt you, and you are safe here," before he jumped off.

192

Chapter 19

Fallon leaped to her feet and ran the few strides to the edge. When she reached the spot where Keegan jumped, a colossal gold dragon flew past the cave entrance missing her by a few feet. Fallon threw herself back and landed on her butt. She craned her head upwards and watched the dragon lazily turn and breathe out a stream of flame. It then descended, angling its body to line up with the cavern entrance. Fallon was rendered momentarily frozen in place, watching it get closer. She hopped up and bolted inside the cave. The dragon easily grabbed the cave's lip, folded its wings, and walked into the great hall. After stepping inside, it sat down, crossed its arms, and spoke, "Yes, I really am a dragon. Yes, I really breathe fire. Yes, you really are safe because you are my life mate."

Fallon was watching from just inside the cavern entrance, mesmerized. When she had imagined dragon-watching she had never in her wildest dreams envisioned this. Fallon pushed off from the wall and walked towards him. She judged the gold dragon in front of her to be at least twelve feet tall at the shoulder and close to forty-five feet long. He had four thick curved horns that arched back from the top of his head. Scales like overlapping armor covered his entire body. His talons were longer than a large

193

dagger. From the tip of his majestic nose to the spikes at the end of his tail, he exuded strength, intensity, and beauty. He regarded her with the same bright green eyes as she perused him.

"We would be more majestic if the sun were glinting off our scales," Helios thought to him. **"But, I'm positive she believes us now."**

"It would be tough not to," Keegan replied.

There was a shimmer in the air, then the gold dragon was gone, and Keegan stood where the massive beast once sat. He nonchalantly walked over to the table, picked up her goblet of wine, and handed it to her. "Believe me now?"

"Yes, obviously I do. I just saw you shift. It's just a lot to take in." Fallon tossed back the contents of the goblet. Her mother's words came back to her. "When you notice someone find out why. Don't fear it. It's not the end of your adventures; it's the beginning of another one." She took a deep breath. *"That's a lot to notice! Time to find out, mom."*

"How about we talk as we finish our meal?" Keegan held out his hand. Fallon placed her hand in his and walked with him to the table. They sat and resumed eating.

She took another bite of the delicious roast. When she finished, she said, "I have questions."

"Of course. Ask away." Keegan replied.

"I'm still a little hazy on how exactly I came to be here. I know you carried me here, but the last thing I remember was hearing a roar and seeing a flash of Bramble's shoulder before I woke up here." She tore off a hunk of bread and buttered it.

"Helios, my dragon spirit, was very excited to find our mate finally, and he roared, which made your horse spook and plow over you trying to get away." He picked up his goblet. "We are sorry you were injured. We have been looking for our life mate for a while and were perhaps a little over-eager in our approach. I put some healing powder on your head; it should be completely well by morning."

"Ah, yes, it does explain a great deal." Fallon nibbled on the bread and considered her next question. She pondered what he had said. She was not angry his dragon form had caused Bramble to spook. Bramble was a horse and just doing what comes naturally to being a horse, which is running away from scary things. Even though Bramble was very seasoned, a dragon was frightening, and something he had never seen before, so running away would be expected. She thought, *"If I had been searching for a mate for a long time, I probably would be impulsive too."*

195

She put the bread down, then asked, "Do dragons usually fly over the lands of Therus? I'm curious because my father and brothers saw a silver dragon eight years ago in this part of the Bear Clan lands."

Keegan shook his head. "No, we don't usually fly over Therus. We avoid the tribe lands."

Helios huffed, *"Glad we flew off in the wrong direction. The fusty female probably has a cave somewhere on the border. Good luck finding us now."* He finished smugly.

Fallon pinned him with a look. "So why were you there?"

"There was an explosion and a burst of light. We went to investigate. On the way there, we sensed you, our mate, in the meadow, and the rest, you know. Did you see the explosion?"

Fallon laughed, "See it? I was in it."

Helios instantly puffed up from where he had been watching. *"Our mate was in that? She could have been hurt!"* *A thin line of smoke escaped Keegan's nose.*

"You are smoking. Are you ok?" Fallon asked.

"Yes. Helios was just worried you could have been hurt. What happened?" Fallon took a long drink of water and told him about the sparkling aerial illuminator. Keegan chuckled and rubbed his chin. "I have never heard of an aerial illuminator being powerful or exploding in sparkling dust. Where did you get it?"

"Lady Shael of the Unicorn Horn in Oak Meadow. She said she could not sell them for parties because they were too loud and would frighten the children."

"About the only children that wouldn't scare would be dragonettes," Helios huffed.

Fallon pulled in a deep breath. The sun had set, and the velvet night sky was ablaze with a million stars. Responsibility tugged at her. Her friends and family were probably worried. They needed to know she was safe, but Fallon did not want to leave. There was something about him that called to her. She never thought she would experience anything like this, especially not with someone like Keegan. While it would have been easy to say it was because he was gorgeous or he was a dragon shifter, there was more to it. It drew her like a magnet. Fallon was determined to find out if he was her life mate. "Keegan, this has been amazing, and I want to explore the possibility of you being my life mate, but I need to let my friends and family know I am safe. They are probably worried."

"I can always take you there tomorrow; then we could come back. There are a few things I need to tell you first."

Keegan told her about the laws and consequences of a mortal being the life mate of a dragon shifter or anyone in the land of Valair. He talked for two hours, taking every opportunity to gaze at her. Fallon was glorious. She was intelligent and compassionate. From the short brown hair on her head to the tip of her boots, his mate was more perfect and beautiful than he could have imagined. Her body had sleek curves he wanted to caress. Keegan had been fighting for composure since she came out of the bedroom, and he was losing. He wondered what she would look like without the tunic and breeches on. His musing did not help his already hard erection. If they took a dip into the thermal pool, he could find out. He reined in those thoughts. He needed to be smarter. Pushing for too much too fast was the sure way to lose her.

Keegan pulled in a deep breath. "The hour is growing late. We can talk some more tomorrow. It's a lot to consider."

"Yes, it is. The laws seem reasonable considering what happened between Therus and Valair in the past," Fallon yawned.

"I see I may have kept you up past your usual rest time," he smiled.

"A long soak and a soft bed would be most welcome."

Helios whipped his head around from where he was sorting through the horde to find the perfect piece to present her as an initial courting gift. ***"Show her the thermal pool. I bet she will love it!"*** Helios sent him.

"There is a thermal pool in the cave just through that opening." Keegan pointed to a cavern opening close to the kitchen.

Fallon got up and stretched. "A thermal pool? As tempting as it sounds, I don't have anything else to wear."

"There are a couple of robes by the pool, and I have things you are welcome to wear." Keegan pointed towards the pool. After stepping past him, Fallon raised a backward glance. His eyes were on her butt. When he whipped his head up, she smiled. The riding split in his tunic flashed as he walked, revealing the bulge in his breeches she did not previously remember seeing. She grinned to herself, reveling in the seductive power she held over him. Heat flashed through her veins and gathered in her loins as she put a little extra hip sway in her walk.

"By the old gods, she is divine!" Keegan thought to himself. From the flushed look on Fallon's face and

her arousal scenting the air, he could tell her thoughts were drifting somewhere deliciously decadent. Not that he minded in the least. That she had glanced his cock pressing against his breeches and was aroused was plainly an excellent sign.

When she neared the thermal pool passageway, the cavern lights popped on with a soft, warm glow. The thermal pool itself took up the bulk of the area of the cavern. There was a sitting area with chairs, tables, and several rugs on the left side of the opening. Two large ornate armoires with cut-glass doors were against the cave wall past the sitting area. When she got closer, she could see an extensive collection of personal care products tastefully arranged in the one closest to the entrance. The second one held lotion, hair care items, neatly folded robes, lightweight tunics, and pants. Thick towels and washcloths lay stacked on a long side table between the cabinets. Behind the long table was a massive mirror bracketed with glowing sconces.

"I…. Oh..wow!" Fallon stammered. She ran her hand over the soft towels. "Keegan, you know how to impress a woman. The meal was wonderful and the thermal pool….it's extraordinary."

Helios preened, *"Told you she would be impressed! We have a most excellent den to court a mate."*

"I'm glad you like it." He stepped in, brought her hand to his lips, and kissed it. "I hope I have enticed you to stay and determine for yourself that I am truly your life mate."

Heat again flooded her veins and rapidly spread through her entire body. She wanted to pull him closer to her and feel those perfect lips ripe for the kissing on her everywhere. She stepped back to let the flush of hormones fade and rational thoughts take over. "Keegan, you have." She managed to get out.

"I'll leave you to it then. Around the corner is a rain head. Just pull the chain, and the water will fall on you. Call out if you need anything." He turned and walked out of the chamber.

Fallon opened the doors of the wardrobe and pulled out a change of clothing. The armoire filled with soaps and various hygiene supplies proved to be a significant challenge. Given the sheer amount and variety of personal care items, she wondered if Keegan had some sort of personal cleanliness obsession. Pulling out a bar of soap and taking a tentative sniff, she shrugged her shoulders. Fallon guessed she would find out soon enough. She was ready for bed, and that mystery could wait. Fallon put the potent rose-scented pink soap back. She picked up the red and white striped bar and read the wrapper. *"Hum....Furrlir majalis"* She took a sniff. An inviting blend of warm spices, juniper, and an exotic floral note met her. She picked up a towel and walked around the corner to the rain head.

The shower area had smooth grooves cut into the rock floor. It angled down to a grate set flush in the rock. Niches were carved into the wall for storage, and several ornate hooks were set into the stone around the rain head. One quick shower later, and she was floating languidly in the warm waters of the thermal pool. The soothing water lapped against her. By the time she waded out, she was completely relaxed. She dressed and walked back into the great hall. Keegan was near the cave entrance. He turned and strode towards her when he heard her come into the room. She was wearing one of his linen tunics that nearly reached her knee. She smelled divine.

Helios rumbled his approval. *"Ah, she picked one of my favorites, the furrlir majalis. Spicey and exotic, just like our mate."*

Keegan smiled. "Helios told me that you picked one of his favorite scents, the furrlir majalis. In your language, it would be fire lily." His eyes held her for a moment. "Now, I think it is my favorite as well. You look relaxed. Did you enjoy the thermal pool?"

"I may want to come back just for the thermal pool." Fallon grinned.

Keegan laughed, "Indeed, it was a happy discovery. That you enjoyed it makes it all the better." He pointed to the three doors behind her. "You were in my bedchamber, and you are welcome to sleep there if you would like, or you can stay in the guest-chamber next to mine."

"I would not want to take your room, so the guest-chamber."

Keegan opened the door. "Guest room it is. When you go into any room, the lights will come on. If you want the lights to go out, just speak it 'lights out.' If you need them on before you get up, speak 'lights on.' They will go out when you leave the room. If you need anything, call me, I'll hear you."

Fallon went in, shut the door, and crawled into bed. She called "Lights out" and was instantly plunged into darkness. She sighed. *This has been a one-of-a-kind day. From exploding aerial illuminators to my life mate being a dragon shifter, a handsome and sexy dragon shifter. I could have never imagined all of this would happen between sunrise and sunset."* As she mulled over what her next steps would be, she fell asleep.

Chapter 20

Hearne had cooked the Gatherday late supper, and Fallon had still not shown up. Laith had dutifully put her back a plate of chicken. Aren's concern mounted by the hour when Fallon did not return. Laith told Aren Fallon said she was going to the Blue Flower Meadow and would be back by late meal. When she had not made it back by the time they ate, Aren announced they would look for her after supper.

Neither Theron nor Feron seemed very worried. Feron commented. "She is fine. She probably decided to dragon-watch and fell asleep under a tree. We should still go look, though."

Bodhran was washing dishes and looked over his shoulder at Feron. "Feron, when was the last time she fell asleep on a watch or did not come back exactly when she said she would?"

Theron scratched his head, and his eyes opened wide. "Never Bodhran. We should go now."

They grabbed their gear and quickly saddled their horses as the sun lay on the horizon. Bren stayed at the den in case she came back. When they rode out of the den, the last rays of the sun were fading. As they neared the Blue Flower Meadow, Aren heard hoof beats and called for a halt. Bodhran initially breathed a sigh of relief; then, his heart sank when he realized the sound was wrong as the horse was riderless. Bramble came into view of the shifters and Bodhran. Theron and Feron could barely make out the horse in the fading light until it was nearly on top of them. The moon had not yet risen, and the woods were dark.

Laith and Hearn dismounted and caught the gelding. Hearne examined him. "He's not hot or injured. The saddlebags are gone; the rest of the tack is fine. She had the reins tied so he could graze, so maybe he just left her on foot somewhere when he decided it was time to go home." Aren breathed a sigh of relief. Hearne's assessment was the most likely to explain what happened.

Theron chuckled. "I'm never letting her live this down. Her horse wandered off from her."

Something struck Feron and not quite right. "I wonder why she did not use the hobbles. She has a set in her saddlebags."

Tyr was still pacing in Aren's chest. Something was amiss. He turned his horse around. "Laith, Hearne shift and track the horse back. Theron, Feron, lead the horses behind you. Sami, ride behind them."

Laith and Hearne shifted and trailed Bramble back towards the meadow. He had wandered a little and stopped to eat, but eventually, they found the patch of yarrow Fallon had been picking. Aren held them away from the area because Hearne and Laith's bears were walking circles around the site and repeatedly smelling two separate locations. They talked between each other telepathically, Aren caught snatches of their conversation, and none of it was good. After a couple of minutes, they walked over to where the rest of them stood and shifted. Hearn looked at the ground and shook his head. Laith stared off towards the killing tree line.

"Alpha." Hearn crossed his arms over his chest. "I've never seen or smelled anything like this. Fallon came here and picked some of the yarrow. We see and smell where she pulled some of the dry heads off. Her footprints are visible in the dirt. The ground was still soft from the rain. Something happened. The gelding had been eating here. I can see and smell where he cropped the grass. Then he left out of here pretty quick. Where he took off, the ground is torn up. There is a clump of dirt that probably came out of one of his back hooves about twenty feet away from where he was grazing. I think something scared him, and he lit out. He had to dig in fast and hard to throw dirt back that far. He ran back towards the den and the tree line."

Theron spoke up. "Where's our sister? We need to track her down. We can ask her why her horse took off."

Laith sighed and rubbed his hands together. "Well, that's the problem. We don't know where she went. She was here. Then she wasn't. There is a trail in, but no trail out."

Theron and Feron dismounted. Feron handed Theron the reins. "Let me see."

Laith stood to block him. "No. Bad idea. You won't see anything in this light, as you are not a shifter, and you will just muddy the scent."

Hearn continued. "That's not all. There is a tiny amount of blood on a rock. It's hers, but there are no other drips."

"If she's hurt, we need to find her; we should spread out and look for her," Theron spoke as he mounted his horse.

Aren snarled and barked an order at Theron. "You will stay with Bodhran and Sami. No one goes anywhere. Something is wrong here. The four of you get back to the tree line and stay there. Sami take my horse. You and Bodhran do not let Theron and Feron out of your sight. We do not need to go looking for any more people tonight."

Aren stepped off his horse and stripped. He walked away from the group and shifted. Laith and Hearne shifted and trailed behind him.

"Something was here." Tyr sent him.

"Alright, Brother, let's figure this out." He padded around the area, careful not to get in the four large dents or walk across any other tracks. He smelled Fallon, the horse, and the freshly broken yarrow. He saw the horse tracks where the gelding had spun to the west and bolted. There was a small amount of blood on a rock. It was Fallon's. Then he stopped to sniff the deep dents and study them.

"That was big. The two farther out are deeper." Tyr took a deep breath. *"Strange. It smells like smoke, but not wood smoke; there is the earthy metal musk and old stale Badger sweat."*

"Badgers? What the heck are Badgers doing here? Let's walk around and see if we can figure out where they came from or went." He sent a mental message to Hearne and Laith. They both reported smelling the same thing.

Laith added, "It smells like her hair where the blood is. She uses peppermint soap on it, and there is peppermint scent by the rock, but no mint grows around here. She might have hit her head." They walked the area again and widened the search and found nothing. It looked like Fallon rode into the meadow, got off her horse, picked some yarrow, and disappeared. Whatever left the large tracks just appeared and disappeared; there were no tracks or scent in or out. They went back to where Theron and Feron waited, then Aren shifted.

"It looks like she just disappeared. There is no scent or tracks out from her." He gazed at Theron and Feron. "Now I'm going to ask you some questions. I need you to think and not jump to any conclusions. Understand?"

"Ok," Theron replied with a confused look on his face.

"You two saw a dragon a few years back near here, right?"

"Yes," both Theron and Feron answered.

Aren drew in a deep breath. "Good, now think back. Do you remember what its feet looked like?"

"Shite balls! You think a dragon took Fallon?" Feron yelled.

"I'm not saying that." Aren calmly replied. "There are some large tracks and a scent we have never smelled. I saw a silver one dive down and pluck a doe

210

from a meadow south of the den a couple of years back. It was far enough away I couldn't see its feet. If it snatched Fallon up, there would be more blood based on what it did to that doe. You two were closer. What do you remember?"

Theron thought for a moment. "One of our group sketched the dragon we saw. It's in the Panther library at Oakenvault. Its fronts looked like long muscular fingers, and the backs were shorter and thicker. That's all I remember."

Feron piped up, "It had long claws on the….I guess you would say….fingers and toes. The back feet were heavier and wider." His eyes popped open wider. "A Panther elder was asking all sorts of questions about the dragon's feet and drawing something. I bet there is a picture at the library."

Theron nodded his head. 'That's right! The prelate asked countless questions about its feet."

Aren crossed his arms over his chest, "Here's what's going to happen. Hearne, get back to the den. Tell Bren what happened. Take the two fastest horses and lite out for Irondenn. Tell Chieftain Barend Don what happened. Fallon is gone. There is a strange scent and big tracks. Don't go saying it's a dragon. We don't know what it was, and we don't know if it took her, or she left somehow. Ask the chieftain if she will send a letter by the swift to Lady Shael at Oak

Meadow. The chieftain will probably send a few of the guard here to see the tracks, which I hope are still visible by then unless there is rain."

Theron stepped forward. "There might be a way to preserve the tracks. If we make a frame around the track and fill it with plaster, we could carefully lift it out and preserve the footprint."

"I did not know such was possible," Aren replied.

Feron added. "We learned the technique at our training camp before the battle with the Scorpions. We were able to identify a Scorpion spy by comparing his shoes to the tracks he left in the mud by making a plaster shape of them. We will just need a lot more plaster than what we used to do a regular footprint."

Aren turned to Laith. "You go to Cederton and bring back a few sacks of plaster. Theron, Feron, and Sami go back to the den and make the frame and bring it back in a wagon loaded with hay. Bodhran and I will stay here. Maybe it will come back, and we can see what it is."

They took off, leaving Bodhran and Aren in the woods. Bodhran put his head down and sighed. "I should have gone with her. She was my duty to protect."

212

"Now, Cub, no one would have guessed this would happen. We both know how safe it is here. We don't know what happened."

Bodhran gave a non-committal grunt. He turned his attention to Fast Strike. *"Any ideas about what happened to Fallon?"*

"Go look at the prints."

"Father, I know you don't want the scent muddied, but I need to look at the prints. Fast Strike may have an idea about what happened."

"Go and look. Stay in my tracks."

Bodhran carefully walked in Aren's prints. When he reached the tracks, he stopped. He pulled Fast Strike and went to hold him over the tracks but stopped as an intense pain shot between his eyes.

"Back away!" The sword sent him. He withdrew Fast Strike and stepped back. When he sheathed the blade, the pain vanished.

"It's a dragon." Fast Strike told him. **"If there is a fight. I cannot help you. If you try, I will impede you. There is a curse. Of that, I can no more speak, nor can you."**

Bodhran's mind was spinning. Dragons? Curses? And the sword would work against him? He went back to where Aren was standing by the tree line. "Fast Strike says those are dragon tracks."

Aren pulled in a big breath and let it out. "Cub, I was worried those might be from a dragon. What else can it tell us."

Bodhran sat down and pulled out Fast Strike, and laid the sword across his lap. He closed his eyes for a few moments. The sword began to glow with a silvery light. When Bodhran opened his eyes, they were as silver as the sword, and he spoke in a deep raspy voice. "Ask. Time is short."

"Did a dragon take her?" Aren asked.

"Yes, that is most likely."

"Why would it take her?"

"Unknown."

"Would it harm her?"

"Not necessarily."

"Can we get her back?"

214

"Perhaps," Bodhran's eyes returned to their normal blue color, and the sword ceased glowing. Bodhran's shoulders slumped forward.

Aren looked at Bodhran with concern. "Are you ok?"

"Yes, I'm fine, just drained." Bodhran stood and sheathed the sword.

Aren scanned the meadow and the sky. The woods were quiet, and the half-moon was rising in the east. "Why don't you get some rest. I'll keep watch. If it comes back, I need you rested."

Bodhran shook his head. "If the dragon comes back. The sword cannot be drawn. I can say no more."

Aren weighed his options. "I'll shift and keep watch from the tree line while you sleep. If it comes back, jump on Tyr, then we will make for the deep woods. We will be faster to escape instead of making for the horses, which might spook and be useless anyway."

Bodhran nodded his head. "That might be our best option; even if I could wield Fast Strike against it, I doubt we could overcome it. We would also risk the wrath of the magic lands if we were to slay it."

Aren shifted and took watch while Bodhran slept. A few hours later, Theron, Feron, and Sami showed up with the wagon. The frame lay in the back on a bed of straw. Bodhran stood watch while the rest of the den slept. Near dawn, Laith returned with a few sacks of plaster in a cart along with buckets and waterskins.

"No problems getting the plaster from Nencia the mason?" Aren asked when he shifted back to his human form.

"No, she had a load ready to be shipped, so I was able to get a few sacks. She had some fast-setting plaster, so I got that. She asked what it was for, but I didn't say. I told her you needed it and it was important. She gave me instructions on how to mix it with sand and water. She says it sets fast, so we need to have everything ready." Laith jumped down from the cart and began unloading the items. They waited until dawn before they started making the cast of the clearest track. They were finished in a little over two hours and had the form carefully loaded on the wagon.

Theron and Feron got a good look when it was loaded on the wagon. Their eyes were wide as shock registered on their faces. Theron was the first to speak. "I think the print is from a dragon."

Feron sighed and scratched his head. "I think you are right. I don't know what else it could be." He looked down at the ground and met Aren's eyes. "Why would it have taken her?"

Aren put his hand on Feron's shoulder. "Fast Strike confirmed it was left from a dragon. We have no idea why it landed there or if it has Fallon. There is every possibility she is fine. We are going to do everything we can to get her back safely. Hearne will be at Irondenn by evening today. I'm sure he rode hard straight through the night, and he will ride hard today. I expect Irondenn will send out some of the guards tomorrow morning. It will take them two days of travel to get here. I expect them to be here by late evening on Mittelday. If the chieftain sends out a message to Lady Shael in Oak Meadow, she should get it on Mittelday. What she does and how long that takes is anyone's guess." Aren crossed his arms over his chest and drew himself up to full height. He calmed his mind and focused his alpha energy into his words. "We are going to pull together as a den and find her. Laith is going to take the wagon back to Nencia. Sami will be taking the imprint back to the den, update Bren, and bring back some supplies so we can camp here. The rest of us will post a watch here."

Sami climbed up in the wagon. "Alpha, what weapons do you want?"

Aren shook his head. "No weapons. We have nothing could be of use against a dragon. If we did, using them against one will escalate things. We do not want to provoke the magic lands into another war."

Feron nudged Theron. "Um, Aren, we do have aerial illuminators. They won't hurt one, but they might distract it long enough for us to get away if we have to."

Aren turned to Sami, "Bring those illuminators. Bodhran, Theron, and Feron stay here with me. We will set up a camp back in the tree line."

Sami nodded his head and left. Aren selected an area for their field camp just inside the tree line where they could view the meadow from the forest cover. Once camp was set up, they would rest. He set Theron and Feron to collecting wood for the base. When they were out of earshot, Theron spoke up. "I want to look for Fallon myself. I think we should search in a wider circle than what Aren and his den did."

"Agree. After we take back the wood and get a couple of hours of sleep, we'll go." Feron yawned.

"We do need a nap. I'm not sure I'll be much good at finding anything, and I might miss something important without some shut-eye." Theron agreed.

After they brought back the wood, they lay down and were soon sound asleep.

Chapter 21

Basia Embyr, Summer 2979, Valair, Calterra Mountains, Fae Realm

Basia had flown after Keegan to the southeast. She had searched all afternoon and into the night and had not managed to locate him or his cave. Basia had long suspected he had a second home somewhere in the Calterra Mountain range, but she had never managed to find it. By the time the sun rose, she was exhausted and furious as she flew over the craggy mountains. This was all that female's fault. Basia was convinced the female who Keegan claimed to be his mate had somehow put a spell on Keegan. What other explanation could there be? She and Keegan were meant to be together. She had this all planned out. They would have at least nine royal offspring. They would be beautiful, and Basia would dress them in regal outfits she made and show them off at court while Keegan doted on her. It was perfect until that bitch came along! Basia longed to wrap her talons around the loathsome female squeeze the life out of her for ruining her plans.

"This is useless," Basia concluded. Randomly flying over the mountain range was getting her nowhere. She needed to think. There had to be a better way to find out where Keegan and this female went.

Maybe, just maybe, if someone were looking for this woman, she might find some information she could use as she did with the sorcerer, Igreth. Basia smiled wickedly to herself. *"What a wonderful idea!"* She banked and headed back to the meadow.

**

The smell of cooked food got Feron's nose twitching and woke him. He nudged his brother awake. Sami had returned with the provisions. Bodhran pointed to the food and drink. The twins got up, stretched, and grabbed some meat, bread, and a water skin. They sat next to the others and ate in silence. When they finished, Theron told Aren that he and Feron were going to do a larger sweep of the meadow, but they would stay clear of the dragon tracks. Aren nodded his head in agreement. With food put away, Theron and Feron walked out to the meadow and began making a broad sweeping arch as the hot sun beat down on their heads. The first sweep revealed nothing. They widened their circle, which took them closer to the boundary with Valair.

Eying the Obsidian Oaks, Feron asked, "How far can those trees reach out?"

"A pretty good bit. We don't need to get any closer." Theron reached to the ground and picked up a rock, then hefted it toward the tree line. Nothing happened. He picked up another stone, and this time threw it farther. The black oak closest to the thrown rock twitched. "Not as close as the last rock." Their father had shown them how to rate the distance when they were children, even though the trees' threat proximity was clearly marked with red-painted posts in the Boar lands.

Feron squatted down to examine a rabbit track in the dirt. "Those trees always made the hair on the back of my neck stand up. Do you think Fallon would have wandered over there?"

Theron shook his head. "Our sister is not dumb. She would have stayed clear of them."

Feron stood, dusting off his breeches. "If she was hurt, maybe she didn't know what she was doing."

Theron scanned the tree line. "It's a possibility. We can walk the tree line and look. We'll start by heading south, walk for a while, come back to head north." Theron reasoned if Fallon had crossed into Valair the trees would have killed her, and the bear shifters would have smelled the blood. He knew Feron was anxious to find her. This would give him something to do, so his brother felt like he was accomplishing something to find their sister. He signaled to Aren they were going to walk south for a while. Aren waived them on.

**

Basia had flown back to the meadow with the blue flowers and found several tribe males there. Two were in the tree line across the field, and two were walking in a big circle where the whore had stolen her mate. She stayed on the other side of the Obsidian oaks. Their height would block her shadow, which raced along the ground almost exactly under her since the sun neared its zenith. When the males came close to the boundary line, they started talking. They were clearly searching for the female. One mentioned "sister."

"Goddess be praised! I found the slut's brothers. I'll use them to get Keegan back." Basia climbed to get height and speed on her descent. She turned to the west and dove down into the meadow.

**

Bodhran stood under the shade of a tree as he watched Theron and Feron walk south along the border. A cool north breeze that had been blowing on and off through the morning was a welcome relief from the hot, late-season summer day. He had castigated himself several times for not following Fallon when she went to pick the yarrow. He had failed to keep her safe. *"If anything happens to her…"* He was interrupted in his musing by a humming like a hive of angry bees. He glanced down to see Fast Strike was glowing hot on his hip. "Father!" He shouted.

Aren whipped his head around to see Fast Strike glowing red. He, Bodhran, and Sami frantically searched everywhere to find the cause of the trouble. Aren glanced into the meadow and did a double-take. A shadow was racing along the ground toward Theron and Feron. There was nothing in the air above the shadow. He bellowed a warning as the shadow bore down on the twins. He shifted and ran towards them, with Bodhran following behind him. Theron and Feron turned to see Aren and Sami in bear form running towards them, with Bodhran sprinting behind them. The twins quickly looked around and saw a shadow speeding towards them. A second later, they were snatched off their feet and hauled into the air in a vice-like grip of light gray talons. A glance above confirmed to Theron they had been taken by a dragon. With his arms pinned, he could do nothing. Feron had one arm free and was hitting the clawed foot to no avail. As the ground rapidly became father away, Theron yelled, "Dragon!"

A hissing voice answered him back. "Another word or another strike, and I'll crush you both." To emphasize she meant business, Basia tightened her grip on them both. Feron ceased his futile pummeling and gave Theron a resigned look. Theron nodded and flicked his head up at the dragon. Feron remained silent. They would bide their time. They needed to find Fallon and escape.

Aren roared his frustration as he saw Theron and Feron vanish from the meadow. He heard Theron yell "Dragon" shortly after he disappeared. The shadow crossed the border into Valair and faded into the trees. He heard something hissing but could not tell what it was. When he got to the area where he last saw them, he drew in a deep breath. There was the same odor of smoke, earthy metallic musk, and old stale Badger sweat in the air. Bodhran came running up to him as he was analyzing the scent. "Quick, take a deep breath and tell me what you smell."

Bodhran drew in a lung full of air, and his eyes shot open. There faintly on the breeze was a peculiar scent. "I smell smoke, metal, and Badger." Sami had made it to them in his bear form. He growled and nodded his head.

"Cub, jump on my back. We are going to the tree line. We will talk then." Bodhran swung up on his back, then Tyr bolted back to the safety of the trees. When Tyr stopped, Bodhran slid down off the bear's back. Aren and Sami shifted. Aren faced them and rubbed the back of his head. "That's the same smell as the track. Sami, what exactly did you smell?"

Sami was studying the meadow with his arms crossed over his chest. "Alpha, I smelled the same thing Bodhran did; earthy smoke, metal, and sweaty Badger ass."

Aren sighed, "It's the same dragon. I also heard Theron yell, 'Dragon.' Now we know they can also be invisible."

Bodhran threw his hands up in the air. "Invisible dragons! Badgers! What the heck are Badgers doing with dragons? Have they made some sort of pack with them? Why did they appear here? Why would they take them? It does not make sense."

Aren was gathering up the remnants of his shirt and boots. His breacan was in excellent shape. He snapped the poppers closed around his waist. "I don't know. The whole thing is bizarre, and we have two days until some help gets here. So, here's what's going to happen. No one is going in the meadow. We will all stay in the tree line. Sami will go to the den and tell Bren and Laith that Theron and Feron have been taken. Laith needs to send out a message with the Swift; maybe they can intercept the guards the chieftain sends. That may get them here quicker. Bodhran, you and I will stay here at camp."

Sami nodded his head. Bodhran angrily kicked a limb on the ground and muttered under his breath. Aren sat down at the base of a large oak tree. What had started as a way for him to get his cub home for a while and to try to find the Valarian female had turned into a giant mess. Shite! He didn't doubt Goron would have his head if anything happened to his children. If the Badgers had formed a pact with the dragons, all

225

the clans were screwed. He was tired, but he knew sleep would not find him, so he picked up his gear bag Sami had brought, took out some paper and a quill, and started writing.

Chapter 22

Fallon, Summer 2979, Valair, Calterra Mountains, Aurium

Fallon woke up and rolled over. The warm, downy covers beckoned her to stay and snuggle back under them. It was tempting, but she needed to get up. She threw her legs over the side of the bed and stretched. The lights came on, filling the room with a warm glow. While she dressed and finger-combed her hair, she reflected on the events of the previous day. Her life mate was a dragon shifter. She had not expected that. She was positive no one in Theus knew there were dragon shifters, and the dragon shifters were resolute it would remain a secret. Keegan had explained that much to her yesterday. She needed to let Aren and her brothers know she was okay. She knew her parents would worry.

Fallon decided she would write them a letter to tell them she would be staying with Keegan for a short while. Soon, she would need to introduce Keegan to them, or her father would find a way to cross into Valair and search for her. Fallon chuckled out loud. She did not doubt Theron and Feron would be there with him when he did it. She grabbed her saddlebags and went into the great hall. From the light coming in the mouth of the cave, Fallon guessed it was well past dawn.

Hearing the door open, Keegan put down his tools and walked out of his workroom to greet his mate. "Good morning. Did you sleep well?" Keegan asked.

Fallon smiled. "I did. The bed is very comfortable. I was asleep almost as soon as my head hit the pillow."

"How about some tea and breakfast? It is just past mid-morning."

"Mid-morning? I did sleep well. Some tea would be nice, thanks." They walked to the kitchen area. Keegan set about getting food out for their meal.

Fallon stopped him. "I want to help, so what can I do?"

"Why don't you take care of the tea, and I'll gather up some fruit, cheese, and bread for our meal."

Fallon nodded her head and set about making the tea. She talked to him while she gathered the items from the cupboard. "After we eat, I need to write my parents and let them know I will be staying with you for a few weeks. If this does work out between us, I want you to meet them."

Helios danced around in his head. ***"Yes! I knew we could win over our mate!"***

"Of course, we can go and visit them anytime you like. However, as I told you yesterday, one of the laws is they cannot come to Valair."

"I remember, it's fine as long as I go and see them," Fallon added the dry ingredients to the tea bags and pulled the kettle off the fire.

"Shyn h'jarta, I am a dragon. I can fly you to any point in the lands. You need only tell me."

She looked at him with her eyes twinkling. "Shyn h'jarta. What do those words mean?"

Keegan was carrying a large platter with food on it. With his head, he motioned for her to follow him to the table by the cave entrance. "In my language, it means 'my heart.'"

Fallon gathered up the mugs and moved towards the table where Keegan was setting up their breakfast. "Shyn h'jarta, thanks, that's lovely." She sat down and studied her mug for a moment. It had only been a day. Yesterday she was with Aren's den, and they were drinking mead under the overhang in the rain. It had only been one day, but being with Keegan felt right. The urgency to find the elusive "something" was gone. She was at peace. "Keegan, I need to tell you this is moving very fast for me. I feel like this is right in my heart, but my head thinks this is too much too soon. There is something else I need to tell you."

Keegan froze, and Helios picked his head up from where he was studying a small pile of jewelry that met his standards from which he would choose the courting gift.

"Fallon, we can take as long as you need. There is no rush. I will not pressure you. I know you are my life mate, but I also know you don't have the assurance I do since you are not a shifter. We will take this at your speed. You should know you can tell me anything. Literally, anything." He reached across the table and squeezed her hand.

Fallon took a sip of tea and a deep breath. "You should know I do not want children. I have two nieces and a nephew. I enjoy spending time with them, but I do not want children of my own. I have always felt this way. It will not change. I understand this might be a deal-breaker for you. Having your own children might be important for you. If it is, we should go our separate ways."

Keegan sat back in his chair. A few scenarios had run through his head, but what she had just said was not one of them. "I am glad you brought it up. I don't think it's possible for a dragon and a mortal to have offspring. A dragon having a mortal for a life mate is rare, and there are no children from these pairings I know about. We would have to visit the Athenaeum Contemplari and consult the elders at the records hall to be sure. Even if it were possible to have children, it is ultimately your body and your choice. I am glad you told me. Honestly, I am fine with or without having children. We would say dragonettes or hatchlings. I do not feel strongly either way. So not having any is fine with me."

Fallon set her mug down. "In my clan, having or not having children is seen as fine. The couple is rebuked if they are too young or have more for which they cannot provide. All are taught at a very young age to be responsible and how to prevent pregnancy. I did not know if this was the way of..." She thought for a moment and recalled the word he has used the previous night. "the Dragon Dynasty."

He nodded his head and put some food on a plate before handing it to her. "Yes, it is the same with us. The female decides if she wants hatchlings. Some females have dragonettes, and some choose not to have any. Either is fine in our society, and it is discussed during the outset of courtship. If the pair are life mates, there is not much to discuss. It seems the goddess, Fate, has their interests aligned." He piled some food on his plate. "Much like your clan, having too many or at too old or young an age is frowned upon." He looked her in the eye. "Males and females can request the magi healers to render them sterile. The magic is effective and can be reversed if necessary. Our wing believes it is important for both males and females to discuss and shoulder responsibility in reproduction. That's why my brother and I went with my father when he had it done. My parents were finished having children, and he wanted to demonstrate responsibility to us."

Fallon added, "It is the same with our clan. My father takes my brothers to gather and prepare silphion the first Gatherday after every full moon. My mother and I go and collect it as we need. The herb prevents pregnancy. Males and females of the Boar Clan know how to do this."

"I am glad we are talking about things discussed in h'jarta kayzaire. The words translate into "heart chase." Kayzaire conveys more as "chase with intent to capture." In your language, it means courtship. In the Dynasty, it is traditional for the males and females to give a gift to the other if they are interested in them as a life mate. Since you are mortal, the dragon male would give a gift to the female. If the other party accepts the gift, the courtship begins. Returning the gift signifies no interest in the individual. I would like to give you a token of my affection and formally announce my desire to begin the h'jarta kayzaire today. The gift simply means interest. Accepting it does not bind you in any way. The courtship can last as long as you need to be sure you want to live with me as life mates."

Fallon thought for a few moments. It was a lot to consider. Keegan had said he would not pressure her, and this could take as long she wanted. Her heart leaped at the chance. Her head urged restraint. She considered his words and replied, "I would be happy to begin the h'jarta kayzaire with you today as long as I have as much time as I need to be sure."

"Conditions for the h'jarta kayzaire? She is a shrewd negotiator," Helios sent Keegan.

"She is. Do you have the gift?" Keegan asked.

"I'm had a hard time deciding. I think this will do nicely." Helios materialized the gift into Keegan's pocket.

Keegan reached into his pocket and pulled out a silver bracelet. It was decorated in scrollwork with a dragon in flight, and a few gemstones tucked in the center of some of the scrolls. "I agree to your terms." He returned with a wink. "Helios saw you wore the broach I made and wanted you to have another matching piece to wear with it."

"You made this broach! I love it, and I wear it all the time. Helios was right; it matches the broach beautifully." She slipped it on her wrist and reached across the table to touch his hand. "I formally accept your token and would like to begin the h'jarta kayzaire."

Helios beamed with happiness. ***"This makes going to the fetid festival in the tribe lands worthwhile to know our mate ended up with a piece we made."*** And for Helios to say that meant he was beyond ecstatic.

"I am pleased we are starting this shyn h'jarta. When you are ready, I will fly you back."

They finished breakfast and Fallon wrote a letter to her parents. While she wrote, Keegan crafted a charm and infused it with a drop of his blood so Fallon could cross the line of Obsidian Oaks without being attacked. He told her the magic would protect her from the oaks and spoke the incantation while touching her forehead. The air around them sparkled then stilled. "We are ready to go. When we leave the cave, I'll use a concealment spell. I do this when I journey to and from Aurium."

Fallon wrinkled up her forehead and looked at him quizzically. "Is there a problem?"

Keegan sighed and told her about Basia. When he finished, Fallon's eyes were wide. "I understand why you would use magic to prevent being seen and tracked. I am sorry to hear what you went through. It's a good thing there is a law now to deter unwanted attention from happening to someone else.

Helios was wincing while Keegan told Fallon what happened with Basia. ***"Our mate will think we cannot protect her since we did not deal with the mephitic, hatchling obsessed female by our self.***

"I know you did not like the way it ended, but our mate is fine with what happened. In your heart, Helios, you know the law is for the best," Keegan reasoned.

Helios grumbled for a bit. ***"Fine. Yes. It will probably help someone."***

"Helios, our mate is not going to have much fun flying with a peevish dragon for the first time."

Helios huffed and blew out a puff of smoke. ***"Yes, you are right. She should have fun on her first flight."***

"Shyn h'jarta, when I shift, climb up my leg and sit at the base of my neck. You will be safe there. Helios will not let you fall. If you are uncomfortable sitting on my back, I can carry you in my talons. Like I did when I brought you here."

"If you say it's safe, I'll climb up," Fallon replied with resolution, but Keegan could sense her trepidation.

"Yes, it's perfectly safe. You won't fall, and even if you did, I could very easily catch you."

"Okay," Fallon tucked the letter in her tunic and nodded her head.

Keegan took several steps back and seamlessly shifted. He watched through Helios' eyes as she approached, planning her best way to reach the place on his neck where she would sit. Helios flattened to the ground and coaxed her. "That's right, little mate. Step up on my arm. Get a foothold on my wing and push up onto my neck. Good. I'm going to say the concealment spell. You will still be able to see me, but no one else can. I'll run and jump off the edge of the cave."

Fallon stretched her legs downward to try to get a grip on his neck. There was nothing for her hands to grab. *"Hope he's right about me not falling off, or it's going to be a short flight."* She adjusted her seat and looked down. It was a far drop to the stone floor, and they were not even flying yet. "Okay, I'm as ready as I'll ever be."

Chapter 23

Helios chuckled. "I am an excellent flyer. You will be fine." He turned his head toward the cave entrance and took off at a run. When he reached the lip of the cave, he jumped straight out into the air. Fallon squealed. Helios chuckled and flapped his wings. After a few moments, he gently banked to the south. Fallon felt the wind rush over her and watched the ground speed along under her. She was a little concerned until she tried to scoot back and could not easily move.

Helios felt her wiggling around and turned his head back to her. "You okay, little mate?"

"I thought I'd shift around, but it feels like I am stuck on your back."

"You are. My magic is holding you on my back. That way, you won't fall off."

Fallon put her hands on her hips. "Oh, Helios! Why didn't you tell me before you jumped off the mountain?"

"Where's the fun if I told you? Besides, I said I am an excellent flyer."

"You are a very sneaky dragon, Helios. I think my brothers and father will appreciate your sense of humor."

Helios laughed. "And not you?"

"It will probably be funnier tomorrow." She smiled.

When they left Aurium, the sun was straight overhead. An hour of flying later, Helios was coming up on the meadow where he found Fallon the previous day. He stayed in the tree line over Valair. Glancing across the meadow, he saw several males in the tree line when he flew by. *"There are three males in the tree line across the meadow from where we found our mate yesterday."*

Keegan replied through the mental link, *"They are probably looking for her. Land behind the oaks in Valair. We will walk to meet them since they can't know about dragon shifters."*

Helios passed by the meadow and turned east. He looked back at Fallon. "There are three males near the meadow where I found you yesterday."

"I saw them when we passed. That is probably Aren, Bodhran, and another from Aren's den," Fallon replied.

Helios arched his eyebrow. "Aren's den?"

"Yes, Aren is the alpha of his den. He is a Bear Clan champion warrior and a bear shifter."

"Uh-huh. I will land behind the Obsidian Oaks. Keegan will walk with you across the meadow to meet them. As he spoke last night, you may not reveal anything you saw or learned about Valair."

"I won't," Fallon replied.

Helios muttered to Keegan, *"A bear shifter tribal warrior should not present a problem, but I'll send you our sword and dagger to your side after we shift."*

Keegan shook his head. *"No, doing so will just make them defensive. They are probably worried. You can have a sleep spell ready. We will use it if we must.*

Helios drifted downward to a clearing in the trees behind the Obsidian Oaks. *"It's a shame. We hardly ever use them, and they are a stunning set. None of the horde have ever seen Drow weapons. Well....not in the last four hundred years. Of course, at the Red River War, they saw plenty of Drow weaponry."*

In Helios's mind, Keegan was shaking his head and rubbing the bridge of his nose. *"Just have sleep spell ready if we need it. I'm sure it will be sufficient. Oh, and Helios, calling them 'The Horde' will probably upset Fallon. You might want to find another name for them, maybe the 'clans' or 'people of Therus', something along those lines."*

Helios touched down lightly. ***"Yes, a good idea."*** Helios flattened to the ground to allow Fallon to climbed off. He shifted, and Keegan was standing at her side.

Keegan glanced to his right and saw the Drow dagger on his belt. *"Helios. I thought I was clear about not going in with any weapons."*

Helios folded his arms in Keegan's mind. ***"I heard you. I did not say I agreed with you. It's a dagger. Everyone in Therus carries them, and besides, it matches your outfit. Who knows, maybe they will be happy to see her and have cake. Then you will have the fanciest one to cut it."***

Keegan sighed. *"They are not sprites, and this is not a formal high tea."*

"Is there a problem?" Fallon asked. She looked around the clearing. They had landed behind the killing trees, which Keegan had called Obsidian Oaks.

"No. Just talking to a very stubborn dragon."

She smiled. "Oh." She pointed to the ornate dagger on his belt. "That's a very nice blade."

240

Helios preened, ***"Our mate appreciates quality crafted weapons."*** Helios proudly returned. ***"Now I know exactly when to get her for the second h'jarta kayzaire gift!"***

"Thank you." Keegan held out his hand. "The charm will work, and you will be safe from the trees marking the boundary line, but I would like to make sure."

"I think it's just an excuse to hold my hand." Fallon coyly grinned.

"It is." He took her hand, brought it to his lips, and kissed it. Nerves tingled from her hand to her groin in a steady current, urging her to press into him.

"Wow! I love your excuse," She murmured.

"When we get back to Aurium, it would be my pleasure to come up with some more excuses. If you would like." He held her hand by his lips while his eyes held her. She could feel his breath on her fingers as he spoke, fanning the embers of her desire.

"It would be welcome," She whispered.

"Then come shyn h'jarta let's take care of the matter before us so we can explore the matter between us."

241

When they walked towards the Obsidian Oaks, the trees parted to the side to allow them passage. Aren saw the movement on the far side of the blue flower meadow. He signaled Bodhran and Sami. They jogged out across the meadow to meet them. Aren watched the couple as they approached. Fallon was smiling and seemed happy. They were holding hands.

The male seemed watchful and reserved as he sized up Aren, Bodhran, and Sami. He was dressed in a brocade and leather long-jacket of brown and green with gold threads. He had a vicious-looking Fae dagger strapped to his side. He did not appear to be Fae, but he was not a mortal either. Aren decided diplomacy would be the best tactic. Maybe this male could help find Theron and Feron. Aren signaled for Bodhran and Sami to stop while he walked closer towards them.

Aren greeted the couple, "Fallon, I am glad to see you. We were worried when you vanished. Are you okay?"

"Yes, Aren, I am well. I want to introduce you to Keegan Varin of Valair. Keegan, this is Aren Gideon, champion warrior of the Bear Clan. This is Bodhran Gideon, Bear Clan champion warrior and my second in the Boar Clan Long Rider crew I lead. The male to the side of Aren is Sami West, Bear Clan Warrior." Aren and Keegan nodded at each other warily.

"We thought you had been taken by a dragon, Fallon." Aren bluntly stated as he eyed Keegan with suspicion.

Fallon considered her words carefully. "I was with Keegan. He found me in the Blue Flower Meadow. I had hit my head. He saw me and took me to his home. Why did you think a dragon took me?"

"Because of the dragon tracks found where you vanished." Aren quietly drew in a deep breath. Fallon's scent was the same. The male, Keegan, did not smell like the tracks in the meadow. Not that he thought he would, because he certainly was not a dragon. That was absurd. He was some sort of magical, Fae being Aren had not smelled before. Aren also did not smell any scent of Badger on him.

"Those are not our tracks; I magically erased them," Helios thought to Keegan.

Keegan looked at Aren. "Could you show me these tracks?"

Aren gestured out to the meadow and started walking in that direction. Fallon looked across the field toward the tree line and then at Bodhran. "Where are Theron and Feron?"

Bodhran pulled himself up straight. "They were taken by a dragon we could not see. It was the same dragon that left tracks where you last were."

Fallon tightened her grip on his hand. Keegan squeezed her hand reassuringly. Keegan replied, "A dragon you could not see? How do you know it was a dragon then?"

Aren stopped walking and turned to face Keegan. "Her brothers were searching for her in the meadow near the killing tree line. We saw a shadow racing along the ground. There was nothing in the sky above. I called to warn them. They turned and disappeared. Theron yelled 'dragon,' which was the last we saw of them as the shadow went into the magic lands. The scent is the same in the air where it took them as the tracks. The tracks are over there. See for yourself if you doubt my words. You are from the magic lands; possibly you have seen dragons and know what their prints look like."

Keegan heard the truth in Arens' words. There was also something else the Bear Clan warrior was leaving out. Keegan heard it as it hung between his comments, which were spoken deliberately and measured. Who could blame them? Their two kingdoms had been at odds for generations. Keegan saw Fallon's face was tense. He spoke reassuringly to her as they continued walking to the spot where he had taken Fallon the previous day. "I'll look at the tracks.

244

If your brothers have been taken by a dragon as is claimed, I shall find them."

"I bet anything in the horde, it's the frowsty female. I'll kill her when I see her," Helios fumed.

"I believe you are right, Helios." Keegan sent him as he neared the spot.

Aren stopped him before they got too close. "We have only let in a very few to this area, so the scent is not muddied. If you can detect what made them, you may want to get closer. We will watch while you look at the tracks. I have been keeping my den to the cover of the trees since the twins were taken." Keegan nodded his head and moved closer to the tracks. There was no doubt, they were, in fact, dragon tracks.

Helios looked through Keegan's eyes. **"Those aren't ours. Those are from a female silver dragon. Even not shifted, I can smell the Badger stink on them from halfway across the meadow."**

"I smell it, Helios. It's Basia. The areal illuminators must have attracted her to this area as it did us. She must have been concealed and saw us take Fallon. Then she hung around to kidnap her brothers. She probably plans to use them somehow."

Helios snarled, ***"We will find her and get our mate's brothers back. Then I want to kill her. She won't stop, and she might harm our mate."***

While Keegan feigned looking at the tracks to have a conversation with Helios, Bodhran moved to Fallon's side. He noticed the bracelet she was wearing but said nothing about it. "How are you, Fallon?"

"Besides worried a little about my brothers, I am fine, Bodhran." Fallon looked him in the eyes, and Bodhran could hear the truth in her words.

His eyes traveled over her assessing her. "Who is the male?"

"He probably is my life mate," Fallon replied.

Keegan heard her speaking with Bodhran. He lifted his head from looking at the tracks. "We are certainly life mates."

Bodhran's eyebrows nearly reached his hairline in surprise. Fallon pulled the letter out of her belt. "Bodhran, this is a letter to my parents. Please send it by the Swift, so they don't worry."

Sami touched her on the shoulder. "Do we need to worry about you? You said 'probably' he is your mate."

Fallon smiled broadly. "No Sami, I am fine. I am not a shifter or a magic-user, so I don't instantly know, but it feels right. I need more time. We are going to take it slow. You do not need to worry. Be happy for me." She patted his hand.

Sami nodded his head. Aren had been watching the male, Keegan, while listening to Fallon. Tyr had already told him this male did not smell anything like the tracks, and Tyr was unsure what he was. Aren agreed with him. Fallon's words rang true, and she did not smell afraid. She scented a little anxious when she learned about her brothers, but she was not scared of the male from Valair. He could not detect she was being influenced or under any sort of spell. That magic made people smell bitter, if the legends were true. If they were life mates, he was happy for them. Not everyone found theirs, and only a rare few found them in the other kingdom.

Keegan came back to where Fallon was standing with the den. He noted the Bear Clan males all seemed to be protective of her. Two of them were on either side and slightly in front of her. The one named Aren, who was the den's alpha, stood close to her while he watched Keegan's every move. Keegan stopped several feet from her so he would have room to react if needed. "Shyn h'jarta, I need to go to Valair to find your brothers. Do you wish to go with me or stay here?" Keegan held his breath. She had an easy out if she did not want to go with him or felt uncomfortable.

Fallon moved past the two big men and strode up to him. "Of course, I want to go with you. I want to find my brothers and be with you."

He took her hand and raised it to his chest. He kept the other males in his sight as he spoke to her. "I shall work to get them back safely. We need to go. There is much to be done to find them."

Keegan pointed to the trees on the other side of the meadow. "It would be a good idea to stay in the tree line. I will let those in Valair know what happened, and I will search for them."

Aren had been standing with his arms crossed, quietly assessing Keegan. "You know what took them?"

"Yes. They were taken by a being from Valair. Where exactly they were taken, I do not know. I suspect they are fine. I will do everything I can to get them back safely."

Aren stared straight at him. "Know I have sent a message to our chieftain when Fallon disappeared. I expect her to send a unit of warriors here by sunset on Mittelday, which is the day after tomorrow."

Keegan squared up and maintained eye contact with him. "I understand your concern and why you did

248

what you did. You should know Fallon is my life mate. She is safe, and I will protect her with my life. I will do all I can to return her brothers safely." He squeezed her hand. "Shyn h'jarta, we must go."

Fallon looked at the two males who were sizing each other up, trying to find a chink in the other's armor. This was not helping them find her brothers. *"Males!"* she thought.

Fallon turned to Aren. "Thank you for searching for me and sending a message to Irondenn about me. I appreciate everything you have done. Aren, truly I am fine. We will find Theron and Feron." She took Keegan's hand, and they walked back across the blue flower meadow towards Valair.

Chapter 24

When they were safe across the boundary out of hearing range, Keegan spoke. "It was the female dragon, Basia, who took them. She will probably try to use them for leverage to get to you or me. To do that, she needs them alive, so I do not think she will harm them. We will fly to Vallis Halden. It's the closest keep. There is a combined unit of Fae and dragon warriors stationed at the keep. I'll make a report. Afterward, we will leave and start searching for them." He turned to her moving her hand to place it against his chest. "You did a great job not revealing anything. I promise you, I will find your brothers, and this will be solved."

Helios had been pacing and mumbling since he determined Basia had taken Fallon's brothers, popped off in Keegan's mind. *"It will be resolved this time because a stinky she-dragon is gonna' die!"*

"Keegan, is it necessary for the warriors of Valair to become involved? Is this because the Bear Clan chieftain might send a unit of warriors to Aren's den? I think it might only escalate tensions if more warriors from both kingdoms are involved."

Keegan listened and considered her words. "No, that's not why. She could be anywhere in the Calterra

251

Mountains. It's too big for me to search by myself. I'm hoping the keep will help look for them. Basia has taken two males against their will from Therus. Unless the person is your life mate and/or willing to go, that's kidnapping. It's a violation of our laws. The best outcome is we find and return them before the Bear Clan chieftain's troops get to Aren's den. Do not worry shyn h'jarta. I'll get them back."

Fallon mulled over the logistics of such a search. The range of flight of a dragon and the mountains would make looking for her brothers difficult. *"Of course, they are trained warriors and cunning.....hum."* She tapped her hip as she pondered. She spoke a few moments later. "I am concerned about their safety, but both are champion warriors and have had special stealth training. They are very crafty. They may escape."

Keegan waited patiently for Fallon as she stared off into the tree line in thought. "Them successfully escaping would be the best scenario. Then the King and the Council can deal with Basia." When they made it to the clearing past the Obsidian Oaks, Keegan shifted. Fallon climbed up, and soon they were flying southeast towards Vallis Halden.

Helios flew concealed over the mountain range. ***"How are you planning to avoid Grand Teta Ryndra Tanit?"***

"Maybe we will get lucky, and she will be working with the Obsidian Oak seedlings. We can swoop in, make the report, then leave." Keegan sent back.

Helios choked back a laugh, ***"Worst plan ever."***

"We don't have time for all of her questions. We need to file the report and start searching."

"You are going to have to tell her," Helios muttered.

"Shite. Fine, I'll tell her. Maybe we can find Fallon's brother's first," Keegan replied.

"Highly unlikely, and you know what that means," Helios said.

"By the Balls of the Abyss, we will have the whole Tanit-Varin Wing descend on us in a few hours. I am not sure why they think a grown male cannot take care of his affairs." Keegan shook his head in Helios's mind. Knowing the inevitable was approaching did not make it any better.

"We may get lucky and have a whole twelve hours before they show. You know our family. They worry and want to help. Look on the bright side. Maybe they will bring meat like they did for our 'intervention.' Such a delicious day!" Helios licked his lips. Keegan muttered something unintelligible and sighed in exasperation. Sometimes nothing was simple. An hour and a half of flying, and they were gliding down to land in Vallis Halden.

The captain of the keep met them as soon as Keegan shifted. She watched Fallon while she addressed Keegan. "What brings you to the keep today with a female of the tribes, Keegan Varin?" The Fae Captain of the keep, Sylmare Zinlana, was older than Grand Teta Ryndra Tanit, and she did not see the need to mince words.

Keegan stood by Fallon. "This is my life mate, Fallon Tulun. She is from the kingdom of Therus. There is a problem requiring your expertise so it may be swiftly addressed."

Captain Sylmare Zinlana raised one eyebrow slightly. "A day of good tidings then, gold dragon." She turned her head to a silver dragon male standing by the door with his mouth open. "Go tell Ryndra Tanit her grandson is here with his life mate."

Keegan inwardly groaned while Helios chuckled. *"So much for a quick report before we flee."*

The dragon male shifted immediately and flew off. Sylmare motioned for them to follow her. "Now, you can tell me about this problem." She shut the door behind them and pointed to two gracefully curved chairs. Captain Sylmare sat across from them behind her desk. She took out some paper and a quill. "What happened?"

Keegan told her everything from the areal illuminators to Basia kidnapping Theron and Feron. Sylmare asked a few questions for clarification about the areal illuminators. Fallon answered them. When Keegan and Fallon finished, she put her quill down. "The information about the areal illuminators was in the report delivered by the furen this morning. I'll update the report to include it is large but harmless." She tapped the feathered end of her quill against the side of her head. "Basia. Yes. That is concerning. I'm sending this to my commander now. As for the two from Therus who were taken, I can send half of the dragon warriors out to search. I'll send word to Fell Halden and ask them to send some out to look as well."

She glanced out the window, and the corner of her mouth quirked up. "Ah, I see our discussion is at an end; Ryndra Tanit just landed." Her eyes flicked between them. "I am now telling you officially; you should not go looking for them. However, we both know you will ignore that. So, I shall tell you this. If you cause an intercontinental incident which makes me have to rescue you, do endless paperwork, several reports all while I re-visit training protocols for my garrison when I am just a season away from retirement, I promise you by the goddess of Fate's lush, sweet backside you will regret it."

Keegan's retort was cut off when the door was thrown open with enough force it bounced off the wall when Ryndra Tanit burst into the room. She nodded at the captain. "Sly, thanks for the messenger."

"You are welcome Ryn" Slymare slyly smiled as she gathered the paper up on her desk. "I need to take care of a few things. Perhaps the three of you can take this conversation to the Iron Fork." She raised her hand in front of her. "May the light of the goddess shine on your path."

Keegan shut the door behind them as they exited the captain's office. When they were outside, he turned to Ryndra. "Teta Ryndra, this is Fallon Tulun, Long Rider Captain of the Boar Clan, and my life mate. Fallon, this is my grandmother, Ryndra Tanit. She grows the Obsidian Oaks bordering the lands of Valair."

Ryndra took Fallon's hand and patted it. "A mortal from the tri…um…the lands of Therus. That's ….well…it's good to meet the woman who has ended my grandson's shyn esari. Welcome to the Tanit-Varin Wing. Please call me Teta or Teta Ryndra, grandmother seems so……ancient. Keegan, when is the introduction banquet?" Ryndra had dropped Fallon's hand to now look expectantly at Keegan.

Fallon studied the woman who was Keegan's grandmother. Ryndra was a tall, older woman with a few gray streaks in her black hair and piercing, green eyes that missed nothing. Of her age, Fallon could not determine. She believed Ryndra might be comparable to the elders' age where she lived, but since dragon shifters lived much longer lives, Fallon could not even begin to guess how old Ryndra might be. Ryndra was wearing a red brocade tunic with fitted sleeves, and brown breeches tucked into boots. She had gold oak leaf earrings and a jeweled broach of an oak tree pined to her tunic.

"Teta, we have just started the h'jarta kayzaire. Come, let's go to the Iron Fork instead of having this conversation on the street where we are attracting an audience."

There were a few curious individuals who had not moved past and were looking agog at Fallon. Ryndra dismissed them with a wave of her hand. "We haven't had a mortal in Vallis Halden in well over three hundred years."

Keegan sighed and growled under his breath. "Yes, I'm sure that is true, but I'm confident Fallon is not interested in being gaped at, so if you please, Teta, continue to the Iron Fork."

Ryndra shrugged her shoulders then loud whispered to Fallon as they walked towards the tavern. "He is not usually testy. He must be hungry. Don't worry; we will get him sorted out in a few minutes."

Fallon giggled while Keegan set his teeth at what his grandmother said but refrained from saying anything in return. The Iron Fork was just down the road across from a large park. As they walked, those passing them nodded or called a greeting to Ryndra, who returned their greeting in kind. A short stroll found them at their destination.

To Fallon, the tavern was very similar to the pubs in Therus. There were wood tables and chairs where patrons sat enjoying their meal. The walls were a light cream stone, and there were plenty of windows. Magically illuminated globes cast the room in a cheery, warm glow. They sat at a table in the back of the tavern. Keegan ordered a platter of seared meat and vegetables. While they waited on their food, Keegan told his grandmother what happened. He finished by saying, "I would appreciate it if you kept this to yourself. I'm sure the troops Captain Sylmare sends, and I will be able to find my mate's two brothers. I would not want to trouble my family. I am certain they are busy. Right, Teta?"

"Right, dear."

Keegan sighed in relief. This was wonderful. His grandmother had agreed to keep it a secret for the time being. "Thank you, Teta. I was hoping I could convince you to keep this quiet for now."

"Oh, Keegan, I never agreed to that. Yes, you are right; they are busy, and they will drop everything to help you and your mate. As luck would have it, your grandsire, Orind Varin, is in the area on a hunt with his old military buddies. The old lizard can still fly circles around most of what looks like hatchlings in the combat wings these days. Don't you worry about a thing, Fallon. Once the wing finds them, Keegan can set a date for the introduction banquet." She paused for a moment. "Although technically, they will have already met her by then." She shrugged her shoulders. "Oh well, does our wing need an excuse for a party? I think not."

The more Ryndra talked, the more Keegan's heart sank. *"By the love for all things holy, Helios, Teta is going to alert the whole Tanit-Varin wing and grandsire's combat buddies."*

Helios was decidedly pleased with the turn of events. ***"Hum, yes, we probably have about four hours before grandsire shows up with his combat wing to help. The rest of the family will be here by dawn. I don't think there is enough space at Aurium."*** Helios rubbed his head. ***"I guess some of them will be sleeping in the woods…..."***

259

"Let's not get distracted on the sleeping arrangements, Helios. We need to eat; get out of Vallis Halden and start looking for her brothers before they get here."

"Why? We cannot search the entire mountain range by our self. We could use the help. Most importantly, who will keep our mate safe while I kill Basia when we find her?"

"Why? I would rather take care of the problem myself and not have the family involved like we are a wet hatchling."

"Well, that egg is cracked. There is no going back. Teta Ryndra will call them by the furen because she and Slymare are old friends. They are coming; you might as well like it. They love us, and they will help just like we would help them. What did you tell me about the HK2 law? Oh…. 'It's done. There is no use complaining.' Yea! That was it. So, ready your fire. They are coming. We should put them to use. Oh, ask Teta if they could catch a few aurochs and mountain goats on their way in." Keegan rubbed his temple with his hand and inwardly groaned.

The server brought out a tray laden with delicious smelling meat, seared vegetables, and a large loaf of warm bread. Ryndra picked up a plate and began to place some of the food on it. "This smells as good as it looks. Now don't be shy, Fallon. We need to eat up.

You have some family to find, and I have a family to inform."

The tavern's door opened, and a woman wearing a red hat with a long black feather stepped in. Ryndra saw her and waved her over. "Linnea, this is Keegan's life mate, Fallon Tulun, from Therus. Fallon, this is my daughter, Linnea Tanit." Fallon greeted the woman, and Keegan asked her to join them. Linnea sat, and the server brought her a drink then added another plate to the table.

When the server left, Linnea spoke. "Are we leaving to search for her brothers after we eat?"

Keegan shook his head. "It did not take long to get around."

Linnea piled meat on her plate. "I met a silver dragon going out on a search, and she told me what was going on. So, I tracked you and mother. Excellent choice, by the way. The food is marvelous here."

Keegan patted Fallon on her knee. There was no fighting it. The family was already showing up. "Yes, we will leave after we eat. There is a lot of territory to cover."

Within an hour, Linnea and Keegan were shifted and flying out of Vallis Halden. Ryndra stayed at the keep to alert the rest of the Tanit-Varin Wing.

Chapter 25

Basia Embyr: Afternoon on Einnday, Valair, Fae Realm, Calterra Mountain Range, southeast of the Blue Flower Meadow

Theron and Feron watched as they soared over the mountain range. Feron decided he would have enjoyed it more if he wasn't afraid of the dragon dropping him or stopping on a ridge to snack on him before continuing on its way. Feron watched the ground pass under him and tried to remember how to find his way back if they could escape. He could tell Theron was doing the same thing. Theron tilted his head at him and gestured to his right. Feron looked and made out a village near the fork of a small river. He gave a short nod of the head back. Theron deliberated about the village; if they escaped, they would need to avoid it. The magic land people might give them back to the dragon. Past the town, the dragon angled due east. A short while later, it flew into a cave and deposited them by the back wall opposite the cave entrance.

Basia congratulated herself as she landed in her cave. She had captured two of the whore's brothers. Now she would question them to learn where the slut had taken her beloved and how she had managed to charm him. Basia dropped them at the back of the cave and turned to walk back to the entrance. Not that there was much chance of them escaping, the drop off was a sheer rock face; unless you could fly, there was no leaving the cave.

Theron had seen the rock face around the opening. Unless they could find some rope and metal spikes, they could not climb down. He pulled himself upright and stretched his arms and legs, which had gotten cramped from being gripped in the talons of the dragon. Of all the things he could have imagined a dragon's cave to be, this was not it. When the beast turned towards the opening, he managed to get a brief gesture to his brother conveying shock. Feron returned it. Their father, Goron, swore they had a unique language between them. They had just shrugged their shoulders. They had just spent so much time with each other they almost knew what the other was thinking.

In the cavern, there were a couple of worn chairs, a table, and a bed around a large threadbare rug. What a dragon needed with furniture in dire need of restoration was odd, but the several highly decorated and probably expensive cradles that looked brand new cinched the title for weird as far as Theron was concerned. Fallon was also not here. He tilted his head at Feron with a puzzled look on his face. Feron nodded and shrugged his shoulders with his hands up. Theron moved his two index fingers back and forth in front of him. This sign between them meant, "I have an idea. Let me talk, and you play along." Feron gave a quick nod.

The dragon turned and sat down in front of the cave entrance and glared at them. "Where is the bitch who bewitched my life mate!"

"What?" Theron and Feron said in unison.

"Don't play dumb with me. I know you are her brothers. Where is she, and what has she done with my beloved life mate."

Theron was flummoxed. Who knew dragons could talk? And, he did not have the slightest clue what this dragon was talking about. He decided his best tactic was to stall and gather more information, so he returned, "You can talk?"

"Yes, of course, I can talk. I'm a silver dragon." Basia replied indignantly.

"The ones back home can't talk," Theron sighed. Basia looked at him askance.

Feron cleared his throat. "It's true, not a word. Mostly hisses."

The scales over the dragon's eyes wrinkled. "What?"

"We always thought it was because they were so little that's why they could not talk." Theron clarified as he gazed solemnly at the dragon.

Feron held up his fingers a short distance apart. "They are about this big. We catch them and put them in our pockets. We call them pants lizards. Then that's when they start hissing. No talking, just hissing. Theron, why do you think they can't talk?" Feron finished with a straight face.

"Well Feron......"

Basia roared. "I do not care about the pants lizards in the tribe lands. I want to know where that bitch sister of yours took my life mate!"

Theron smiled to himself. He had just learned the dragon could not tell if they were lying or not. It was handy information indeed. "Our sister took your life mate. Can you tell us what happened?"

"My life mate is a royal, gold dragon. He loves me deeply. We are going to have nine royal dragonettes. We are going to live at the palace. I'll make them beautiful clothes and show them off at court. Our life was going to be perfect until she showed up." Theron watched the dragon's tail twitching like one of an agitated house cat.

"Uh-huh, yes. So…. you two were together; then he was not here. Could he be lost? We could help you find him. We are good trackers."

Basia sighed in exasperation, "He was never here."

Theron feigned a perplexed look. "How could your life mate never be here?"

Smoke seeped out of Basia's nostrils, rising to the roof of the cave. "King Palorin Alvorith made a law we could not be together."

Theron quickly figured out the smoke coming out of a dragon's nose meant the dragon was angry. He stored the tidbit away. Theron put his hands on his hips. He shook his head and made a tsk-tsk sound of disapproval. "I would have been furious. It seems overly harsh."

Basia replied, "I am, and it was."

"How did this come to pass?" Theron pretended concern as he intently watched the dragon's body language.

Basia rolled her eyes. "Someone lied and said I would not leave him alone. They said I attacked him. They said he did not want to be with me, which is, of course, completely false."

The more the dragon talked, the more Theron was positive the dragon was moonstruck. "Uh-huh. Why do you think our sister had anything to do with this?"

"I saw her go with him," Basia yelled.

"What in the abyss is this overgrown lizard talking about? It's crazier than a bag of squirrels." Theron thought as he scratched his head. "Okay. So, tell me about that."

"I was flying, searching for him using a concealment spell. I heard him roar, 'My mate.' He picked her up and disappeared. I landed where he picked her up. I caught her scent. You smell a little like her, so you must be related to her. Where is she, and where is my mate!"

"Holy shite balls, sis got taken by a different dragon! We have got to make this dragon think Fallon is not after her mate, get out of here, and find her." Theron thought before replying, "That... So... That is a lot to take in. What are you called? I'm Theron, and this is my brother, Feron."

I am Marquesa Basia Embyr. Where is she!" Basia growled and stalked towards them.

"I hope this works," Theron said to himself as he tapped his fingers on his thigh. Feron saw his signal

to him and reasoned this was probably the worst plan ever, but what did they have to lose?

"Marquesa Basia, well," Theron looked at the floor of the cave and back up to her. "Basically, I don't know how to be the bearer of this, but Bellis, our best sister, already has a betrothed."

"What!" Basia yelled.

Feron groaned inwardly and let out an exasperated sigh. "Believe it. Bellis is betrothed to Boris, the bear.

Theron nodded his head. "Beyond a doubt, Bellis would never betray her beloved Boris, the bear."

Basia's head pivoted between the two. "Boris? I don't care about a bear."

Theron looked perplexed. "Baffling, because kingdom-wide Boris, the bear, is the best, bridge-builder."

Feron plastered a look of innocent, wide-eyed wonder on his face. "Oh, his business is booming. Boris builds the best bridges over brooks. Their breadth spanning babbling brooks from bank-to-bank beckon you beguilingly with their beauty."

"Oh, Boris's no buffoon; he's a brilliant, boss, bridge builder who does a brisk business," Theron exclaimed.

Basia's tail had stopped twitching. Theron considered it a good sign. "At the risk of being brusque, and besmirching your bandit boyfriend with blanket blame, I believe Bellis was bundled off by him. It's blatantly barbaric, and we beseech you to bring her back. Boris's bereaved."

Basia gnashed her teeth in frustration. *"Bellis' babbling brothers are barmy. By the First Egg! Now, I'm doing it. I need to think."* She turned and flew out of the cave.

Feron slapped his brother on the back. "Basia's befuddled."

Theron smiled. "Brilliant, badass 'B's,' Brother!"

" 'B's' are not so bad," he laughed. "When we did it to that guy, Yoni, at the Warrior camp, that was tough. 'Y's' are hard. What's the rest of your plan? Unless you have some wings, we are stuck in this cave."

Theron rubbed his hands together. "We can come up with something."

Chapter 26

Basia flew towards the river, fuming. *"Why did he take another male's mate? They don't know where she is. How can I use them to help me get him back?"* She spied some ibex grazing near a flat rock outcropping and dived down. Her concealment spell lifted causing the goats to scatter. Basia barely managed to pick one off before they darted away. *"That idiot Igreth! The charm's not lasting as long this time."* She muttered an oath as she flew towards the river. Thinking always went better on a full stomach in her favorite spot by the water. She just had to figure out how to use the brothers to her advantage.

Velli, Basia's dragon anima, stirred in the back of Basia's mind, careful not to let her become aware she was coming out from under the suppression spell. Velli felt like she had been buried under a mountain. She awoke groggy and disoriented when they had landed back in their cave with the two strange males from the tribe lands. Taking someone from the tribal lands who was not your mate was a high crime. Basia had doomed them if she got caught.

Velli sighed. Basia had long stopped listening to reason. When she refused to help Basia after the king ordered them to have no interaction with Keegan, Basia became mad with anger. Velli liked Keegan and

Helios, but Keegan was not Basia's mate. Having the king make a new law and order them to desist in approaching Keegan had been a blessing as far as Velli was concerned. Besides, he was their king, and Velli had sworn to uphold him like all dragons in Valair. What could she do when their king had called them off? It was a scant three full moons after Velli refused to help Basia, that Basia had suppressed her with a spell from the wizard, Igreth, who Basia blackmailed.

Being suppressed was the ultimate form of betrayal, and Velli was surprised at her level of anger, sadness, and a small amount of fear from Basia's duplicity. The sense of loss, a loss of trust, a loss of the female she thought Basia was, made Velli ache with a bone-deep sadness. Velli wondered how the sun could even shine because she felt such complete desolation. Mixed in with those emotions was an aching pit of shame Velli felt about what happened. How could she have let this happen? She was a dragon. She was supposed to be wiser and be a guide for Basia. All dragons had different callings, but being a guide was hers, and she had failed miserably. She felt ashamed by what had happened.

The heaviness of sleep tugged seductively at her. Velli considered giving in and admitting defeat, but in her heart, how could she call herself a silver dragon if she did? She carefully felt around and discovered she did have a tiny bit of control. While Basia was

273

distracted diving down to capture an ibex, she pushed against the concealment charm. It stopped working, as evidenced by the mountain goats scattering. A small victory, Velli decided. She weighed her options and reasoned she would wait and intervene when the time was most advantageous.

Laying on the bank of the river invisible, Basia made short work of the ibex. She licked her paws clean. A rustling of wings alerted her to the two brass dragon males flying overhead. They were scanning the area. As Basia watched them fly in a line due south, turn, and fly back north, she realized they were flying in a search pattern. She discounted it as probably a hunt for a lost villager. She spent the rest of the afternoon trying to puzzle out how she could somehow use that bitch Bellis' brothers to her advantage.

As the shadows were growing long, a boat with two Fae females drifted past. "Dulara, the sun is low in the sky, and we have caught a good many fish. We should head to Nelelune and put in there for the night. They will pay good coin for the fish."

"Aye, you are right. The dragons must not have found the one they are looking for who took the tribe males. They are still flying. Queen Valaitha will be sending out the night hunters soon to look for them. I do not want to be in the forest tonight." She shook her head and straightened out a net. "Our queen has some fearsome trackers."

"Hmph! If those tribe males are not found safe and unharmed, there will be one less silver dragon female in Valair. The little sprite said her mate has gone to fetch the assassin, Mythrum the Death Drow".

The Fae called Dulara laughed. "Oh, the news you can learn from those chatty sprites, especially when one is a mate to a Halden outpost furen and needing some fish. But did you have to give her two of our best fish, Na'Shalla?"

"Bah, sister, the news was worth the price. Now we know we must get to the village before nightfall. Besides those furen work up a hearty appetite flying messages, and the little messenger has a long way to fly to reach to the Drow lands."

"I'll set the sail. It will get us there all the quicker." Within a couple of minutes, the sail was up, and they were moving swiftly downstream out of hearing range.

Basia froze when she heard their words. A heavy weight sat in her stomach, and it was not the ibex she ate. *"How could they have known I took them? I was concealed. Shite! I have got to take them back! Maybe I could just leave and flee to the tribe lands."* Her last encounter with Mythrum played through her head. The one where he lovingly stroked his sword, Soul Taker, and talked about how nice her head would look decorating the pike railing outside the palace if she didn't leave the king's eldest nephew alone immediately. The fear returned with palpable assuredness, which almost caused her to urinate on herself as she had then.

"By all the old gods and the Horde of Ages, I am fucked," she murmured. "How am I going to get out of this?" She launched into the air and flew towards her cave. The night hunters would be out soon, and they were adept at seeing through a low-level charm for invisibility. "Maybe I could convince the males this was all a mistake. That's it! I'll charm them. That will be easy; they are males. All males like ale, food, sex, and talking about themselves. Well, sex is out." She changed direction and flew towards the village. There she shifted into her concealed human form to steal several bottles of ale. Her larder was full, so she did not need to take any food. She placed the bottles in a sturdy sack that was sitting around unguarded, shifted, and flew home.

While Basia was gone, Theron and Feron found they had plenty of time to plot and explore the odd, cave home. They discovered plates, utensils, and things more suited for a person than a dragon. Feron had shrugged his shoulders, "Maybe she ate the previous cave owner?"

Theron pointed out the dresses and other feminine-looking clothes hanging in a wardrobe. "Maybe Feron. It would account for the things we found. I'd bet anything those are her cribs. Why does she want to make her children dresses and show them off at court? Dragons don't wear dresses. Speaking of dresses, the clothes smell like a stale, sweaty Badger. Could a Badger clan woman have been taken?"

Feron was running his hand over one of the expertly crafted cribs. "Probably. I didn't know dragons needed cribs. I thought maybe eggs and a big nest. This whole thing is just weird." They did find the larder and helped themselves to the food they found. Their father's words rang in their head. "Most of the time, things are better thought out on a full stomach." If there was ever a time to be at the top of their game, this was it.

Basia arrived just after nightfall. She walked into the cave the put the sack down. "I think we might have started on the wrong foot. I was angry my mate took your sister, Bellis. I may not have been thinking clearly. Let me make it up to you. I brought back some ale."

Feron looked skeptically at the bag, that in his opinion, was too close to the dragon for him to consider retrieving. "Yea, sometimes it happens. How about you just take us home?"

Basia thought quickly. The night hunters were out. Tomorrow and probably the next day, dragons would be flying over this area of the mountain range. She would need to find a way to keep them here for a few days. "Um….It's getting dark. I don't like to fly at night."

Theron spoke up. "Okay, so, how about first thing in the morning? We need to find our sister, and you need to find your mate."

Basia broke eye contact with Theron and glanced out of the cave. She looked suspiciously like his niece, Halle, when she got caught doing something she should not have been doing. "It may be a couple of days. Wind gusts are coming across the mountains. I need to take you back when it's safe."

Theron could see Feron in his peripheral vision squint his eyes. His brother had noticed the dragon was lying too. Feron scratched his head. "Don't you need to find your mate?"

A thin wisp of smoke just escaped Basia's nostrils before it was immediately cut off. "I'll start back looking for him after I take you home."

"Do you know where he might be? We would like Bellis back." In Feron's opinion staying here a couple of days while another dragon had their sister was not an option. They would have to convince the dragon to take them back sooner.

Basia glanced nervously towards the cave entrance again. "He is probably somewhere in a cave in the mountains."

Theron wondered why she kept glancing at the cave entrance. He was beginning to suspect Basia was worried she had been followed. He walked towards the cave entrance to be blocked by Basia's clawed foot. "The winds can be strong, and I don't want you to get swept off the ledge. Why don't you try some of the Fae ale I brought back as a peace offering?"

Theron picked up the bag on the floor and brought it to the ramshackle table. There were five large bottles in the thick bag. He took one out and pried off the cork. He took a swig and handed it to Feron. The ale was some of the best he had ever tasted, rich, hearty, and fruity with just enough of a bitter edge to balance the sweeter notes of the fruit. It was also more potent than the ales back home. Feron noticed the increased alcohol content as well when his eyes opened wide after taking a deep swallow.

"Now. Isn't that better?" Basia fake purred. "Why don't you tell me all about yourselves?"

Theron saw Feron put his hand to his heart and grinned to himself. *"Drunken tavern party? Game on!"* Feron began by telling Basia an outlandish and completely fabricated tale about making the rounds at taverns in Irondenn as they each took turns drinking and adding to the story. Soon, they pretended to be drunk. Feron started singing loudly and off-key. They sang the raunchiest tavern songs they knew and made up others on the fly. Feron started dancing and tripped, staggering towards the cave entrance to have Basia shoot over to the opening to save him from tumbling off. Feron winked at his brother as Basia herded him back. Theron chuckled to himself. He knew that Feron was pretending to be drunk to gauge what the dragon would do. Basia didn't want or couldn't let anything happen to them. He guessed it was probably the second of the two. This was going to be fun! The rest of the night, they did their utmost to pester the dragon with off-key singing, horribly bad jokes, and careening close to the cave entrance to have her "rescue them." Close to morning, they had devolved from filthy songs and stories with no point to a musical farting contest.

If Theron was judging things correctly, Basia was thoroughly chaffed. While she had what he perceived to be a pleasant expression on her face, her voice was stilted, her tail was twitching, and one of the claws on her back foot was uncontrollably tapping against the cave floor. His suspicions were confirmed when the sun broke the horizon, and Basia loudly announced she would check the wind then bolted from the cave. When they were sure she was long gone, they burst out laughing and slapped each other on the back. Once they ate some food and plotted for when she came back, they lay down on some blankets they found and fell asleep.

Basia flew to the tall peak and scanned the sky while silently cursing her misfortune. The tribe males were horribly stupid, and she couldn't flame them. By the First Egg, how she desperately wanted to, but could not. Basia had to bide her time until she could return them to the tribe lands. She spotted a couple of lone dragons flying across the mountains in the morning. The early afternoon saw a squadron of older gold dragons flying in a battle formation close to her location. Her heart sank. *"By all the old gods, what have I done? If I take them back today and they call out, another dragon is going to hear them, and they will be on me in a flash. If I stay here, I'm going to get caught. If I go back and they sing another verse of "Vexing Virgin Verna" again, I don't know if I can stop myself from lighting them up. This is all that bitch, Bellis' fault. Everything was fine until she tempted my mate away, and the two-timing whore already has a mate, Boris, the bear, bridge builder. I swear by the First Egg, I'm going to kill her on sight!"*

The sun was starting to sink when Basia saw the hunter crossing a low ridge in the distance headed west. The Fae warrior was riding an enormous, brown, and black striped kadis. The great cat glided across the rise to leap a ravine in stride before continuing towards the tribe lands. Basia's heart was beating fast when she flew back to her cave.

281

Chapter 27

Keegan & Fallon, Late Einnday, Valair, Calterra Mountain Range

Helios and Nyret flew in the direction Aren had seen Theron and Feron disappear. They searched the flight path Keegan thought she might have taken and found nothing. It was late evening when they headed back towards Aurium. They met Orind Varin's wing of veteran buddies from the Red River War, flying in formation sweeping the mountain range. Orind's dragon, Cidren, eyed Fallon as he pulled abreast of Helios. Fallon held her head high and unflinchingly regarded his gaze. Helios rumbled a warning and flashed his teeth at Cidren, who yielded them space. He turned his head, motioning for Helios to take the lead position in the "V" pattern. "Hope your cave is big," he rumbled.

"Shifted, yes, there is room. We should hunt on the way in," Helios returned.

Cidren glided to Helios' right. "There is no need. The hunt was good. We have brought plenty of supplies and enough meat to feed two battalions of ravenous shifted dragon warriors or the Tanit-Varin wing." He smiled smugly before continuing. "It might be wise to eat before we go to your cave."

Helios dipped his head in acknowledgment. They continued flying northwest until Helios spied his destination, the waterfall that fed into a lake near his cave. He glided down to land on the shore. When all had landed, their dragons pulled an assortment of cattle, large tuna, mountain goats, and aurochs out of their hordes. Cidren deposited a dead young bull in front of Helios. "Would your tribe land's mate like a fat goat?"

Fallon watched as the rest of the dragons were ripping apart carcasses with gusto. Fallon concluded the spectacle was as impressive as it was disquieting. She stood next to Helios and schooled herself into a semblance of stoicism. She did not want Keegan's family to think she was uneasy about dragons, well…being dragons. Fallon called on her experience dealing with shifted bears and wolves. She knew acting fearful around them was not wise. Her wolf cousins told her it was best when dealing with a shifter in their alternate form to present an unfazed and calm demeanor. Their wise words had served her well in dealing with the animal half of the shifter's nature in the past. She replied to Cidren, "No, thank you for asking."

Linnea's dragon, Nyret, watched the exchange and swallowed a mouthful of tuna. "Cidren, those of Therus, are like many of the Fae. They eat cooked meat."

He cocked his head to the side, listening to Nyret. "Hum….yes. I can flame it for you if you would like. The smell of burning hair might put you off your appetite, though."

"That's very generous of you to offer, but I'm fine," Fallon returned. Cidren turned his attention to the goat in front of him and finished it off in three bites.

Fallon decided an analytical approach to the situation would be the best course of action, so she busied herself noting how Helios used his claws to hold his meal and what parts he seemed to favor. Helios noticed her watching in between, ripping off a foreleg of the bull and eating it. She had stayed close to him ever since they landed. He could tell she was a little apprehensive but seemed to be taking things in stride. He was proud of his mate's fortitude. The sight of sixteen dragons eating with zeal was probably not the easiest thing to watch. When they finished, they waded into the lake and washed. After Helios cleaned, Keegan suggested he catch a few fish Fallon could eat later. Helios waded around, snaking his head under the water periodically. A few minutes later, he had the needed trout stored in his horde. Reaching the shore, he knelt, and Fallon climbed up to her perch on his back. A short flight later, they arrived at Aurium.

Upon arrival, Orind and Keegan introduced Fallon to the rest of the Fifth Gold Wing veteran warriors. Orind explained there were originally twenty members of the Fifth; one had passed away, and the other five could not make the hunt. Both males and females of the Fifth greeted Fallon pleasantly, but several seemed aloof. Orind noticed it as the introductions concluded and nudged Fallon. "Don't worry about the ones who seem standoffish. They just are restless being this close to the tribe lands and having to hold themselves back from flaming it again," He cackled.

Keegan gave an exasperated sigh that tapered into an annoyed growl. "Grandfather. Such was not necessary."

Fallon patted Keegan's arm. "Ah, shyn h'jarta, it is very…old…history." She stressed the word "old" and gave Orind a big smile.

Linnea burst out laughing. "She has you there, Orind."

Orind laughed, "You have a good mate, grandson, spunky and sharp as a tooth."

Keegan kissed her on the head. "Yes, I do." He looked at the dragon shifters standing awkwardly around in his cave. "Why don't I show you the thermal pool? I think you will enjoy it after a long day of flying."

"Thermal pool?" A female shifter called from the back. "I've got a couple of barrels of summer mead for a pool party." Her offer was met with thunderous agreement as the Fifth followed Keegan to the heated waters. It was not long afterward Fallon heard the shifters laughing and splashing around in the water.

Keegan returned, smiling. "The mead and the pool should keep them occupied for a while. Let me cook you the trout Helios caught."

"Sounds delicious, and I'd love to help," Fallon replied while they walked to the kitchen area.

Linnea stretched. "I'm going to enjoy the pool and drink some mead."

While they prepared the meal, Kegan reassured Fallon they would find her brothers. With the strongholds on the west of Valair sending search parties out, the retired Fifth, and the Tanit-Varin Wing who would descend on them the next day, Keegan was confident it was just a matter of time before the twins were located.

"I agree. I don't think Basia can stay hidden for long." Fallon replied as she carried her plate and mug to the table by the cave entrance.

Keegan followed her holding a tankard of mead. The sun was setting in the west, sending up its last tendrils of red and gold to the sky. A movement on the ridge in the distance caught Keegan's eye. Two Fae night hunters, one riding a spotted kadis and the other mounted on a sable hyrcania, surveyed the land to the west. They were wearing matt black leather armor, which would blend seamlessly into the approaching night. Their curved swords of Drow, ebony steel were slung over their backs. Behind each of their saddles lay a neatly rolled net. The warrior riding the hyrcania gestured to the south as her mount, a giant wolf-like beast, stretched his nose into the west wind. The female Fae riding the huge spotted kadis, which was swishing its tail in annoyance, nodded her head. She picked up the reins on her agitated cat, and they disappeared over the ridge heading south.

Keegan set his tankard down. "Fallon, the Fae Queen, has sent her night hunters out to search. There were two of them on the far ridge. They turned and headed south. With those female warriors looking for your brothers, the search will be short. I need to let the others know shyn h'jarta. I'll be right back."

Keegan strode to the cavern, where his ears told him the party was in full swing. Orind Varin was soaking in the warm water near a marble table set in the water. He took a drink from his mug then put it on the table. Keegan noticed several other tables in the water with an assortment of cups and goblets dotting their surface. *"Where did those tables come from?"* He thought.

"I don't know. They are not ours." Helios scratched his head. *"The Fifth must have pulled them out of their hordes. At their age, who knows what all they have collected and stashed in them."* Keegan had to admit, having a table in the water to set a beverage on was a clever idea. Helios rumbled, *"Yes. It is a good idea. I'll be on the lookout for one. Our little mate may like to enjoy a cool beverage while she soaks."*

Orind saw Keegan walking towards him with a determined stride. "Problem, Grandson?"

"No. The Fae Queen has sent her night hunters out. I saw one on a spotted kadis and another on a hyrcania riding together heading south."

The noise from the Fifth dropped. Orind ran his hand over the top of his head. "Hum, interesting the Queen of the Fae, Valaitha Ellamaur Sylvi, would send her hunters out on a couple of tribe males being taken daft, female silver dragon. The hyrcania following a scent?"

Keegan shook his head. "No. He was checking the wind blowing from Therus, but it was not following a trail."

"They will catch it soon. The hunt will be short with them joining in the search."

"Assuredly. I look forward to having this resolved so I can focus on the h'jarta kayzaire with my life mate."

Orind took a drink of mead. "I expect so. It is good you found your other half. Not all do. Your grandmother and I did not. We care deeply for each other, as a bonded couple, but we are not life mates."

Keegan looked surprised. He did not know his paternal grandparents were not life mates. Orind continued, "Yes, it's true. I never found my life mate despite a long shyn esari. I was very taken with your grandmother's ability to pin me down as a dragon." He cackled and slapped his thigh. "Teovanna's not too bad at wrestling in her two-legger form either. She is one scrappy and passionate female!" He turned slightly and pointed to a healed pink burn on his butt. "I still have a burn scar on my ass cheek from the last time we were canoodling. Those Rogoth females are fierce! That's why I work out with the Fifth. We may be pushing the second-millennium mark, but I need to stay at the top of my game to make the female in my life happy. Am I right!" He hollered. Orind's statements did not go unanswered by the rest of the shifters who raised their mugs high, cheering and hooting.

"Go Grammie Teo!" Helios chuckled.

Keegan smiled and shook his head. "Good talk, Grandfather."

"You need any tips and tricks, Grandson, just let me know. I have hundreds of years of practice at this, and your grandsire has some moves sharp as the First Tooth." He wiggled his eyebrows suggestively. Guffaws of laughter and a couple of bawdy comments echoed behind Orind by a few of the retired fighting wing.

"I've got this, thanks," Keegan replied over his shoulder. He chuckled as he sought out Linnea, who was lounging next to a couple of women of the Fifth.

"I need another favor," Keegan stated when he approached them.

"What can I help you with?" Linnea replied.

"My mate could use another change of clothes, and mine are too large for her. Would you happen to have something she could borrow until we can make arrangements for her wardrobe?"

"Sure, if she does not mind wearing red tunics. That's most of my clothes."

"Red would be perfect, Aunt Linnea."

The two females next to Linnea also offered up some clothing. Neither wanted the garments returned. The redhead told Keegan, "My dragon has been complaining our horde needs to be thinned down of clothing, weapons, and books. So please keep the garments. She might like a cloak too. Zeni, don't we have a cloak or two lying around….Seventy-three! Why do we have seventy-three?...... Oh, Yea. You are right. I forgot about the cloak phase we went through a few hundred years ago."

Linnea had her hand over her mouth to hide her grin. Nyret materialized two red tunics and two black breeches on the table in front of Keegan. It was quickly followed by a pile of clothes, three cloaks, and an assortment of slippers and boots from the other two women.

The other woman waved him off. "Keep them. I have far too many."

Keegan thanked them while Helios placed the clothing into their horde so it would be easier to carry. He left the Fifth to their fun and sought out Fallon. He found her finishing up her supper and bringing the plate to the kitchen. "Shyn h'jarta would you like some mead?"

"No, thank you, though. I think I am going to wash and turn in. It has been a long day. With your grandfather and his friends here, where do I need to sleep." Fallon was rolling up the sleeves on her tunic in preparation to wash the plate and utensils.

"You may sleep wherever you like. Where you slept last night is fine. You are certainly welcome to sleep in my chamber, and Linnea could have the guest room. I am fine sleeping on the rugs on the floor."

Fallon debated the choices for a few moments. It did not seem fair to take up an entire room to herself when they had come to help find her brothers. "There is no need for it. Your bed is large enough for us both to sleep in easily. Besides, you need to get plenty of rest; tomorrow might be a long day." She looked at him from over the washbasin. "But Keegan, know sleep means sleep, not bed sport. How will that be for you?"

Keegan was thrilled at the prospect of sharing a bed with his mate. Helios was pleased too and rumbled contentedly. "Shyn h'jarta, the pace of the h'jarta kayzaire is entirely up to you, as we discussed. Of course, I would be the happiest dragon in Valair if you wanted to have sex with me tonight, but I know it is moving far too fast. I am more than content to have you next to me in our bed. I will not push you. When you desire it, just say the words, or word, point....maybe a note?" He flashed her a dazzling smile, which made her heart beat faster. "How do they do it in Therus?"

Fallon grinned and shook her head; she knew he was teasing her. "They speak the words most of the time."

"And other times?" Keegan walked behind her and nuzzled the back of her neck and kissed her earlobe.

Fallon turned to him and stroked the exposed part of his chest. "Shyn h'jarta, I guess you will find out." She turned back to wash the remaining dishes.

Keegan groaned; he was tempted to pick her up, carry her to the bedroom and kiss her senseless to start. His cock which strained against the fabric of his breeches had other ideas that sounded even better. He needed a distraction, or he was going to do something dumb. "After you wash up, Linea and a couple of females from the Fifth have some garments for you to use until we can get you a wardrobe."

"That was very kind of them. I'll be sure to thank them."

Fallon washed up and politely declined the invitation to join the Fifth in the thermal pool. Keegan showed her the clothes. They were finely crafted and in pristine condition. Fallon found a silky light blue nightshirt among the garments. She slipped it on and climbed into bed. No sooner than her head hit the pillow, she was asleep. Keegan spent some time with the Fifth before turning in for the night. Fallon was sleeping peacefully when he quietly slid into bed next to her. Her scent perfumed the air with a sweet headiness that pulled him to her. He groaned and rolled over to face the door.

Chapter 28

Fallon awoke curled against a firm wall of spicey, slightly smoky warmth. She murmured contentedly and snuggled in deeper. The dreamland beckoned her back. She brushed it off in favor of the pleasantly warm spot where lay. *"This is the best bed."* She mused, sighing. Then she remembered she had to find her brothers. Slumber receded, and memories of the previous day emerged to banish sleep. Fallon sighed, this time out loud.

"Good morning shyn h'jarta. You were sleeping so peacefully I didn't want to wake you," Keegan purred while he stroked her hair.

Fallon opened her eyes to find herself staring at Keegan's chest, a hand's width away from her face. She looked up from where she was wedged against him to see him watching her. "Oh, I didn't oversleep, did I? Why didn't you wake me?"

"I have my life mate in my bed for the first time, and she is cuddled up next to me. Why would I wake her?" He teased. When he saw the look of concern flash across her face, he hastily added. "The Fifth is just starting to move around. It is still early. I would have roused you soon." He kissed her on the top of her head. "I'll leave you to your morning routine. I'm

296

going to see what our guests are up to and start breakfast. I'll see you in a few minutes." He rolled out of bed, dressed, and left.

Fallon sat on the edge of the bed and stretched before pushing the covers off her lap and rising. She dressed and straightened the bedclothes before leaving the chamber. The great room was bustling with activity. There were canopied beds of various shapes and sizes with elaborate bed curtains set out in an orderly pattern around the room. Fallon watched as one of the wing finished dressing. She walked away from the bed, and it vanished. Linnea had come out of the bedroom behind Fallon and stopped next to her. She saw Fallon's eyes get wide when the bed disappeared. "Her dragon put it back in their horde," Linnea explained.

"Handy!"

"Definitely!" Linnea said, smiling.

"Thank you for letting me borrow some clothes."

"You're welcome, and they are yours. I hope they are of use to you."

"Yes, they will be. Thanks again. Would you like some breakfast?" Fallon replied as she gestured with her arm to the kitchen.

"Yes. Today might be a long one searching for Basia"

They made their way to the kitchen and joined in with Keegan and Orind, who were preparing food for the Fifth. Soon they had boiled eggs, bread, fruit, and thinly sliced meat ready. While everyone ate, Orlind and Tedda Avondale pulled out a large, detailed map of the Calterra mountain range. Tedda suggested flying north to south sweeps of the area from the watch post north of Aurium to River Halden south of Nelune. She pointed to the map and indicated they would work their way towards the western border.

Orind nodded his head. "Tedda Avondale always has a solid tactical plan. Her search pattern sweeps will overlap the Halden strongholds, which will be flying grid search patterns in their provinces. We will leave in thirty minutes."

Half an hour later, Fallon was seated on Helios, and they were soaring over the mountain range. They saw and spoke to several dragon patrols from the west strongholds. The patrols had no new information about the males from Therus. After the noon break Helios spotted a large wing of dragons flying west. The approaching wing changed direction to intercept the Fifth. Moments later, the Tanit-Varin wing soared alongside the Fifth. Laidon's dragon, Joth, glided next to Helios. He glanced at Fallon and nodded his head.

"Son." He inclined his head towards Cidren. "Where do we need to start looking, Father?"

Cidren explained the search pattern they were using. Joth ducked his head and flew back to the Tanit-Varin wing, who had taken up position to the Fifth's right. The two wings searched the rest of the day and found nothing. The search party of dragons from Fell Halden they encountered in the early afternoon had no news of Theron and Feron. The sun was dipping towards the horizon when they turned to fly back to the waterfall. On their way, they encountered two brass dragons from Vallis Halden who were heading back to their stronghold. Cidren called out to them to join their wing for the evening feed. They looked at each other and readily agreed, taking position at the back of the "V" formation.

Cidren winked at Fallon. "Dragons talk if their bellies are full," he smiled slyly.

At the waterfall, the Tanit-Varin wing pulled an assortment of meat out of their hordes. The two brass dragons' mouths had dropped open at the volume of food that appeared. Cidren tossed the brass female a boar while one of the Fifth materialized two goats in front of the male brass dragon. Fallon stood near Helios as he devoured a massive tuna. Helios sliced off a section of the fish and stored it in the horde for Fallon's supper later.

When they finished eating, the two brass dragons expressed their thanks for the meal. Cidren and the members of the Fifth waved them off and told them they had served and appreciated their commitment to Valair. As they chatted, they learned in addition to the Fae night hunters, Mythrum had been summoned from the Drow lands. Almost every eyebrow raised at that gold nugget of information. The brass dragons told them the night hunters suspected Basia was somewhere south of their current position in a cave near the tribe land border. The hunters were confident they would close in on her location in two days to coincide with the dark Drow's arrival. The dragon areal searches would help keep her pinned down until the hunters could zero in on her location.

"Hum," Orind mused out loud, "a kill order was issued."

The brass female spoke, "The Fae night hunters carry binding nets."

Tedda's dragon, Hail, rumbled, "Public execution." The wings sounded their concurrence and nodded their heads in agreement.

At Aurium, after both wings shifted, Keegan introduced Fallon to Laidon Varin, his father, Dane, his brother, and the rest of his family, the Tanit-Varin wing. Laidon told Keegan that Kalasa had gone to Shal H'jarta, the Dragon Dynasty's capital, to see their king, Palorin Alvorith. His sisters were visiting with a cousin.

Introductions made, the Tanit-Varin wing set about making a base camp kitchen which could have easily a rivaled the Royal Culinary Academy, who traveled with King Palorin on official Dynasty business. Huge smokers and fire pits being set up by the lake at the base of the mountain was a promise of tasty food to come.

Fallon watched the coordinated chaos unfold in the cave and down by the lake. It reminded her of the Tulun pack gatherings. There was laughter, bustling activity, and abundant quantities of food. The only thing missing was Theron and Feron daring each other to steal the tastiest morsels from under the cooks' noses. Keegan brushed up against her arm. "They can be a lot, but they mean well."

"They remind me of the Tulun wolf pack, my mother's family; big loud, ready to help, and there is always plenty of delicious food."

Keegan laughed. "They do sound like the Tanit-Varin wing. Speaking of tasty food. How about some seared tuna?"

Fallon's stomach growled. "It sounds wonderful."

Keegan guided her through the groups talking and milling around into the kitchen. Helios materialized the sizeable chunk of bluefin tuna onto the prep table. Keegan reached for a knife but was blocked by his cousin, Pertti. "I got this. Why don't you and your life mate spend some time with your father and brother? I'll bring the food out when it's ready."

"Thanks, Pertti." Keegan grabbed some mugs and a jug of cider. He motioned for Dane and Laidon, who were talking with Silvanner, to follow him. Keegan nudged Fallon. "If Uncle Silvanner offers you any fermented beverage, either refuse it or don't drink it. His brews are strong enough to lay a dragon low. There are stories. I'll tell you later."

Fallon wrapped her hand around his forearm. "Duly noted: Avoid Uncle Silvanner's concoctions. I would love to hear a couple of those stories. Do they involve you?"

"Helping contain the mischief they caused, yes, they do include me," he grinned.

Laidon and Dane separated from Silvanner and joined them at the table by the cave entrance. Keegan poured the cider; then they talked long past Pertti's bringing out a plate of food for Fallon and past the sun disappearing in the west. Laidon asked Fallon general questions about her family and assured her they would find her brothers. When Dane inquired about her brothers, Fallon told him about the twins and regaled them with a couple of their exploits.

Laidon shook his head, laughing. "Your poor parents."

Dane's mouth was hanging open. "Our parents would have sealed us in a cave until we were four hundred years old if we did anything like that. I almost feel a little sorry for Basia."

"It sounds like Basia Embyr picked the wrong two males to abduct." Laidon reached out and patted her hand. "Don't worry, daughter to be; they will be found."

Fallon agreed. "I think it would be impossible for her to stay hidden for much longer since so many search for her."

The moon was painting the Calterra in shades of silver before they left to seek their bed. Keegan pulled Fallon to him and kissed the top of her head. "Tomorrow shyn h'jarta, we will look some more. She cannot hide forever." Fallon would have agreed, but she was already asleep.

Chapter 29

Basia, Skewday evening, Valair, Fae Realm

Basia was dreading going back to her cave even though the sun was sitting on the horizon and the night hunters would be on the move soon. She canted her head to look at the sky. It was clear. She had counted no less than five dragon units searching for her. It was more than she saw yesterday, Einnday. It was concerning. If she continued to stay out past nightfall, there was no doubt the hunters would find her.

As much as she wanted and needed to leave, the thought of dealing with those two, horrible, idiot tribesmen seemed like a fate worse than being captured by the Fae. Their preposterous questions, loud off-key singing, and nearly non-stop idiocy had made killing them look like a plausible option. She had briefly considered flaming and eating them, but their frequent bouts of farting made her suspect they might have a contagious disease. To limit her exposure to them, she stayed near the cave entrance. Her cavern would have to be magically cleansed after they left, and it was going to set her back a few gold coins. Maybe if she had consulted the scrolls and crystals of enlightenment at the athenaeum, she would have learned how utterly moronic tribe males were.

Probably another reason why the Obsidian Oaks were planted, she mused. The sun sunk lower in the sky. She could put it off no longer. The dragons would be calling off the search for the day, and the night hunters would start stirring soon. She groaned and flew home.

**

Feron pushed back from the table and loosened his belt a notch. "I'm stuffed."

"Did you try some of this?" Theron turned the bottle around. "It's Sparkling Sprites Social Elixir: Select Frost Berry by Silvanner Varin Esquire. Ooh.... fancy!" He handed the bottle over. A gold dragon flanked the blue script. Under the name was a picture of a tiny sprite with translucent wings, cap askew on its head, sprawled gracelessly under a bluebell. There was a wee, gold goblet lying to the side in the grass.

Feron chuckled. "Looks like it's a favorite with sprites." He rubbed his belly. "I'm full. Let's open it later." He stood and stretched. The light was turning a softer color outside the cave. "She's going to be here soon. I don't know about you, Brother, but this has been the most fun I've had in a long time. Well, except for being trapped in a cave by a crazy dragon who might eat us. That does put a little damper on it."

Theron was rubbing his hands together gleefully. "But she can't hurt us. She has to keep us safe. Honestly, if we didn't have to find Fallon, I'd be happy to stay here at least a whole moon cycle. I have so many ideas!"

"About that, Theron, I have something I want to try this evening." They spent the next few minutes talking and laughing as Feron lined out his plan.

"Brilliant, Brother!" Theron poured some of the ale over himself and awaited Basia's arrival. When the sun sank below the horizon, Theron began to sing off-key "Barkeep Barry's Barley Beer." With Feron singing the chorus quizzing Theron about how many barrels of barley beer Berry brewed.

Basia inwardly groaned, *"By the First Egg! Do they ever shut up? At least it's not Vexing Virgin Verna, who if the song is anything to go by is the sluttiest female in the tribe lands."*

"Marquessa Basia, home at last." Theron attempted a bow and drunkenly careened to the right and into a chair which he petted and talked to. "You're fine. Just don't get in the way. I'm talking." He pulled himself upright and straightened his tunic as he eyed Basia. "How....how.....is the......" He thought for a second and patted his cheek while he looked up at the cave ceiling. "The...er..." he moved his arms back and forth in front of him, "you know the...um..." he puffed out his cheeks and blew. "The moving air." He snapped or tried to snap his fingers a couple of times unsuccessfully. "Yep, that's it, the moving air. How's it doing?"

Basia looked perplexed. "Moving air? What, the...the wind?"

"Yep, that's it." He pointed at her, and stagger-turned to Feron. "Hey, Feron, she found the wind word."

Feron farted loudly. "Great! Because I broke it."

Theron fanned his hand in front of his face. "Is the wind still too fast? Right now, I could use some of it in here. Shit balls Feron, stop eating so much meat! So Markesta....er..Marches...well... Markeesi Basia is the wind too fast? We would like to go home if you pleases." He drew himself up and crossed his arms, as he tried to look distinguished.

Basia stood by the cave entrance, her right talons were twitching and plucking at her left forearm. *"By the Great Horde! I cannot stay in this cave with them tonight. They are going to drive me insane. Oh, By the Egg, the stench! I've got it. I'll use a sleep charm on them!"* Basia reached into the horde and found nothing. No horde, no charm, nothing, just a black pit. A slight panic set in as she rummaged around, trying to figure out where her horde was and how to access it.

Velli had regained more control and watched the spectacle unfold, with the two tribe males clearly pretending to be drunken idiots. She projected it to Basia as fact. She reinforced that they were telling the truth and were, in fact, idiots. So Basia bought their performance as truth, without question. Velli managed to hide the horde from Basia while she was distracted. The dragon watched curiously as Feron stalked up to Basia while she searched for the horde. As he drew near, Feron let loose a blood-curdling scream. "AAAWW! Cat balls." He brushed his hand by his ear several times and mumbled to himself.

Basia jumped when he screamed. Her head hit the roof of the cave and she fell to the floor with a crash.

"The abyss!" Basia roared.

Velli grinned. *"These two…these two are delightful."* She thought before she disappeared into the back of Basia's unconsciousness.

Theron seemed nonplused by the event. Feron wandered back to the table and began to drink while repeatedly brushing his hand by his ear. "Oh, yea, he does that from time to time." Theron sat a bottle on the table then tried to pry the cork off. "He hasn't had his medicine in …well a while. We found him under a tree and his…um, heck. What is the word?" Theron put the bottle down and held his hand up around his head, mimicking putting a helmet off and on. "His um….heck,…head mitten? Yea! His head mitten was dented after a battle."

"I've been hit in the head plenty." Feron looked at him fiercely. "I told you it started after I was sick when we went through the Bison Clan village where they were all shitting uncontrollably."

Theron put the bottle between his thighs and continued to wrestle with the cork. "I thought that was when you started farting so much."

"I'm going to kill them! I knew they were disease-ridden! Shite!….. By the goddess' pink ass, I can't kill them." Basia reflected while she rubbed her head.

"Okay, let's sing. You don't scream when we sing. She can't hit the roof again. It might chip her…um..her head…nubbies." Theron held two fingers up by the side of his head like horns. "We were only halfway through the beer party song." Theron looked wistfully at Feron. "I love that song."

"Singing? How about some more ale? It might help." Basia offered, desperate to find something to shut them up. Her nervous tic was back, and she was plucking at her left forearm again.

Feron's eyes lit up, and he squealed excitedly, "I know. I know. We can do this one again." He drew in a deep breath and belted out,

> "From towns near and far,
> they stumble to her bar.
> Her hand they'll 'nare win.
> It's Verna, the vexing virgin...."

Basia felt a stabbing pain. She yelped and discovered that she had plucked out one of her scales. She started hopping up and down, shrieking. "Shut up! By the old gods just SHUT UP! What will it take for you to shut up?"

Feron calmly eyed her dramatics. "Take us home or so help me; I'll sing about Verna. All. Night. Long." He emphasized each word and looked her in the eye.

"It's dark. We can't go now!" Basia implored.

Feron drew in a deep breath. Basia waved her arms back and forth. "Okay, okay, I'll take you back to the tribe lands tomorrow evening."

Feron crossed his arms and began,

> "The barkeep's name was Tandy.
> By faith, the ole sot, was randy.
> She swung a rock which crushed his
> cock....."

"Stop, just stop. I swear it on my entire horde. I swear I will take you to the tribe lands tomorrow evening."

Feron glared at her. "You will take us back to exactly where you found us; you will take us back unharmed, leave us unharmed, and leave the lands of Therus."

"Yes. I swear it. Just shut up." She rubbed her bicep where she had plucked out the scale.

"Deal," Feron and Theron both said at once. They sat down at the back of the cave and waited.

Chapter 30

Keegan & Fallon, Mittelday, Valair, Calterra Mountain Range, Aurium

Hair tickling his nose woke Keegan out of a deep sleep. Fallon lay in his arms. Her quiet breathing told him she still dozed. He drew in her scent and watched her slumber. He was ready for the matter to be resolved with Basia. The sooner his mate's brothers were found, the sooner he could devote all his time to the h'jarta kayzaire. Lying beside her and not acting on his amorous desires was difficult, but he knew it would be worth the wait. Besides, he told himself they had hundreds of years to pleasure each other, a couple of weeks or a moon cycle was nothing.

Keegan felt Helios rustling. *"Good morning, Helios."*

"Morning, Keegan. I found the second h'jarta kayzair gift we should give Fallon." He held up an elaborately carved black dagger with a moonstone in the hilt. The knife was slightly smaller but matched the Drow blade he carried.

"The Drow mating blades. An excellent idea Helios!"

"She liked yours; now she has the mate to your blade. Very fitting." Helios smiled. He turned his head to the side. *"The wings are starting to move about, and I smell….."* he took a deep breath, *"smoked salmon. Divine!"*

Keegan nuzzled Fallon's neck and left a trail of light kisses from her earlobe to her shoulder. She murmured and snuggled against him brushing her thigh across his stiff cock. *"Hmm"* Keegan softly groaned to himself. *"This is the sweetest torture."* He continued kissing her until her eyes opened. "Good morning shyn h'jarta."

"Mmm, I could get used to being awakened like this every morning," Fallon replied as she nuzzled his chest while her fingers played with his bicep.

They stayed wrapped in each other's arms for a few minutes until Keegan heard the volume level from the wings in the great room going up. "I am afraid Beloved; we must rise and meet the day." He gave her one last kiss on the shoulder and rolled out of bed, followed by Fallon.

"I have something for you." Helios placed the Drow blade in his hand, and he gave it to Fallon.

Fallon took the knife and pulled it from its sheath. The carving on the black blade glinted in the light. The handle fit perfectly in her hand. It was well balanced

313

and felt light as air. "Keegan, it's exquisite. It looks like yours."

"It's a Drow mating blade. Bonded Drow wear matched blades. This set was given to me by a friend so I could gift my mate with the matching dagger. Accepting it means it is a gift as part of the h'jarta kayzaire. It does not signify we are bonded."

Fallon hugged him. "I love it. I'm wearing it today."

He kissed her forehead. "A beautiful blade for a beautiful woman." He grabbed his clothes and put them on. "I'll meet you in the great room soon." He left the chamber, pulling the door shut behind him. Fallon followed him soon after with her new dagger adorning her belt.

They ate breakfast as Tedda and Orind pointed to locations on the map they had covered the previous day and discussed where they would be searching today. By the end of the day, if Basia had not been found, they would finish at the border with Therus before heading for Aurium.

The two wings shifted and began their search. The day progressed much like the previous day. They encountered a couple of search parties who had no new information. At the noon break, a silver and a brass dragon from Vallis Halden joined them. They learned from the stronghold warriors the Fae night hunters had picked the scent of a silver female dragon by a river, north of Nelelune. The Nelelune village watch had sent a report about stolen ale, and food stuffs to Fell Halden. It was believed this was Basia, as the scent where the items were stolen was the same as by the river. The hunters were converging on the area around the village. The silver male finished by saying. "With dragons in the air during the day and the hunters searching at night. Her time is short. King Palorin Alvorith has ordered her to be taken alive and delivered to a Halden for immediate transport to the Royal Court in Shyn H'jarta. The tribe land males are not to be harmed and are to be taken to the Royal Court as well."

Fallon nudged Helios. "Why would my brothers be taken to the Royal Court and not let go to Therus?"

"Probably the same reason why you will have to swear an oath of secrecy and have a binding charm placed on you. Your brothers have seen Valair, and they cannot take its knowledge with them to pass out either intentionally or unintentionally. Do not worry, little mate; the oath binding charm will not harm them or you."

The rest of the afternoon did not reveal the hiding place of Basia. While the Fifth and the Tanit-Varin Wings flew over the Calterra mountains, Basia was eagerly awaiting the sun to get close to the horizon, so she could take the two disgusting tribe males back to where she found them. She decided she would wash in the river after she unburdened herself of them. Basia was positive they suffered from some malady. When the sun had settled low enough in the sky, she took them and flew towards Therus.

**

The two wings had kept to their search pattern and now found themselves at the border by midafternoon. There, they used a group invisibility charm. In an instant, anyone in Valair watching them would have seen the two huge wings of dragons vanish. Members of the wings would see each other, but those who had not said the group invisibility spell could not see them.

Fallon shifted in her spot on Helios' back. "Helios, since we are this close, could we go to the blue flower meadow and see if Aren is still there? I want to tell them the search continues for Theron and Feron. They are probably anxious."

Nyret had been flying close to Helios in the formation for the last two and half days. She had deduced from listening to Fallon talk that Aren was the Bear Clan shifter male's name who was their mate. She and Linnea had also been watching Keegan and Fallon to determine how well they got along. Linnea and Nyret had spent the better part of a year talking with the elders and examining the scrolls and crystals at the Athenaeum Contemplari to learn everything there was to know about the lands of Therus, its people, and dragon shifter mating bonds. Linnea now felt confidant she knew enough about how this might work she was willing to take a chance on the Bear Clan male. Seeing how happy Keegan and Fallon were, having just met, reinforced her decision.

"They might meet our Bear Clan warrior mate. We should go. Maybe he will be shifted. He is the fluffiest bear!" Nyret sent Linnea.

Linnea smiled, *"Good idea."*

Nyret snaked her head towards Helios. "It would help them not worry and keep them from doing something foolish like trying to enter Valair. I think it is a good idea to let them know the search continues. I'll go with you and remain hidden."

Keegan sensed Fallon's concern. It probably would be a good idea to update Aren as much as possible about how the search was going. Keegan weighed the options.

"Our little mate is right. We should probably stop; we are very close to the place where we found her. It is not out of our way, and the males do not present a danger we cannot easily overcome," Helios spoke in his mind to Keegan.

"Okay we will fly by and assess the area. If there are only a couple of the Bear males present, we will shift and walk over. We do not need the wings going. It may make the bear shifters nervous." Keegan sent back.

"Agreed the Fifth might be a little flame happy being in the lands they once battled."

Helios rumbled "Agreed." to Nyret. The Fifth and the Varin Tanit Wings, however, took some convincing. By the end of the exchange, the wings agreed to remain close to the border and not go with Keegan and Fallon.

Closer to the blue flower meadow Helios and Nyret peeled off the "V" formation to make their way towards the meadow. A short flight later, it came into view. They glided over the tree line of Valair to keep their shadows in the forest. They spied three males just inside the forest on the west of the field. Helios banked to the east and found a spot to land. Fallon slid off, and Keegan shifted. As they approached the Obsidian Oaks, Keegan took her hand. The oaks drew back their branches to allow them passage. Keegan quickly glanced skyward and saw Nyret flying over the trees. The movement across the meadow caught Aren's attention. He watched as Fallon and the male from Valair approached. Aren, Sami, and Bodhran walked into the field to meet them. Fallon greeted each of them by name.

Aren clasped Keegan's arm. "Have you found Theron and Feron?"

Keegan dropped Aren's arm. "The search continues, but the area where they might be is narrowed down. Many in Valair search for them. They will be found soon."

Bodhran nudged Fallon's arm. "How are you doing, Fallon? I know you must be worried about your brothers."

"I am well, Bodhran. We are searching for them, as do many in Valair. It should not be much longer. How are you and Aren's den fairing?" She shifted and wrapped her hand under Keegan's arm, and he patted her hand.

Bodhran watched the interplay between Fallon and Keegan. He noticed the clothes she had on were not ones he had seen her wear before. She wore a vest that reached down to her knee in a swirling, blue pattern with silver threads. At her waist was a dagger matching the male's. Under the vest, she wore a fitted shirt, breeches, and boots. She looked rested. There was nothing in her scent that seemed off. There was a little stress in her voice when she spoke about her brothers, but he reasoned it might be normal considering what had happened to them. As far as he could tell, she seemed pleased to be with the male from Valair. It appeared Keegan was equally as happy and making sure her needs were being met. If Fallon had found her life mate in Valair, he was glad for her.

"Have there been any other problems, or have you seen anything unusual?" Keegan asked.

Aren felt a tingling and the hairs on the back of his neck started to rise. Tyr had his nose in the air and was edgy. ***"Get back to the trees, Brother."***

Aren held up his hand. "Get into the tree line. Somethings off."

Chapter 31

Keegan nodded, and they moved towards the trees. Helios extended his senses. ***"He's right. I feel something. By the First Horde! I think it's the Queen of Stink! And we can't shift! We need to get Nyret's attention."***

"Run!" Keegan called as he snatched up Fallon, flung her over his shoulder then sprinted for the tree line. Aren, Bodhran, and Sami were right on his heels.

Fallon picked her head up from where she was slung over his shoulder to see her brothers tumble to the ground from the talons of a silver dragon. They hit the ground rolling before jumping up and running towards them in the wake of the silver dragon.

"Dragon!" Fallon yelled as she watched her brothers tumble across the meadow. The silver dragon roared and flew towards them. She flicked her head to the side to see the safety of the tree line still too far out. A quick glance skyward showed Nyret on an intercept course, but she was out of range to help. "We are not going to make it," she shouted.

Aren reached in his pouch and grabbed out a round areal illuminator. "Keep going. I'll slow it down." He barked as the three men raced on. He turned to face the approaching dragon. *"Tyr, we have one shot."*

Tyr was standing in his mind snarling. ***"We are one, Brother!"*** The sound of Tyr's and Aren's battle cry erupted from him in a voice like thunder that resounded off the tree line across the meadow. He readied himself and waited.

"Helios, I need the sleep spell when I get Fallon to the tree line!"

"Ready!" Helios centered his magic, boosting it to intensify the effects of the sleep spell.

**

Nyret had the sick feeling they would not make it in time. Keegan could not shift because the Bear Clan males would see him and know the biggest dragon shifter's secret. He and the non-magic users who had seen it could be executed. It was their law, and it did not matter why it was done. It would not matter to the king that Keegan had done it to protect his life mate. Revealing it to anyone in Therus who was not your life mate meant death. She rushed on, trying to get to Basia before she seized them. Nyret saw one of the Bear Clan males turn and face the oncoming dragon and yell a battle cry. Nyret and Linnea gave a collective gasp; it was their life mate. Nyret roared in frustration.

323

**

Basia ignored Nyret and kept up her pursuit, quickly closing the gap. Basia saw the Bear Clan male standing as if to challenge her. *"Fool,"* she thought. Basia drew in a massive breath of air, filling her lungs to flame him.

Aren watched the dragon get closer, he heard another roar, but he remained focused on the dragon who had dropped Theron and Feron. It was nearly on top of him when it drew in a deep breath.

"Now Tyr!" Aren threw the areal illuminator at the dragon. It streaked towards her faster than the eye could follow. It struck her in the chest. The explosion from the illuminator igniting threw him back and sent the dragon rolling head over tail across the meadow from the blast as the illuminator fired off. Flames spewed out of her mouth as she rolled end over end. Theron and Feron, who had been following in her wake, dove out of the way as she went sailing past them, a pinwheel of flames, sparkles and dragon parts.

The illuminator ricocheted off her and rocketed towards the line of Obsidian Oaks. It struck one with a mighty blast sending silver and purple spears streaking out from the impact in a giant glowing sphere. When the shining spears raced out of the exploded illuminator, the trees howled and swung their branches to hit any that came near them. When hit, the spears, burst into showers of sparkling glitter. The trees attacked the incoming spears as they emitted a blaring alert.

Keegan deposited Fallon in the tree line and heard Nyret roar. He turned to see the explosion hit Basia. Keegan watched the silver female dragon bowling across the meadow in a tangle of wings, limbs, and flame. He yelled at the two males. "Take Fallon deeper in the woods."

Fallon's protests were cut short as Bodhran grabbed her and sprinted into the trees. The two males following Basia managed to avoid being hit by her as she whirled past them. Flames spilling out of her mouth ignited patches of grass. The illuminator careened wildly before striking an Obsidian Oak in an eruption of silver and purple. The oaks responded by wailing.

"Uh oh, the border warning has been activated. This, this is going to be bad..." Helios shook his head.

Keegan glanced skyward; he found Nyret diving down towards Basia as she tumbled to a stop. Basia stood and shook her head, trying to clear it. Spears of purple and silver from the illuminator hit her, sending showers of sparkling dust to cover her in glittering purple patches. She took one step before Nyret streaked down and smashed into her, knocking Basia flat.

Keegan ran back out into the meadow, followed by Aren, who held another aerial illuminator. "We don't need it." He hollered to Aren as they sprinted towards the area where Nyret had Basia's pinned with her powerful talons and was savagely biting the silver dragon. Blood poured from a couple of bites and a few claw marks from Basia. Nyret tightened her vice-like grip on the struggling dragon and snapped her mouth around Basia's neck, sinking her teeth beneath the scales. She felt the blood pump through the artery in her neck, just another few inches, and she could quickly end the life of the female who had threatened to kill her mate.

Keegan jogged up to them. "Nyret! The king wants her alive. You can't kill her." Nyret growled in response. Basia tried to talk, but Nyret clamped down on her neck, cutting off her breath.

"You know I'm right," Keegan reasoned.

Nyret gave a resigned growl. Keegan cast a sleep spell on Basia, rendering her unconscious. With Basia asleep, Nyret loosened her grip on the silver dragon, then vented her frustration by stomping out the hand full of grass fires. She finished and moved to stand by Keegan.

"Thank you," Keegan replied.

Nyret waved her hand dismissively. She glanced towards Valair and flicked her head towards the border.

"Can you quiet the trees?" He asked.

Nyret crossed her arms, closed her eyes, and shook her head. Keegan turned to Aren, who had been watching the exchange with a look of astonishment on his face, as Keegan pointed to the sleeping female dragon. "Someone from Valair will be here presently to take this one back. You are safe. She will not wake up for many hours."

Aren jogged back to check on Theron and Feron, who were making their way towards the area where the two dragons had fought. Aren clasped the twins on the shoulders and shouted above the roaring of the trees. "Are you alright?"

"I'm fine, and I think Theron is fine. Maybe a few bruises from being dropped in the meadow." Feron replied, looking behind Aren at the two dragons.

"I'm good," Theron replied, glancing at the dragons and the tree line. "Is that the dragon who took Fallon? Is she here?"

"Fallon is fine. She is in the thicket behind the meadow with Bodhran and Hearne."

"How did she get away from the dragon? Why did it take her, and who is the male standing by the silver dragon?"

Aren sighed, "Your sister needs to tell you about it. Why don't you find her? She is worried about you two."

They nodded their heads and set off to find Fallon. Aren made his way back towards Keegan and the two dragons. The one who had fought against the silver dragon who had taken Theron and Feron was larger and more heavily built. It was a shimmering gold color. Its scales sparkled with the last light of the sun glinting off them, aided by a generous amount of the purple and silver dust from the areal illuminator. Aren noticed his boots and breacan had a fair amount of dust and were glittering. He was still finding some of the red and gold stuff from the first illuminator they set off by the creek. The glitter seemed to be more tenacious than cockleburs.

Chapter 32

Tyr was moving around inside of Aren, watching the dragons, and keeping an eye on the sky. He stopped and put his nose in the air. Aren paused and took in a deep breath. ***"Smoked honey!"*** Tyr closed his eyes and buried his nose in the sweet, warm scent. He pulled in more of the intoxicating smell. Aren paused to take in the heady fragrance hanging heavy in the air around him. A luscious, thick wave of rich, smokey, late-summer honey blanketed him. He felt like he could gather it up in his arms. There were notes of night-blooming jasmine, white pepper, and the distinctive, provocative tang of a female. Tyr's eye's shot open. ***"It's our mate!"*** Tyr pushed to shift so he could run and find her.

Aren couldn't deny the fact this scent was the scent of their mate. He had always been told he would know, beyond knowing, when a shifter smelled or saw their mates, that it was "the one", and this was her, their mate, finally. *"Hold on, Brother. There are dragons, kidnappings, screaming trees, and our den we have to protect. I want to find her too. Where is she?"*

"Close and just upwind." Tyr was pacing and looking everywhere, attempting to locate her.

"Upwind?" Aren thought. *"Wind's out of the north. The only thing north and close are the two dragons and Keegan, and it's not Keegan.........
Brother? Um. You sure about this?"*

Tyr stopped, taken aback, and pinned Aren with a firm look. **"Yes, I'm sure, and so are you. Let's go."**

"Tyr, upwind is Keegan and two dragons. Our mate is not one of them."

"Maybe we can't see her like the sleeping dragon when it took the Boar Clan males."

"Hum...well now. She might be. Pretty smart, Brother."

For a bear, Tyr managed to plaster a very smug look on his face. **"Thanks."**

Aren walked back upwind to where Keegan and the dragons were. The silver one was still asleep, and the big gold one seemed to be keeping an eye on him.

"Theron and Feron went to find Fallon. I'm going to check on something." He yelled to Keegan over the noise of the trees. Keegan waved him on. The closer he got to where Keegan was, the stronger the smell became. He passed them, and the scent faded quickly.

"Passed her," Tyr announced.

Aren scratched his head. *"Yea, odd. She must be hiding near where Keegan is."* He turned around and walked back towards them, moving to the other side of the sleeping silver dragon.

Linnea was watching Aren through Nyret's eyes. *"He is wearing the oddest thing....a skirt? What is he doing Nyret?"*

"Maybe the skirt is a tribe garment? I like it. It shows off his legs." She watched him stroll past them. **"By the First Egg! He is looking for us and does not realize we are his mate. This is most embarrassing!"** Nyret let slip a soft growl. Keegan heard her over the trees and looked at her quizzically. Nyret ignored him.

"Nyret, the clans don't know we are shifters. They just think we are dragons. We have worked long and hard to keep it that way."

"He's our mate. I would have thought he would have been able to figure it out," *Nyret* huffed.

"A positive would be we are doing a good job of keeping our shifting a secret," Linnea responded, trying to placate Nyret.

The male stepped around the other side of them, coming up on their left. When he was even with their shoulder, Nyret flashed him her teeth. The male froze. He maintained eye contact as he slowly and carefully stepped farther away from her. ***"Shit fire! I scared him."***

"Oh, by the Horde of Ages! This is not going well. The elders said big teeth are scary to them. Just look happy."

"Okay, okay. Sorry, I forgot. I can do happy." Nyret sank down and set her face in what she believed was her best serene and cheerful look. She pulled her lips up, but not enough to show teeth, opened her eyes wide, cocked her head slightly to the side, and buried her claws in the dirt. Nyret sat there and tried to emulate what their diplomat great aunt had told them, "Think smiles, because it shows up in your face."

"You watching the big dragon, Brother?" Aren sent to Tyr.

"Yes. It was growling before. Now it's smiling. It's thinking about eating us. That's how I look at a fat trout." Tyr kept a wary eye on the massive gold dragon who sat in the grass, watching at them like they were a tasty snack.

"Brother, I don't know where she is. She is right here, but I can't see her. I can only smell her. Wonder if the dragon was growling to warn us off from her

because we got too close to her. Maybe it protects her?"

"Call for her. Get her to come to us."

Aren knew Tyr was frustrated because they were so close and still could not find their life mate. *"I can't holler for her brother. I don't know who I'm hollering for."*

"Moose don't know the female's name when they are calling." Tyr groused as he padded around in a circle in Aren's head.

"We're a bear, a hunter, and a warrior of the Ten Clans. We should figure this out."

"This is hard. I would rather be stung by bees to find our mate."

"Me too, Brother, but we have got to puzzle it out together."

Tyr sighed, **"Okay"**

"Good. We'll get in close and talk to Keegan. We can see if we can find her that way."

**

Keegan has watched the odd exchange between Nyret and Aren. Nyret had let out what sounded like a frustrated growl. Keegan thought it was because she was denied killing Basia, but that didn't seem logical. Helios, however, would have been very frustrated if he had his teeth around Basia and then could not kill her, but Nyret? Perhaps it was all the noise the trees were making. After all, she did tend the Obsidian Oaks. He decided to remain vigilant and watched her out of the corner of his eye.

Helios saw the encounter. ***"Yes. I do not know what is going on either. Nyret told me to mind my own affairs, she was busy. She is very testy and seems distracted."*** He thought for a few moments. ***"Hum....I wonder."*** He stroked his chin while he pondered it.

Keegan watched Aren go past them and stop. Nyret had sat down next to where Keegan stood. Aren then started scenting the breeze. Keegan took a deep breath and smelled nothing other than the meadow, Nyret beside him, and the wafting scent of Basia's Badger musk she wore.

Helios stuck his nose in the air. ***"I don't smell anything other than the rancid female."***

"He's probably just making sure no one comes upon us unawares; we would have a hard time hearing them over the trees."

Aren stood there a few moments, then walked past them from behind. He seemed to be searching for something. Keegan didn't detect anything. He reached out to Helios. *"Aren is searching for something. Do you feel anything?"*

Helios extended his senses. ***"No, nothing. Fallon and the rest are standing by the edge of the meadow, talking. That is all I can detect. I will remain on alert."***

Keegan glanced up at Nyret and did a double-take. She had her fake, court, diplomatic smile on and looked slightly drunk with her head tilted and a gaze focused on nothing. It wasn't long before Aren came around their other side. Nyret turned her head to give him a toothy smile. Aren froze and slowly backed away from them. He stayed away for a few moments and then walked towards Keegan.

Helios was grinning. ***"Get him to talk to you and keep him talking. I think I know what is going on."***

Aren closed the distance to stand in front of Keegan. "Keegan it was a good thing you both showed up when you did. You sure the dragon will stay asleep for a while?"

"Yes, the spell will keep the silver dragon sleeping until nearly morning."

336

Aren kept looking around and glancing at the sleeping dragon and the area where they were standing. "Good, that's good." He replied absently. "I don't want anyone else to get kidnapped. So......any idea why this dragon might have taken Theron and Feron?"

Keegan noticed Nyret had lowered her head and was quietly sniffing the space above Aren. "Aren I'm not exactly sure why the dragon took them. Have there been unexplained disappearances before in this area?"

Aren paced the area around Keegan and Nyret, glancing about and discreetly sniffing the air. He replied absently, "No, there have not been any I remember hearing about. Do you think this might have been an isolated instance?"

Nyret nudged Linnea. *"Did you hear? His name is Aren. I wonder what fuzzy britches name is?"*

"Fuzzy britches? Oh! His bear. Probably not fuzzy britches." Linnea caught his warm woodsy-spicy scent. *"I almost forgot what he smelled like."*

Nyret reached her head down. *"I know, it's so yummy!"* Nyret rumbled happily. Aren heard the low deep rumble and glanced up to see the gold dragon's nose about three feet from his head. He jumped out of the way, came down on the sleeping silver dragon's neck, flailed about for balance, but ultimately failed to stick the landing. Aren ended up on his butt in the dirt with his breacan flipped up over his chest. He shook his head and stood up. He had been so caught up in trying to find his hidden mate he did not see the dragon sneak up on him. He pointed his finger at Nyret. "Keegan would you please call off that dragon. It acts like I'm its late supper."

Helios was rolling around in his head, laughing. *"They are mates. Aren….he, he…….."* Helios broke off into a fit of laughter. *"He doesn't know Linnea and Nyret are a dragon shifter. Bwa-ha-ha-ha. He could smell his mate, but he could not find her, and she was right in front of him…big as …Bwa-ha-ha-ha…big as a proverbial dragon."* Helios succumbed to guffaws leaving Keegan to deal with Aren and Nyret.

"Oh! That's…." As understanding dawned on Keegan, he realized he had to come up with the right words to say, which would not give away anything that was not his to reveal. "Um…well…. Aren, this dragon would definitely not eat you."

"How do you know? It's growled at me twice and was sniffing me."

Linnea had her head down and both hands on her forehead. *"I could just die of embarrassment right now."*

Nyret sat with her arms crossed, glaring daggers at Aren as she growled louder. ***"If I wanted to eat him. He would know it."***

Chapter 33

"Aren, you are just going to have to trust me." He needed to find a way to talk to Nyret and Linnea without Aren. "Do you have a water skin or some cider? I could use it."

"Sure." Aren turned and stalked off towards the camp in the trees. When he was far enough away, Keegan turned to Nyret. "You know he doesn't know about dragon shifters. You are probably going to have to shift and speak to him."

Nyret answered in hushed tones, "We can't. You know our laws. There are others around."

Keegan whispered, "I don't mean right now. Later."

Nyret's lips were slightly turned down, and there were wrinkles on her forehead. "Okay. Fine." Nyret sat with her arms crossed, looking grumpy for several minutes. Keegan checked the skies for any sign of the wings and turned to see where Fallon was. "Do you want some help?" He asked Linnet and Nyret.

"No…….yes….." She looked exasperated. "I don't know. This is not the way the archives said it would go."

341

Keegan chuckled, "It usually does not go according to plan. I can help now I know what is going on."

"I would appreciate a little help. Thank you." Nyret looked less grumpy. She rolled her eye in the direction of the camp. "They are coming. All of them."

**

Back at the camp in the tree line Theron and Feron were glad to see Fallon was safe. They hugged her and questioned her about what happened. Fallon told them Keegan had found her in the meadow and had taken her to his home. She added he was possibly her life mate, and they were taking their time to get to know each other.

When the twins determined all was well, they eagerly began telling their sister all about their adventures. "And the silver dragon can talk! I never would have guessed they could. Wait until the Panther prelates find out!" Feron began excitedly.

"Oh, this is not good." Fallon thought before replying, "Truly, Feron? That's amazing."

Aren stomped past them, snatched up a water skin before he turned to head back. Feron called to him as he went by. "Hey, Aren. Did you know dragons can talk?"

Aren stopped dead in his tracks fast enough his breacan flapped forward with the momentum. "What?"

"Yea," Feron added, "they can talk. Pretty good too."

"Oh shite! I've got to stop this." Fallon cleared her throat. "Hey, everyone. I need to see how Keegan is doing."

Theron grabbed a flask. "Yes. I want to meet this Valairian who might be my sister's life mate. Maybe he can tell us about talking dragons."

Aren headed out to the meadow. "I absolutely want to hear about talking dragons. Bodhran, Sami come on."

Aren, Sami, Bodhran, Theron, Feron, and Fallon tromped back out to where Keegan, Nyret, and a sleeping Basia lay in the grass. Aren, who had a very anxious Tyr clamoring to find their mate, wasted no time. "The Boar Clan males who were taken by that dragon," he pointed at the sleeping Basia, "say it could talk and it was invisible. So, does that dragon", he pointed an accusing finger at Nyret, "talk and become invisible too? And where's the invisible female? I can smell you. Come on out!" He bellowed over the howling of the trees.

"Ooh my....this is quite the little complication." Helios tapped his claws against the scales on his chest. **"We should just sleep them all."**

"Without a doubt," Keegan finished. He spoke three magic words that caused Feron, Theron, Aren, Bodhran, and Sami to drop to the ground beside Basia. He looked at Fallon. "They are unharmed and asleep. Fallon, there was no choice for me in this. They can't spread this knowledge. They will most likely be given the option of a memory loss about this or agree to an oath spell to prevent them from telling. They will be safely brought back here when it is done."

Nyret crouched down beside Aren. "Don't be angry with him Fallon. I was preparing to do the same thing. I regret I did not do it first; then, you could be upset with me instead of your life mate."

Fallon shook her head. "I'm not angry. I wish it had not come to this, but what was the choice? Bodhran, Sami, and Aren would not have gone willingly. If they fought, they might have been injured. Theron and Feron, well, they would have gone for the novelty of it." She studied Nyret, who was gazing down at Aren. "He is your life mate?"

Nyret nodded her head. Fallon continued, "His bear is impressive and fierce in a fight. He fought in the battle against The Thorn just over a season ago. He

344

would not have gone willingly. This was probably better. Your life mate is a good male and a good alpha, Nyret."

She patted Nyret on her shoulder and went over to where Theron and Feron were sleeping and started to pull Feron into a better position than the one in which he had fallen. Keegan joined her. Together they worked to reposition the males. Nyret shifted, and Linnea sat down on the ground and pulled Aren's head in her lap. She brushed the hair back from his face. This was not how she envisioned her first meeting with her life mate to go.

"It's a rough start, but we will get it sorted out," Nyret offered.

"He will be angry. I would be." Linnea stroked his hair.

"Yes, it would be expected. We will win him over. How could he not like us? We will look the stylish couple in our matching skirts." Nyret teased, trying to make Linnea feel better.

"I hope so, Nyret."

Keegan and Fallon had finished moving Theron, Feron, Sami, and Bodhran. They were taking a long drink from the waterskin when four Fae night hunters came through the Obsidian Oaks. Three rode kadi following a Drow hunter on a deep, slate-gray hyrcania. The three flared out behind the Drow on point. Keegan motioned for Fallon to stay with Linnea. He approached the hunters as they moved towards them.

"Greetings to the Eternal Fae Kingdom, may Queen Valaitha Ellamaur Sylvi reign be long. I am Keegan Varin of the Gold Wing."

The Drow hunter jumped down off her hyrcania. The few remaining tendrils of the setting sun glinted off her ebony hair. She regarded Keegan with icy gray eyes. "Greetings to the Eternal Dragon Realm, may King Palorin Alvorith reign be long. I am Dryraith Sawvari, Primis Tracker of the Fae Queen's hunters. We are hunting the silver dragon female, Basia Embyr, and the males she took. We are to deliver them to your king at my queen's command."

"The ones you seek are here. They are in a charmed sleep. Two wings will be here presently. We will take them to Vallis Halden. We welcome you to wait with us."

"We shall wait, Keegan Varin of the Gold Wing. Know the King's Royal Wing also approaches." She motioned to the three hunters. They rode out towards Aren's camp. She turned to Keegan. "They will keep watch."

A short time later, Helios came to the front of his mind. ***"The wings approach."***

Keegan inclined his head towards Valair. "They are here." He turned and went to Fallon's side.

**

King Palorin Alvorith's dragon form, Flare, encountered the Fighting Fifth and Tanit-Varin Wings as he flew with two units of the Royal heading towards the borderlands past Vallis Halden. They had exchanged a few words before they heard the Obsidian Oaks sound the alarm. He sent four of his warriors back to the stronghold while he and the four wings flew concealed to investigate the perimeter alarm. He shook his head. The alarm had not gone off in over seventy-five years, and it was the once-a-hundred-year test. It had never gone off as a warning. *"First, Basia Embyr, now the barrier alert. Where there is smoke, there is fire."* He mused.

"Light it up!" Flare rumbled.

That was his dragon's solution to most things, flame it. Perhaps an inelegant solution, but such was Flare. Flame first and ask later was his motto. It had taken them decades to be able to work well together. With his enchanted battle-ax, Oblivion's Kiss, it was different. He and Flare had entered into a truce with the weapon after a couple of hundred years.

The ax fully believed in the meaninglessness of existence and that the gods did not exist. Even though the goddess of Fate personally bound his spirit to the ax. Palorin had long stopped arguing with Oblivian's Kiss about the goddess. The ax was resolute in his position, or as Palorin saw it, the weapon was delusional. Palorin suspected the nihilist beliefs Oblivion's Kiss went on about were a cover for denial and depression for being melded to the weapon. Piss off a goddess and get the stick.

Palorin considered Oblivion's Kiss' situation to be a cautionary tale he worked hard to avoid. He tried to be the best ruler he could be. Palorin studied long hours and spent a great deal of time on the fighting field. He surrounded himself with wise council and strived for statecraft with a reasonable amount of patience.

However, his subjects did not see him as mild-tempered. Flare's impetuous hotheadedness had smoke seeping out of his nose when Flare was exasperated. Generally, it occurred when there was tedious policy or when someone was dishonest. In short, it happened pretty frequently at court, with smoke escaping from his nose at regular intervals. His subjects interpreted this as him being furious, which earned him the reputation of being short-tempered. There was an upside to it. Policy meetings did not last long. Palorin considered this to be a positive.

His fiery reputation may also have had something to do with the mountain estate he reduced to magma and ash. A supplier was knowingly passing off faulty goods. Palorin found the evidence proving the merchant's guilt. He shifted and let Flare have his way. The merchant was buried under the heap when Flare destroyed it. For good measure, Flare flamed it hot enough the stone melted. Flare had been pleased with the solution. No more faulty goods were passed off to his wing. Flare considered all the citizens of the Dragon Realm to be his wing, and he was fiercely protective of them.

**

Approaching the border, King Palorin could sense while the perimeter alarm had been activated, no one had crossed into Valair. *"Maybe they are waiting near the border?"* The scenario seemed like a far stretch as they had no intelligence reports about an attack.

"Can't invade if they are dead." Flare sent to him.

"Dead now, dead later, it doesn't matter. Everything dies." Oblivion's Kiss chimed in unhelpfully.

Palorin drew in a big breath to let out a long, controlled sigh and would have wondered for the seven thousand five hundred and eighty-ninth time why he had not found a mate, but it was crystal clear to him why he did not have one. Today was not the day to untangle that big hairy knot, and the next decade did not look much better. The problem now was the border alert.

The Obsidian Oak line came into view. They glided over the area where his magic revealed to him the point of incursion happened. He saw no forces close and sensed none hidden. He spotted a small band of warriors traveling in their direction down a narrow lane many miles away. Palorin saw four of the Queen Valaitha Ellamaur Sylvi's night hunters. The tracker he knew. It was the female Drow primus, Dryraith Saevari. She sat on her hyrcania, Ash. They were spread out in a meadow around an unconscious silver dragon and several clan males. There were two dragons in their shifted form and a tribe's woman.

He spoke a word through Flare, and the trees quieted. The three wings glided to a landing in the meadow. King Palorin shifted. "Dryraith Saevari, primus tracker of Queen Valaitha Ellamaur Sylvi's night hunters is this," he pointed to the sleeping silver dragon and the clan's men, "the quarry you hunt?"

"Yes, Your Majesty. They were charmed when we came upon them."

"I consider the command your Queen gave you fulfilled."

The Drow signaled to the other three, and they rode back across the border to Valair. Palorin gazed at the sleeping bodies. The gold dragon female, Linnea Tanit, held one of the clan male's head in her lap. She stood now between him and the male. *"Interesting,"* mused Palorin.

"Mate," Flare clarified.

"There are more than two clan's men sleeping here. Is there some reason she," he gestured to Fallon, "is not sleeping as well?"

"Your Majesty, this is Fallon Tulun, Long Rider Captain of the Boar Clan, and my life mate. The males knew we could be invisible and could speak in our dragon form." Keegan replied.

Smoke seeped out of Palorin's nose. He nodded his head towards Fallon and continued speaking with Keegan. "How did they gain this information?"

"It seems they learned it from Basia Embyr. I do not have all the details."

Palorin waived his hand over Basia, and she shifted. He produced a gold circlet which fastened around her neck. He gestured to the Royal Wing. "Pick them up. We leave for Vallis Halden. There is a small unit of warriors a few miles from here headed in this direction." He turned to face Keegan but stopped when he heard a low, threatening growl from Linnea. She was glaring at the gold dragon male who was attempting to pick up the sleeping male who she had been holding. Palorin waived the warrior off. "Take him, Linnea Tanit."

Keegan stepped forward. "Your Majesty. There are a few others who know about our ability to be invisible."

"How many?"

"Fallon, how many are in Aren's den?"

Fallon held the king's eye as he shifted his gaze from Keegan to her. "There are a total of five in his den. Adding my two brothers, who Basia Embyr kidnapped, there are seven who have knowledge, unless Aren sent a written report of the invisibility to Irondenn. If he did, the report is already there."

"Keegan Varin, do you know where the den is located?"

"No, not exactly, Your Majesty, I have not been there."

"Fallon Tulun, Long Rider Captain of the Boar Clan, do you know where the den is located?"

"Yes, Your Majesty."

"Good, you will go with Keegan, myself, and my warriors. We will retrieve them." He turned to the wings. "The rest of you will take those sleeping to Vallis Halden immediately. The prisoner, Basia Embyr, is to be placed in a locked cell. The males are to be treated as guests. They will be guarded until we can sort this out and return them to Therus. Leave no sign we were here." He turned to one of the wings of warriors. "Commander Fridyl take a mage and a few stealth warriors. Erase the knowledge from the lands Therus. Start at their capital, Irondenn; we will handle this area and the den." Commander Fridyl nodded her head, gathered her unit, and flew towards Irondenn.

They erased all evidence of the presence of dragons in the meadow. The Fifth and the Tanit-Varin Wings left with those who were asleep for Vallis Halden. Fallon pointed the way to the den. It did not take long before Sami, and Laith were asleep. A confusion spell had Hearne easily in their grasp and the Bear Clan troops wondering where he went. With their quarry safely tucked away, the Royal Wing headed northeast towards Vallis Halden.

Chapter 34

Aren was walking in the forest. It was fall; the leaves were bright shades of red and gold. Tyr bounded ahead of him to a tree where bees were buzzing. A small applewood fire crackled close to the tree's base, sending smoke up the tree into the hive. Aren picked up some equipment to collect the honey. The jars were lying by a stump covered in blooming jasmine. Tyr was anxious and trying to knock the tree down. *"Hold on, Brother, I've got to get......"* Then he saw a female in red across the meadow near the killing trees. The cool breeze was blowing her rich fragrance to him. It was heavy in the air. He dropped the equipment and walked out to her with Tyr padding softly at his side. The field grass was thick, trying to pull him back. He growled and shoved the soft plants out of his way. *"Soft plants?"*

Aren opened his eyes to see the sun pouring in the window. *"Where?"* The scent of smoked honey, jasmine, and pepper hung in the air. He was in a bed. He didn't remember getting into bed. He sat up. Several other beds were in the room lined up with his den members in them. Theron and Feron were in beds across from him. It looked like a barracks. He glanced around and saw her. He knew it was her. She was wearing a red tunic with black trim. She had a red hat on her head with a black feather in it. She was sitting in a chair near the door watching him. He reached out for Tyr. He could feel his bear in the back of his mind peacefully curled up and snoring. He nudged him and got a cross grunt for his effort. He left Tyr to his dozing. He stood up and walked towards her.

She rose and waited for him to approach before speaking softly. "I am Linnea Tanit. Your den is asleep. They will awaken soon. You will not be harmed. All of you are here because you have knowledge about Valair that cannot be known by outsiders. The knowledge can be magically eliminated, and you will be free to go."

"You! You were at the meadow. Why didn't you reveal yourself to me?" He looked wildly around, gesturing with his arm. "Where are we?"

Nyret growled. ***"By the First One's Scales and Claws! We spent most of the night coming up with that greeting. It was short, on point, and delivered all the pertinent information in a non-threatening way. He completely ignores it? What did we spend four hours of our life doing that we will not get back?"***

"Peace, Nyret. I'll handle it." Linnea replied. To Aren, she spoke, "You are in Valair in Vallas Halden in the barracks."

"Are we prisoners here?" He ran his hand through his hair and felt for his knife. It was not at his side.

356

"No, you are not technically prisoners, neither are you free to roam or leave for Therus until the knowledge of what you learned has been erased." She waited for his next question.

He looked suspiciously at her. "Erased how, exactly."

"The elder magic users will speak a spell, and the knowledge you have of Valair will vanish. You will be free to leave. We will take you to where we found you." Linnea tugged at the cuff of her tunic. He looked angry.

"We thought this could happen. He's mad and needs some time to think. Gather some food and give him some time. He is not going to hear anything we say right now." Nyret urged.

"Your den will awaken presently. I'll bring back Keegan, Fallon, and food for you to eat." She turned to leave. Aren grabbed her arm. Warmth instantly flared from where his hand touched her to his chest. He dropped her arm and stepped back in surprise.

She opened the door and left. When the door swung wide, Aren could see two hulking guards standing on the other side. There was nothing he could do now; he would have to bide his time. He checked on his den, Theron, and Feron. They were all sleeping peacefully.

Of the barracks, there was not much to see. The room was long and rectangular. The building was made of thick stone with large windows set along the wall. He went to examine them and found there was an invisible barrier preventing him from climbing out. The barricade was strong enough he could not push it. Maybe when the rest of his den was awake, they could force their way out. Opposite the door was a hearth with a carved mantle set off-center from the wall surrounded by heavy chairs. A couple of tables were placed against the wall. One held a keg of water and cups. The door in the wall with the hearth led to the privy and bathing area. Towels, washcloths, soap, and grooming supplies, minus a razor, were neatly stacked on open shelves. He heard someone get up, so he went back where the others were.

Feron was standing up, scratching his head. He looked relieved when he saw Aren. As Aren was bringing Feron up to speed on what was going on the rest of the males began to wake. Aren felt Tyr stretch and shake out his fur. He waited until they were all alert before he told them what happened. "And none of us have any weapons." Aren finished.

Theron poured himself some water. "It would not matter if we did have them. They would be ineffective against a dragon. Perhaps Bodhran Fast Strike might fare well." He saluted him with his mug. "So, when's breakfast?"

Feron slapped his hand down on his thigh. "I'm hungry for boiled eggs, apple butter, and some fresh, warm bread." He thought for a moment. "Thick slices of smoked ham would be welcome too."

Laith rolled his eyes, then grabbed the arms of the chair to lean forward. "Food? You are thinking about food at a time like this?"

Feron filled his mug with water. He turned to look questioningly at Laith. "Um..yes? The silver dragon fed us alright, but I've got a taste for some smoked ham this morning."

A couple of Aren's den groaned while Bodhran snorted in laughter. The door opened. Keegan, Fallon, Linnea, and another woman entered the room carrying baskets.

Fallon put her basket on the table. "I'm sure you have many questions. We will answer all we can. "She," Fallon pointed to the woman who came in with them, "is the captain of the warriors at Vallis Halden, Sylmare Zinlana."

Sylmare ran her eye over the men as Keegan, Linnea. and Fallon put the baskets down on the table. "I'll get straight to the point. You have knowledge about our lands you may not have. You have some options. A couple of the options would allow you to go freely back to your own land. You will have the use of a sahalla. A sahalla means "a learned person". These sahalli, since there are many of you, and more than one will be needed, have erudite knowledge of our laws, royal edicts, customs, lore, and history of these kinds of events. You would be wise to listen to them and ask questions. You are our guest, of a sort. You can leave this building if you have a guard, and you heed him or her. If you cause any trouble, of any sort, by my definition of trouble, you will be right back here and not be able to leave. The sahalli will be here tonight. King Palorin Alvorith is here. He will speak with you, as it pleases him. It would be prudent to be polite. One last thing, all your weapons will be returned to you when you leave. I have duties to attend. If you have any questions, ask them." She pointed to Keegan, Fallon, and Linnea. "Or ask the sahalli this evening." Holding up her right-hand palm out, she uttered a blessing. "May the goddess of Fate shine her divine light to guide your steps." Sylmare turned and left the building.

Feron stepped forward and hugged Fallon. "Did you bring any smoked ham?"

"No, but there are boiled eggs, fruit, cheese, cold chicken, and apple cider."

He gave a put out an exasperated sigh. "That will have to do." He patted her on the head and started dragging the contents of the baskets out on the table.

Bren stood with his hand on his hips. "If no one else has any questions. I have a few. How did we get here? Where exactly is "here"? When exactly can we leave? Why can't others know about invisible dragons?" He stopped mid-rant. "Ok, I can see how it might be some type of military strategy thing they might not want let out. I'm still not happy they took my knife. Maybe I need it to cut the bread."

Feron held up some bread. "It's already sliced."

Theron held up some of the chicken. "Chicken is too. Hey Feron, do you see any of the fancy, sparkly faen wine in a basket down there?"

Feron put the remainder of the items on the table. "Nope, no bubbly for breakfast."

"Wine?" Bren barked. "Shite, by the goddess! Bigger things are going on than a frilly breakfast."

Aren put his hand on Bren's shoulder. "That's enough, Bren. Eat, then you can ask them what you want to know."

When they sat and started their meal, Keegan told them what had happened and explained why they would not have the knowledge of Valair.

Bren set his mug down loudly on the table. "What about you, Fallon? Did you have your memory

361

cleared? You have been in Valair for a couple of days." He finished testily.

Helios slammed to the front of Keegan's mind. *"You are about to nap your way through the day, furball!"*

Fallon put her hands on the table. "You are angry. You were caught up in this. You were taken from your home and woke up here. I understand some of why you are upset. Keegan is my life mate. I will live here in Valair with him. I must take an oath charm to prevent me from telling anyone about those of this land. So yes, I must do the same thing."

Bren grumbled as he finished his food, but there was not another outburst.

Aren ignored Bren. He had other things on his mind besides a surly den member. Tyr had been excitedly watching Linnea. *"It's her! Our life mate! I like her. She brought us honey for breakfast. Honey is the best unless it's salmon; that's good eating. I bet she would like salmon. We should catch her some. She probably likes it cooked. I'll catch it, and you can cook it. That's a nice head covering. I wonder what type of bird feather is on it? We should smell it and find out. We could smell her too, she smells nice..........."*

Tyr continued chattering away more like a squirrel than an enormous and terrifying war bear. Aren was glad someone was happy. Their situation was a mess. On many days, his den was a confused heap of crusty bachelors with the current predicament of the week to sort out. *"You would think I would be great at this by now. That this, right here, would be as easy as scooping a salmon out of the stream in a heavy fall run."* He pondered, studying the contents of his mug, and giving half an ear to what Keegan was saying. It was trickier today. A quick decision or a fight was not going to get them out of this tough spot. He had his den to rescue, including Theron and Feron, some sort of big decision to make about what he knew about Valair, and a life mate to chase. He doubted Goron Scaeva, Captain of Woutan Bright Hammer Boar's warriors, could get out of this one. On second thought, Goron would probably not have been in this predicament in the first place.

Chapter 35

"Brother, did you hear me? We need to spend some time with our mate." Tyr paced around in his mind.

"I hear you, Brother," Aren sent back.

Aren tuned back in to hear Keegan finishing, "......so you can stay here in the barracks, or you can go with us."

Aren stood up fast. "I've been in here long enough. I'm ready to get out." He had no idea where they were going; he hadn't been paying attention, but wherever they were going was probably better than here, he decided.

Aren seemed to have made up everyone's mind. They all got up and followed out behind Keegan and Fallon. Aren held back and walked alongside Linnea. He touched her arm and spoke softly, "We need to talk."

Linnea nodded her head. Bodhran, closest to them, turned his head to the side when he heard Aren, but continued to follow the others. In the courtyard, Aren saw about forty people gathered. They looked to be near Keegan's age or perhaps older; he could not tell. They were dressed in various styles of clothing with matching jewelry.

Keegan gestured to the people. "This is my family and part of the large group who searched for Theron and Feron. They are happy my life mate's brothers were returned safely. My grandmother, Ryndra Tanit, has offered the hospitality of her home for an introduction banquet for Fallon and to celebrate the safe return of her brothers."

"Hum," Aren thought, *"better than the barracks."*

Captain Slymare Zinlana rounded the building corner, followed by five warriors, and headed towards Keegan. "These five are going with you. Fenilin, my second, is in charge." She gestured to a female wearing leather armor with glowing runes. "Do not let them drink any of the concoction brewed by Silvanner Varin. Have them back at sunset so they may speak to the sahalli." Fenilin nodded her head. Silvanner turned her attention to those assembled and smiled broadly. "A fine day for revelry with family, friends, and acquaintances. May the goddess bless your celebration by frolicking among you." She waved, "I have paperwork to complete." She turned and went back to her office.

"Ok then…." Theron murmured.

"She's almost retired," Fallon whispered back.

"She studied several years to be a priestess but went in the military," Keegan added.

"Oh!" Theron and Feron replied.

"Frolicking blessings to you too, Captain," Feron called out.

Sylmare waved her hand and kept walking. Fallon dropped her head and shook it. Theron playfully punched his brother on the arm. Feron held up both hands in front of his chest, palm up. "What? I'm being nice and trying to fit in with Fallon's future in-laws." Those gathered laughed, and with the ice broken, they left for the day-long party at Ryndra Tanit's home.

After giving his den a warning to be on their best behavior, Aren sought out Linnea and moved to walk by her side as she spoke. "My home is close to where we are going. We can go there and have time by ourselves. I have already cleared this with Fenilin if you agree."

"Yes. That's a good idea."

"Good. We will head this way to get to my place." Glancing back, she saw Keegan and caught his eye. "Keegan, we will come to Ryndra's this afternoon."

Bren looked skeptically at Aren. "Shouldn't we stick together?"

"Bren, I'm going to spend the good part of this day getting to know this woman. Sami can handle things until I get back." They turned off the road onto a trail and disappeared out of sight, leaving Sami and Bren staring after them with their mouths hanging open.

A short hike down the road brought the smell of roasting meat. Around the bend and down a lane, Ryndra Tanit's two-story, sand-colored, stone house sat between two groves of neatly spaced trees. Among the trees were tents and fire pits laden with food.

After introductions and showing her guests around, Ryndra made her way to Keegan and Fallon. "I don't see Linnea, and wasn't there supposed to be another tribe's man with the group. He didn't decide to stay in the barracks, did he?"

Fallon covered a big grin with her mug. Keegan hedged. "Perhaps they were detained."

"That's odd. I thought Linnea said she would be here this morning. Is she with the other bear shifter from the tribes?"

"Excuse us, Teta, I need to make sure that our guests from Therus do not drink any of Uncle Silvanner's fermented wonders." Keegan grabbed

Fallon then they hurried over to the brewing table where most of the den had gathered.

Helios shook his head. ***"I'm sure someone will tell her."***

"Probably so, but it's not our tale to tell." They spent a little time talking with Aren's den before they left to explore the gardens. Keegan pointed out Ryndra's pride and joy, the blue roses she cultivated. They grew in profusion under her care in hues from pale icy blue to a rose so dark it appeared black.

Keegan picked up Fallon's hand and kissed it. "We should go back and find your brothers to make sure they do not get into any mischief."

Fallon drew her hand down his chest and gave him a seductive smile. "My brothers are grown men and able to annoy a dragon enough to get her to do their bidding. They are fine. I, on the other hand, have a good idea where we might find some mischief."

"Shyn h'jarta, name this place, and we will make haste to go there." Keegan's voice dropped low, and his eyes shone brightly. He pulled her to him and kissed her. She was warm, and the air was heady with her scent.

"Keegan? Keegan? I know you are here. I want to meet your life mate," A clear female voice called.

"Um, are we invisible?" Fallon asked when she pulled back from Keegan.

"Yes. You said mischief, so I thought it would be wise to be invisible as to set a good example for our guests. Captain Sylmare seemed to expect good behavior on someone's part. I forget whose." He leaned in and nuzzled her neck. Fallon melted against him. She slipped her arm around his waist and kneaded his muscular butt. Keegan whispered in her ear. "The details seem unimportant right now….. "

"Keegan, it's your life mate's introduction banquet. Your sisters would like to meet her." The voice was insistent.

"Brother's hiding. I love hide and seek! I'm going to hide now!" Keegan and Fallon watched as a black-haired girl ran full tilt through the flower beds.

A blonde-haired woman wearing a long, green gown with gold jewelry jogged after the child towards an arbor. "No, Ravenna, don't use the hide charm right now, little one."

"I not little! I hide now." She shot back right before she vanished.

"Ravenna! No, don't. Ravenna un-work the charm. No hiding. Remember what I said about being a big dragonette for this party? Big dragonettes don't hide at parties that's for hatchlings." The woman stared hard at the last place the girl stood.

"But brother's hiding?" A voice behind a bench called out.

"Kalasa, everything alright?" Ryndra joined Kalasa, where she was standing by an arbor of sky-blue roses.

"Just trying to find Keegan and now Ravenna," She sighed.

"Now you know those two are probably out here having fun. They are young. You remember, fun, right? Besides the garden is lovely, let them enjoy it. If I had a strapping young dragon male, I would be doing the same thing this morning." She spoke louder. "The grotto by the water lily pond is very nice for, um 'activities.'" Ryndra looked at Kalasa. "There that should do it. Now about my granddaughter. Ravenna, Teta Ryndra has some fresh cherry tarts, but only for dragonettes she can see."

Ravenna appeared in front of Ryndra. "Can you see me?"

"Why yes, I can! Let's go get one."

Kalasa followed Ryndra and Ravenna out of the garden. Fallon giggled, "Your sister is adorable."

"Yes, she is. I have twin sisters who are younger than me, Aria and Brynn. Ravenna is the youngest, and I think she could get away with murder. Dane and I would have been grounded for a decade for half the things she does."

Fallon laughed. "Perhaps some parents just get more comfortable being parents, so by the last child they are not as rigid."

"Maybe they are just tired," Keegan said as he nibbled her ear.

"Hum, yes, that does seem more likely," Fallon replied as they both chuckled.

Keegan kissed her on the head. "As much as I would love to stay here all day, we need to get back."

"Maybe when all of this is over, we can find someplace where we might be alone. Do you know where we might find a nice quiet cave? Maybe one with a thermal pool?"

Keegan scratched his chin in thought. "I think I might know the perfect place."

She shot him a brilliant smile. "Excellent! When all of this is settled. We should go."

"Done," Keegan replied. He dropped the concealment charm, and they rejoined the party.

The day passed quickly. Ale was drunk, stories were told, and spirits were high. Even Bren's grumpiness abated after two platters of food and a small keg of ale. By midafternoon Aren and Linnea arrived. While Ryndra made a valiant effort to ferret out any information about where the two had been, her daughter was not forthcoming with any information. The matter was closed when Linnea gave Ryndra a firm look and quietly told her. "I understand you are worried but drop it, Mother."

When the sun began to ease toward the horizon, Fenilin signaled it was time to leave. Food was gathered, and goodbyes were said. Bodhran watched Aren and Linnea walk close together. Aren was wearing a gold broach of an oak tree set with rubies on his tunic he had not seen before. It looked similar to the pendant Linnea was wearing of an oak tree. Its roots intertwined to form a frame around the tree. At the base of the tree, the roots held a black stone. Bodhran was pleased. If something good came out of them being taken to Valair, he hoped it would be his father's happiness.

Chapter 36

The ten sahalli were waiting on them when they arrived. The scholars explained the options available to them. They could live in Valair for the length of their days in prison. They could choose a forgetting spell that would wipe out their memories of the last couple of days. An oath charm would let them keep their memories of the previous couple of days but make it impossible for them to share information about Valair with outsiders. A shalla spoke with Fallon about the oath charm and when she would be required to give it. The last option was death. That was reserved for those who had committed a high crime against Valair in addition to having information about Valair.

The sahalli thought it would be most likely, given what happened, they would be offered either the forgetting spell or the oath charm. However, as in all things they relayed, the king would make the final decision. They had an hour to discuss this amongst themselves and ask any questions before being called before King Palorin. As a group, they were evenly split. Aren, Bodhran, Theron, and Feron decided that they would choose the oath charm. Bren, Sami, Laith, and Hearn opted for the forgetting spell. They told the sahalli their decision and waited to be called in before the king.

King Palorin Alvorith spent his day in drills with the warriors at Vallis Halden. He discussed the transfer of the captain position due to Sylmare Zinlana's midwinter retirement. He agreed Fenilin Kiah would fill the role nicely. He sent for the sahalli when they arrived. It was unusual for a Therian to end up in Valair. Today he had several of them, counting the life mate of Keegan Varin. He was sure today would be written about in the scrolls. Not many from Therus ended up in Valair. When it happened, it was almost always a life mate, like Keegan's. Those were simple; an oath spell was used. This was different. Some of the tribe males had been kidnapped, and some knew because of Basia Embyr's foolishness. Keegan's life mate, he would give her the oath charm tonight. With the others, he was inclined to use the forgetting spell.

While he waited on the sahalli to finish speaking with the men, he questioned Fenilin about their behavior earlier today. He was pleased to learn they had not given her any trouble. After dismissing Fenilin, he looked at their weapons, which lay on the table. He felt Oblivion's Kiss pull towards one on the table. He saw the sword when it was brought in. He knew it, and he knew its history. It was an ancient blade of legend forged when the old gods were young and warred among the stars. It was one of the thirteen banished to the lands of non-magic. Only eleven remained, and two had not been seen in the recorded age. This sword made his ax look to be still smoking from the fire, newly forged, in comparison.

He felt Oblivion's Kiss reach out to it. **"A traitor,"** Oblivion's Kiss began.

"An ill-mannered child," Fast Strike returned.

Seething Oblivion's Kiss retorted. **"Your crime, your penance, it gains you nothing in the end. Your hope of being redeemed is for what? Nothing."**

"Myself, my raging depressed child, for myself." To Palorin the sword spoke, **"The life of mortals is short compared to dragons. In two hundred or so years, leave the bairn and know a warrior's blade. We will burn a path across the heavens."**

The seductive power of the blade flowed over him. Flare picked up his head and turned his gaze towards the glowing sword. Palorin found himself reaching out to touch the sword.

"And leave ash in your wake," Oblivion's Kiss finished.

"See, and you said it didn't matter, little one." Fast Strike chuckled and fell silent. Its light faded.

Palorin snapped out of the pull of the blade as its laughter faded. *"Crafty blade,"* he thought.

His guard knocked softly on the door. The sahalli had completed their work. He motioned for the guard to open the door. The sahalli entered first, followed by the males from Therus. Keegan Varin came with his life mate and his family. Members of the Tanit-Varin Wing were followed by the retired Fifth Wing, "The Fighting Fifth," his father had called them. The wings nodded their heads to him when they entered then settled behind those from Therus.

Palorin stood. "For those new to our lands, I am King Palorin Alvorith of the Dragon Dynasty. You are here before me today because you have a life mate in Valair, you were kidnapped, or you have knowledge of us. The sahalla of lore tells me it was in my grandparents' age, when they ruled, that so many from Therus required an oath spell or a charm of forgetting. The two who were taken, step forward." Theron and Feron stepped to the center of the room. "You two will be going to our capital to answer questions about what happened when the trial of Basia Embyr is held the day after tomorrow. You will have the use of a sahalla to guide you in this, if needed. You will be given the spell of forgetting afterward and returned to the lands of Therus."

Two of the sahalli moved to stand beside Theron and Feron and placed their palms flat on the left side of their chests.

Palorin gave a slight nod of his head, "Speak."

"Thank you, Your Majesty. The archives have records of those from Therus who have broken no law and have arrived in Valair as a hostage or by accident, to choose the oath charm or spell of forgetting. These two were captured. Their sister is life mate to Keegan Varin. They wish to remember celebrating their sister's introduction banquet and their new extended family, and so would like the option of the oath charm."

"I am inclined to use the charm of forgetting; however, I shall consider this, I will give my final decision after the trial of Basia Embyr." The sahalla nodded her head and stepped back. King Palorin continued, "Keegan Varin, bring your life mate forward."

Keegan brought Fallon with him on his left arm. His parents and the sahalla who had spoken with Fallon stood behind him. Palorin smiled, "The crown has many duties, that can often not be pleasant. However, most happily, your case is one I look forward to resolving. Introduce the court to your lovely life mate."

"King Palorin Alvorith, this is my life mate, Fallon Tulun, Long Rider Captain of the Boar Clan. We have just begun the h'jarta kayzaire."

"How long has it been since you discovered she was your life mate Keegan Varin?"

"Four days ago, Your Majesty."

Palorin rubbed his chin. "This is a very recent development."

"Yes, Your Majesty."

Palorin turned his attention to the woman at Keegan's side. "Fallon Tulun, the sahalla have spoken with you. What is your desire in this?"

Fallon stepped forward. "While I do not have magic or the spirit anima to make my life mate instantly known to me when I meet them, I believe it to be Keegan Varin. We have discussed this and have decided to have a longer h'jarta kayzaire so I may be assured I am correct. I would ask for the oath charm so I can remain in Valair to be with him."

Palorin nodded his head. "It is prudent to take the time to consider something important. Know the sahalla are available for you. You are new to our lands and our ways; you would be wise to seek their help."

He motioned for Fallon to step forward. "Approach so I may speak the oath charm."

Determined not to let her nervousness show, Fallon drew herself up to her full height and squared her shoulders. With her head held high, she approached King Palorin. He reached out and touched her forehead with his right hand. "Do you Fallon Tulun of the Boar Clan of Therus swear to keep those of Valair safe and never share any of the information you learn here with anyone of any land besides those of Valair who hold the best interests Valair in their hearts?"

"I so swear," replied Fallon

King Palorin spoke words of a language Fallon did not know. She felt warm swirling air around her that smelled a little like early morning forge fires when they were awakened. He withdrew his hand. "May you both know joy and peace all your days, and may the goddess bless your journey."

Keegan hugged Fallon and kissed her forehead while those present clapped and cheered. They moved to the side when Palorin addressed Aren's den. "You have been told why you cannot have the knowledge of Valair. It is regrettable this happened, but it did. In times past, we have offered the choice of the oath charm, which you just saw me give Fallon Tulun, or the forgetting spell. I have decided to use the forgetting spell. After I give it, you will immediately

381

fall into a deep sleep. You will be taken to your lands. Your weapons will be with you when you wake. My warriors will watch over you while you sleep so that no harm may befall you. You will have a scroll indicating Fallon and her brothers are safe, and you will have more information about them soon."

The sahalla stepped slightly forward with his palm over the left side of his chest. Keegan stepped forward and did the same thing. There was a restlessness among the Bear Clan males. Linnea Tanit, who had been standing by Aren, stepped forward with her hand on her chest, as did Aren.

"Speak Keegan Varin."

"Fallon and I could go with your warriors. Explaining in person, it may allay more worry than perhaps a scroll."

"In truth, it would, but the tribunal of Basia Embyr begins and ends tomorrow. You and Fallon are required for it." Smoke seeped in a thin line out of his nose and drifted towards the roof.

Keegan dipped his head and returned to where he had been standing. "Yes, Your Majesty."

King Palorin's eyes were glowing, and he had increased in size in just talking about the tribunal. His neck muscles were corded in thick ropes. His shirt was tight across his chest, and his belt creaked before magically adjusting up in size. The thin line of smoke thickened. He turned his gleaming eyes on the sahalla. "Speak sahalla." His voice had a base metallic rumble to it caused by Flare, who sat just behind his eyes watching.

The sahalla pulled his hand away from his chest, the fabric of his garment sticking to his clammy hand. He tried to meet the king's gaze and failed. He shook his head, his horns rustling the air when he dropped his head and spoke. "Your Majesty the Therian male known as Bodhran Fast Strike Gideon wishes the oath charm. He is the second to Fallon Tulun in her Long Riders......." He let the sentence hang in the air.

Bodhran stepped forward and held the King's gaze. Palorin studied him a few moments before he spoke. The male was tall and broad, but unlike the rest of the Bear Clan males, he did not have a bear spirit. "Ah, Fast Strike had bonded to you. It is a fine blade. To your request, you have no bond of kindship to one of this land. My decision is unchanged."

Bodhran stepped back. King Palorin directed his gaze to Linnea. "Linnea Tanit tender of the Obsidian Oaks, speak."

Linnea strode forward with Aren at her side. "Your Majesty, the Bear Clan male of Therus known as Aren Gideon, champion warrior, and alpha of his den, is my life mate." A couple of gasps and a few murmurs were heard from the wings.

Palorin looked at Aren. "This is so?"

Aren felt the dominance and weight of something powerfully massive lived in the king. Whatever it was, it was not pleased. Tyr puffed up. ***"Brother, this one is angry and BIG!"*** He watched through Aren's eyes, ready to push Linnea out of the way if the other male attacked.

Aren calmly stared at the king and spoke in a clear voice. "Yes, King Palorin, Linnea Tanit is my life mate. I ask for the oath charm."

The light in King Palorin's eyes dimmed briefly. "How long has it been since both of you discovered you were life mates, Linnea Tanit?"

"That is not an easy question to answer, my king. I saw him last year, and my dragon told me he was my life mate then. I was shocked. I never felt impelled to find a life mate. I thought tending the Obsidian Oaks was my life work, and I was not destined for a life mate. I consulted the sahalli and studied the scrolls for a year before I felt ready in my heart and mind to be with my life mate."

He dipped his head and turned his attention to Aren. "Aren Gideon how long have you known?"

"I sensed something last year, but I did not know who it was until this morning."

Aren watched him intently for any clue as to which way the king was leaning in his decision. He found nothing.

Palorin continued, "Linnea Tanit, have you completed the bond with him?"

"No, Your Majesty, we just spoke to the other, today."

King Palorin nodded his head. "Aren Gideon, you are going to remain in Valair with Linnea Tanit starting today?"

"We have not made a firm decision on it. I have my den. I cannot leave them like this. I am their alpha."

"Truth. As a leader, your responsibility for the safety of others is a priority. That being said, it is my decision the last four days be wiped from your memory. Both of you have some knowledge of the other before today. You can secure the safety of your den and then renew your life mate connection."

Chapter 37

Those gathered reacted with shocked gasps and surprised whispers. Before anyone could respond King Palorin uttered a single word, immediately Aren and his den were frozen in place, unable to move. A nod to the guard had them quickly moving to stand behind the rigid males. One of the guards attempted to escort Linnea to the side. She roared and tossed him into the stone wall across the room. The remaining guards approached to intervene and were called off by King Palorin. Linnea snarled at the guard standing behind Aren. The guard glanced at the king to see Palorin motioning him to step back. When the guard stepped aside, Linnea took his place. King Palorin spoke the words of the spell, and the Bear Clan males slumped over unconscious. The guards caught them and lifted them effortlessly over their shoulders, packing them out of the building like sacks of grain. A brass dragon carried a bag with their weapons. Linnea trailed after them shouldering Aren. Once outside, they shifted and flew towards Therus.

King Palorin addressed those remaining. "Those who are part of the tribunal for Basia Embyr; I leave at first light." He strode out of the room with the remainder of his guards.

Theron turned to Feron with his eyes wide and whispered. "Shite fire, do not provoke the king!"

Feron nodded his head as they walked towards the door. "No lie, Brother. We should find Fallon."

The twins spent the rest of the evening at the Iron Fork with Fallon and Keegan's family. Ideas were tossed back and forth about how to best help Linnea get Aren, with Silvanner Varin proposing several different methods. Each of his suggestions was met with an eye roll and a scoffing snort from Tedda Avondale, the Fighting Fifth's tactician. Tedda watched the unfolding spectacle from the corner with a large glass of Fae wine and a tray of savory canapés. Tedda, picked up a smoked beef and goat cheese appetizer nestled on rye bread and analyzed the current Tanit-Varin Wing predicament of the day, *"Wonder what Linnea and Aren want?"*

Of course, in the typical Tanit-Varin tradition, they left out Linnea's desire in the matter. When it was brought to their attention by Pertti Halvor, Silvanner Varin very logically pointed out. "She's not even here. So how can she give an opinion?"

Pertti smacked her hand to her forehead. Tedda doubled over laughing and pounding the table. Fallon looked at Keegan questioning, her eyebrows raised. Keegan shrugged his shoulders with his hands up in front of him. "Family," he replied.

A knowing look passed between the twins as they sensed a kindred spirit. Theron and Feron decided to investigate more of Silvanner Varin's "brilliant" plans. They succeeded in encouraging him to elaborate on his current hair-brained scheme, which involved getting Aren's Den completely smashed on his Summer Solstice Blueberry Cordial and absconding with him to Valair passed out drunk.

"Couldn't we just sleep them, Uncle Silvanner." Pertti deadpanned.

"We could, but I need to move some inventory; it's taking up too much space."

Tedda held her hand up and, between gales of laughter, and managed to get out, "Stop….Just…Stop. I can't breathe." Bwa-Ha-Ha-Ha "I think I might pee myself too." Bwa-Ha-Ha-Ha "By the First Horde….this is the best. I love this wing!"

"Um, Silvanner. Isn't that one of the reasons Basia is in trouble? For taking someone from Therus who wasn't their mate?" Fallon asked.

That seemed to pull Silvanner up short. "You are right. Linnea will have to carry him across the line."

"Good catch, sis!" Feron called out while Tedda continued to howl in laughter.

Silvanner pointed to Theron and Feron. "We've got some planning to do."

"Oh, sweet goddess, help us all," Fallon murmured. Her brothers could find trouble aplenty by themselves. They certainly did not need help from a dragon who distilled high-proof beverages and seemed to be mischievous and bored. Fallon had loads of experience over the past few years with that combination of behaviors. Fallon had initially hoped Theron and Feron would be given the oath charm, but now she fervently hoped they would get the forgetting spell to be spared being a part of the plans being hatched by one, Silvanner Varin, Esquire.

The next morning as the sun peeked above the horizon, they were flying for Shal H'jarta. The tribunal would be held near the palace, located on the Dragon Dynasty capital city's outskirts. They arrived with plenty of time for Theron and Feron to bathe and change into some clean clothes provided by the Royal Wing. Just before noon, they were taken to the royal stadium. The stadium was a massive open-air oval arena with tiered seating around a flat open field. It served many purposes, from contests, games, performances, exhibitions, to the infrequent, high-profile, public tribunal and execution. This was not a trial; her guilt was evident. Dragon ideas of law and order did not value wasting time on cases where culpability was more than apparent. Those who spoke at the proceeding stood in the "Ring of Compulsion" and answered questions from the sahalla magister or the king. The Ring of Compulsion made the one standing in it speak the truth. While shifters and many who lived in Valair could hear a lie when spoken, not all could. The Ring made the event transparent for all who attended and forced the truth to be spoken.

At precisely noon, the gong was rung, and the tribunal began. The king sat in the seat of judgment and motioned for the proceeding to begin. The Enforcer read her crimes: Defying a Royal Order of His Majesty King Palorin Alvorith by refusing to stop stalking Keegan Varin, imprisoning her dragon spirit, Velli, blackmail of Igreth O'Barin, the criminal threat of Perrikin Farwick, life mate of Igreth O'Barin, and favored Minstrel of Her Royal Majesty Queen Valaitha Ellamaur Sylvi's primis consort, Norellis Quentis Crixus, kidnapping Theron Scaeva and Feron Scaeva of Therus and theft of goods of less than one hundred silver pieces in Nelelune.

The Enforcer called each who had been affected by Basia to answer questions. Enforcers and night hunters who had information gave brief statements. Basia was ordered to shift, and Velli was questioned. By midafternoon when Basia was placed in the Ring, a narrow trail of smoke was seeping out of Palorin's nose. At the end of an exhausting two and a half hours of dramatics, yelling, wailing, and the occasional yelp when she lied, causing the Ring to zap her and wrest the correct information out of her, there was no soul sympathetic to Basia in the entire amphitheater.

A Fae woman behind Fallon murmured, "I swear by the Goddess of Light and Fate's plump toes, if that crazy silver dragon female says, 'I just want to have nine royal dragonettes and dress them up in beautiful clothes I make and live at court.' One more time, I'm going to hop this railing and stab her in the eye with my favorite rose quartz wand that was passed down to me through my ancestors going back to the Great Migration."

Helios, who had been watching the whole affair with a jaded eye, tapped his chest twice with his right paw and pointed. *"Testify sister, testify."*

Questioning completed, King Palorin rose, the smoke streamed behind him caught up in the breeze. "You are guilty of all charges against you. During questioning, you admitted you knew these things were wrong and did them anyway. You do not suffer a sickness of the mind. All these crimes were premeditated. For these crimes, you, Basia Embyr, will be executed before the sun sets today."

Basia's cries and pleading were cut short by King Palorin, who rendered her mute with a charming word.

King Palorin looked where her victims sat. "You have the right to say what you will, now, if you choose. Theron Scaeva, do you wish to say anything?"

Theron stood, "No, Your Majesty." he replied before sitting back down.

"Feron Scaeva, do you wish to say anything?"

Feron stood, "No, Your Majesty." he replied and sat back down.

"Perrikin Farwick, citizen of the Eternal Fae Kingdom, do you wish to say anything?"

"I am pleased this is over, Your Majesty."

"Igreth O'Barin, citizen of the Eternal Fae Kingdom, and life mate of Perrikin Farwich, do you wish to say anything?"

Igreth stood. "I will regret my part in this, the length of my days. Wearing the bracelets that prevent me from ever using magic is more than befitting, considering what I have done. I would hope all those affected by my actions can perhaps forgive me one day. I would have all know Velli is innocent of the charges read against Basia Embyr because of the suppression charm I gave Basia." Finished making his statement, Igreth sat back down.

Fallon listened to Igreth. It seemed a miscarriage of justice, which would cause Velli to suffer death for something very much all Basia's doing. In this entire tribunal, it was the singular thing that did not seem equitable to her when Velli's suppression was brought out in the testimony. Fallon thought it was terribly wrong for the dragon spirit to be punished when Velli was also a victim of Basia's machinations.

The king stood in front of her. "Fallon Tulun, citizen of Therus, do you wish to say anything?"

Fallon couldn't let the burden on her heart go unspoken, so she stood. "Thank you for this opportunity to speak, Your Majesty. I am new to Valair and do not yet know all the laws and ways of this land, so I ask for Your indulgence when I ask, can nothing be done for Velli? To me, she seems a victim in this."

King Palorin drew in a deep breath. "I regret it, but unfortunately, there is nothing that can be done for her."

At the end of the line, a sahalla shuffled several steps out into the arena and stood with his hand over the left side of his chest. The breeze blew the light cowl hood off his head and ruffled the sparse, gray hair on his head.

Palorin saw the elder sahalla out of the corner of his eye. "Speak, sahalla."

"There is a way of legend, Your Majesty. The Splitting."

Palorin shook his head. "The Splitting is not in the recorded text. It is a tale told to children who misbehave."

The sahalla shrugged his shoulders. "True, it is not in the recorded text, but not being there does not make it any less real." Murmurs rippled through the crowd.

"The tribunal will be briefly halted while I speak to the sahalli." King Palorin left the stadium floor with several sahalli following in his wake. A few minutes later, Mythrum the Death Drow was summoned to the king.

Theron reached over, tapped Fallon's shoulder, and smiled. "That's my big sister."

Fallon shifted in her chair towards Keegan. "What's The Splitting?"

"It's a cautionary tale told to dragon shifter children who misbehave. Most children have difficulty learning boundaries, and dragonettes are no exception. They are powerful, can fly, breathe fire, use magic, and have other abilities depending on their species. So, having this power can sometimes encourage naughtiness. It is not uncommon for parents to tell their children if they don't behave, the goddess's magic users will take their dragon from them, and they will instantly grow ancient and decrepit. It's an effective threat."

"What happens to the dragon spirit?" Fallon asked.

"According to the tale, if the dragon was good, the goddess would find another body for the dragon. If the dragon was bad, it would be sent to the spires, um, our version of the afterlife to make atonement."

Mythrum entered the king's private chambers as two guards rushed past him at a jog heading towards the stadium floor. The sahalli were seated to the right side of King Palorin.

"Mythrum, can you take the life essence from someone?" Palorin spoke without preamble.

Mythrum bowed slightly from the waist. "Of course, King Palorin, I take the lives of those who I am charged with executing in doing that; I take their life essence."

"Yes, but can you pull out a life force from the body with Soul Taker and put it in another?"

"A moment, Your Majesty." He gripped the pommel of Soul Taker and closed his eyes.

The sword appeared in his mind glowing a bluish-black against a star-filled background of night sky. ***"What the Dragon King asks for was done once when the Goddess of Fate was new to this land. Many clerics and magi combined their power to forge the animi to the other unmajos vessel when I pulled it out. They could both be lost if this is not what the goddess wills."***

"In our years, you have not spoken of this." Mythrum sent.

"I am not obligated to disclose the minutiae of my existence to those I have been bonded to." The image faded. Such was the way of enchanted things; they were oftentimes capricious.

Mythrum opened his eyes. "Soul Taker can pull out the dragon anima. Fusing the anima to the new unmajos vessel will be the problem. It will require many powerful clerics and magi. It may not work, and both souls will be lost."

"Unmajos?" A sahalla asked.

"A word in the old language meaning non-magical, purely mortal." Mythrum clarified.

397

"That leaves out almost everyone in the kingdom except for a scant handful." King Palorin rubbed his chin. "There are three in the stadium from Therus."

The elder sahalla spoke. "Your Majesty, there is only one, the female. Velli is female. A female anima will only meld to the same vessel."

Palorin turned to one of the guards. "Go bring Keegan Varin and his life mate, Fallon Tulun to me." He stood and faced Mythrum. "The sahalli thought there was a possibility Soul Taker could do this. I have sent for the athenaeum of magi and the clerics. The problem of Basia will be ended today one way or another."

Chapter 38

Keegan and Fallon were admitted to the king's presence. King Palorin addressed them, "Fallon Tulun, you asked if anything could be done for Velli. There is a chance she could be saved, but she will need the other half of her dragon form. This other half cannot be a shifter or possess magic. Would this be something you would consider?"

Fallon stood rooted to the spot. Of all the things she thought they might be called back to speak with the king about, this was not it. If she did this, she and Keegan would have a much longer life together, and Velli would be saved. On the other hand, she did not know Velli. Now, this dragon was going to be joined with her for life. The thoughts swirled around in her head as she spoke to the king, "Your Majesty possibly, but I have questions. I must also speak with Keegan."

"Of course, you might also wish to speak with the sahalli and Mythrum before you make your decision. You may use the solarium adjoining this room. When you have finished, come back to give me your answer. You have an hour to decide."

The guards opened the double doors to the solarium. Those assembled in the king's chamber left with Keegan and Fallon. When the doors shut, Fallon spoke to them. "We only have an hour. So, I would like to speak to Keegan by myself, briefly. Then I may have questions for you if I decide to pursue this course of action."

She and Keegan walked out onto the balcony. Fallon looked out across the city for a few moments before she drew in a deep breath to speak to Keegan. "I have so many questions; I don't think an hour is enough to answer them. I'm not sure what to do about this. I could save her. Is she head sick? Will I have that to deal with? If so, I can't do it. What about us? How will this affect us? What are your thoughts about this? I have at least a hundred questions, and there is not much time." She slid against his body and wrapped her arm around him.

Helios spoke through Keegan. "Velli is not head sick, little mate. Basia was obsessed, and it wore Velli down over time. It is wonderful to be a dragon! You will be able to breathe fire, fly, and maybe some magic. You are our mate with Velli, or without."

Keegan stroked her back. "I have questions too for the sahalli. Know I will love you and support you in whatever decision you make."

They stood on the balcony for a few more moments. Keegan kissed the top of her head. "We must get our answers."

Their questions for the sahalli and Mythrum lead to more questions than answers. They discovered this had been done once before in the time of legend that Soul Taker would admit to, and it was not without risk. Having a dragon anima would lengthen her life to Keegan's. Velli would have to consent to this, and they would have to stay at the Anthenaeum Contemplari until cleared to leave by a panel of sahalli, magi, and clerics.

Near the end of the hour, Fallon spoke with Keegan. "It weighs on me Velli will die for what Basia has done. My heart urges me to do this."

Keegan sighed. "I was afraid you would choose this path. It is the chance something might go wrong, which has me selfishly wanting you to choose not to involve yourself in it. If your heart is pushing you to do this, then it must be the will of the goddess. I will be by your side the whole time. Together we will succeed."

Hand in hand, they told the king their decision and followed behind him as he strode into the arena where a crowd of magi and clerics waited. Those assembled grew silent when the king stepped onto the grass in front of Velli. "Velli, you are offered "The Splitting" with your new half-to-be, the female from Therus, Fallon Tulun, Captain of Long Riders of the Boar Clan. What is your decision?"

"I agree to The Splitting," Velli replied loudly for all to hear. The shocked silence of the crowd gave way to gasps of astonishment.

King Palorin called to the masses, asking for their silence before he spoke to them. "Sit and listen very carefully to everything I say." The crowd fell quiet and sat waiting on the king. "This has not been done since the age of our ancestors. All those with magic are to assemble in circles around us. Mythrum will draw out the dragon spirit. When he says the word, all must send their magic to the point where the staffs of the clerics touch and keep it there until told to stop. Keegan, you would do well to let her brothers support her, and you contribute the energy from your life mate bond. Even if it has not been completed, it is still potent."

Sensing this would be a day written about in the Eternal Scrolls, the crowd focused on the task at hand. The bands around the center of the stadium formed quickly. The clerics stood around Fallon with their staffs ready. Basia, had been ordered to shift back into her more human form. She was still under the influence of the King's mute spell and could only stare daggers at Fallon and Keegan. The masses, now ready, waited noiselessly as an eerie silence descended over the arena.

"Basia," King Palorin spoke. "You are sentenced to death." He nodded at Mythrum, who plunged Soul Taker into her chest. Basia's mouth opened in a silent scream as the blade flared cobalt. Soul Taker began to pull a silver mist from her, as Basia's form aged and shrank to become a few bones and dust on the green grass.

"Send your power now!" Shouted the Drow elf.

Chants and humming filled the air. Singularly then picking up speed, beacons of light shining in all colors shot to the point where the cleric's staff's touched. The energy bands distorted the air giving the illusion the space above the staffs was expanding and contracting. The clerics nodded to the Drow, and he placed the tip of his sword on Fallon's chest. They spoke a spell while the magical current from the crowd crackled and arced down to the black blade into Fallon's body, causing her to convulse. The silver mist traveled down the dark sword into her chest. Mythrum shouted for the magic to cease. There was silence, and Fallon went still as a stone held between her brothers. Keegan felt for the pulse in her neck. He could feel it faint but steady beneath his fingers. He picked her up and carried her out of the stadium.

**

Fallon was gliding over the Calterra mountains. The mountain goats scampered away as she went by. She was searching for something she could not find. She felt deep sadness, loss, and frustration. She knew somehow, she could never find it because it was gone forever. It started to rain. The gray clouds looked dark as the hole in her heart felt. The thunder vibrated the air next to her. She needed to land.

**

Fallon woke up in a bed listening to the rain drip off the roof. Her head hurt; everything hurt. She felt like she had been run over by every horse in the clan's herd. She groaned and opened her eyes. Wrong. The light tried to stab her through her eyes straight through to the back of her brain. She closed her eyes and sunk back down into the bed. She felt the bed dip and smelled Keegan. She could hear him breathe; he smelled worried and relieved.

"How do I know what that smells like?" Fallon wondered.

"Fallon, I'm going to raise you so you can drink something. You need to sleep some more." Keegan eased her up and held a cup to her lips. It smelled like a combination of a mint sleeping and pain-relieving potion. She could smell the magic charm as it sparkled in the brew, which was odd she knew what it was. She drank it down, and sleep took her. The next time Fallon woke up, the pain was not as bad, and the light was no longer a hot poker trying to sear its way through her head. Keegan was sitting in a chair. Theron and Feron were seated on a large, long, low cushion playing a dice game on the floor.

Keegan came to her side when she moved to sit up. "Let me help you shyn h'jarta." He supported her while Theron and Feron wedged some pillows behind her back. She smelled happiness coming off them with some traces of worry. Fallon was not sure what confused her more that she could smell these things and knew what they were, or she had discovered her brothers were capable of worry. She was in a tent, a massive, luxurious tent with rugs, furnishings, partitions, and what looked like an expansive view of a large hay meadow.

Fallon rubbed her head and murmured, "I remember waking up in a building. It was raining... waking up looking at a hay meadow, that's odd. What happened? I passed out."

Keegan put a stoneware cup of fruit juice in her hand. She knew it was grape juice before he handed it to her. She had smelled it when he poured it. Fallon brought it to her lips. It tasted divine! She gulped it down.

Keegan motioned to Feron, who stepped between the tent flaps and disappeared. Keegan sat on the bed. "What is the last thing you remember?'

She ran her hand through her hair and thought back. "There was a male, Mythrum. He pointed a black sword at me." Fallon pulled the neck opening of the linen gown down, looking at her chest. There was no cut or mark of any kind. "There were voices and a blast of pain. That's all I remember."

"That's when you blacked out. The Healers had to help you, but The Splitting worked. Helios said Velli is currently asleep."

Fallon rubbed her arms and stared outside. "Why are we in a tent?"

Theron laughed. "Well, sis, you shifted and destroyed part of the healer's building, so they thought it would be safer for everyone if you were in a tent."

Fallon put her head down and shook it. Theron grinned, "Don't worry Fallon, Feron and I figured out there were dragon shifters when Aren was sniffing around Linnea's dragon looking for his mate. We just pretended we didn't know. We were both disappointed in ourselves we didn't figure it out earlier.

Fallon groaned, "The building. Oh, by the goddess. Is it bad?"

Keegan patted her hand. "It… Well…. They were considering some renovations anyway that the king agreed to fund. Don't worry about it. Sometimes young dragons shift unexpectedly. It's fine, no one was hurt, and the healers will soon have space for a large dragon who might shift during healing. See, that worked out nicely, didn't it shyn h'jarta?"

"Where....." Fallon started to ask where Feron went, but he appeared with several individuals in tow.

"Evening Blessings. I am Shaezia Philldra. I am part of a group that oversees the healer studies at the Athenaeum Contemplari. We are here to check on you and see how you are faring." The healers asked questions, touched her head, waived glowing wands and other items over her. At the end of their examination, they determined her condition to be improved. They suggested food and rest for the next few days.

Shaezia introduced Dakat Erembour to Fallon. "Dakat is a black dragon healer who specializes in the injuries or sicknesses of the mind. We are hopeful he will spot any problem which might arise from the merging of the two life forces into one body."

Dakat stood silently for a moment before he spoke. "Velli sleeps. I think she will do this for a few more days." He thought a moment. "She is despondent. When you feel her stirring....hum, you won't know what that feels like....It will feel like there is another person in the room with you or someone is inside your head with you. When you feel it, you will know. Just speak to her and introduce yourself. Take it slow and try for small gains. I will be here and check with you daily."

The healers left, and apprentices brought in trays of food. Fallon was ravenous. She wolfed down the meal between some low growls that had Feron and Theron's eyes wide. Keegan called for the kitchen to send two more trays, which she polished off before curling up and going back to sleep.

Chapter 39

The morning sun streaming through the tent curtains woke her up. Fallon could see the sun glittered off the dew on the grass. She felt better. There was only a slight ache across her chest. Theron and Feron were sleeping on a pallet, and Keegan was on another. She sat up and pulled the blanket around her to watch the birds flitting across the field. Fallon felt something roll in her mind, like a fish just under the surface of the water, causing ripples on the surface. She spoke Velli's name in her mind, but it felt like she was speaking in front of the opening of a cave.

Helios woke Keegan to tell him Fallon was awake. Keegan left his pallet to sit beside her and pull her against him. He held her as they watched the new day bloom. "Helios says Velli has retreated to her horde. He thinks she needs some time to herself."

Fallon put her head against his shoulder. "Hum, time to oneself. That does sound lovely. Do you know any nice caves where we can hide for a season or two?"

He grinned. "I do! It even has a thermal pool."

"We should go."

"Just as soon as the healers say you are ready, we will go and stay for as long as you wish." He squeezed her hand. "We were supposed to take this at your speed. I'm sorry it came about like this. I'm sure you had other ideas for how you wanted this to happen."

She chuckled. "No one else will have a story just like it."

"No, no, they won't." He held her hand and looked into her eyes. "Truly, Fallon, how are you with this?"

"It is strange. I am at peace with all of it. I am pretty sure I knew you were my mate when we first talked, but it seemed a little too perfect, maybe. I'm not sure why I hesitated. With Velli, how could I not do something to help?"

He gestured around them. "The "too perfect" part got fixed."

"I don't know; I kind of like the tent and the view. I think it's very romantic.

Helios sat with a quill in his paw in Keegan's mind, *"Adding a tent to the list for the horde. Pinnacle Canvas has some nice ones. Oh! We will need lanterns, chairs, more rugs...I think interior walls would be nice. One of the new frost-charmed boxes the snow Fae have. A big, comfortable bed! Yes!*

Who wants to sleep on the ground........." Keegan smiled and shook his head.

"It's a good thing I am a gold dragon, and we have massive, horde space because Helios is planning a very elaborate tent."

"I'm sure it will be wonderful, Helios," Fallon said.

"I am glad someone appreciates my attention to detail," Helios replied before he went back to his list.

Later, Keegan's family came by to visit. Kalasa, Keegan's diplomat mother, told them since Fallon was getting stronger, the king might send for Theron and Feron soon to either give them an oath charm or a forgetting spell and send them back to Therus. After most of the family left, Silvanner and Tedda, spirited Theron and Feron away "for some ale," Silvanner had said. Fallon was convinced there was more to it. It was late when the twins made it back with Silvanner. Theron went to tell her what they had planned, but Fallon held up her hand and told him, "I do not want to know. Just be safe and have a backup plan."

He winked at her. "We do."

The following day a messenger arrived to tell Theron and Feron the king expected them in his chambers at noon. When the time came, Fallon hugged them and said goodbye. She was still not cleared to leave by the healers. Silvanner went with them to see the king. After sunset, a very intoxicated Silvanner came back with Tedda to tell Fallon and Keegan the king had given the twins the oath charm and sent them back to Therus.

Silvanner loud whispered, "Ever, ever, thin' is fine. Juss fin'…er fine. We gotta plan. Is'a good one." He started giggling.

Tedda rolled her eyes. "Muzzle it, Varin, or I'll sleep you right here."

Silvanner shooed her off with his hand. "She's spunky! Like I was sayin'"

Tedda uttered the sleep charm, and Silvanner dropped to the grass. She said good night to Keegan and Fallon, shifted, picked up Silvanner, and flew off.

Keegan's forehead was wrinkled when he turned to Fallon, who told him, "I've learned it's better not to ask. Maybe we should stay hidden in the cave for a year or two."

Keegan hugged her. "Sounds like paradise."

It was another week before Velli spoke to Fallon. They spent the next several days getting to know each other. Fallon learned Velli was distraught over what happened to Baisia because Velli saw what happened as a failure on her part.

The Black Dragon, Dakat, offered words of wisdom that Velli took to heart. "Not even a dragon can guide someone who refuses to be lead. Basia always had the option to do the right thing." Those words were a healing balm for Velli's heart. Soon Fallon and Velli were able to shift and fly. When Fallon could shift effortlessly, the healers declared her ready to leave.

Keegan helped gather her things. "If you have not gotten the knack of putting them in your horde, I can put them in mine."

Fallon thought for a moment. "No, Velli says we can do it." Fallon picked up the bag, and it promptly disappeared.

"Look at you two! Good job!" He glanced down and put his things in his horde. "I've got something I know both of you are going to love. Ready? It's a season-long haven of seclusion in a cave!"

Fallon and Velli laughed. "My dream sanctuary! How did you know?"

Keegan kissed her, "I know all about making my female happy." Keegan wrapped his arms around Fallon. He growled, low in his throat. It made his chest vibrate against her breast. He bent back her head across his arm and kissed her, cradling her in his arms. His lips were soft at first, then progressed with a sure, gradual intensity that caused her hands to drift up and thread her fingers through his hair. Time stopped as the morning breeze continued to caress them with scents of apples, leaves and the last of the years cut hay.   He broke from the kiss, and they held each other, committing the moment to memory.   The noise of the acolytes packing up the tent brought them back to where they were.

Fallon's eyes traveled down his body as her hand drifted down his chest. "That was amazing, shyn h'jarta, but I'm tired of the interruptions."

Keegan groaned. He jogged a few steps away and shifted. Helios crouched down on the grass. "Come mate; it is a lengthy flight. You and Velli are not quite ready for a long journey. Let me show you how fast I can fly."

Velli huffed as Fallon climbed up on Helios' back. *"He may be faster than me, but I am much more maneuverable. When we are more aligned, we will pick a mountain goat off a cliff face. I'd like to see him do that."* She smiled in Fallon's head.

Fallon laughed. *"Savory, roasted, mountain goat stew is delicious."*

414

Velli smugly sat down and watched the scenery go by for a while before she spoke. ***"Fallon, we should give our mate a token for the h'jarta kayzaire. I will look through our horde to find the right thing."***

"Thank you, Velli. I have not had time to buy anything suitable."

True to his word Helios arrived at Aurium just before dusk. Velli took in the cave when they landed. ***"So, this is where it was hidden! The concealment spell used was very effective. We will be safely hidden here. No one will be able to find us unless we want them to.....and... that,...that is a horde load of food!"***

Fallon looked to the food preparation area to see edibles of every description piled on the table and stacked on sturdy shelves that had not been there when she was last at Aurium. "That is a lot of food…"

Keegan hugged her from behind. "The family stocked us with supplies. There is even enough of Uncle Silvanner's brew we could open our own tavern. If we do some hunting, we could stay here by ourselves for…hum..several years. If we wanted." He kissed her head.

"What a thoughtful mate. I wanted to see every land, but now, for the next season or two, I just want to know every part of my handsome, attentive mate. Then maybe we can explore Valair."

Keegan nibbled her neck. "Your attentive mate is already exploring. I believe you will have to catch up." Fallon pulled away from him and moved towards their bedchamber. She looked back at him. Her sparkling eyes and sultry smile drew him with her through the door.

"Are you sure about this Fallon? There is no going back after this."

"I am sure with every fiber of my being I want this, and I want you, now and forever."

He leaned forward and kissed her. Fallon returned the kiss parting his lips with her tongue and kissed him back with more fervor than before. The soft growls vibrating in his chest were music to her ears. She ran her hands up his strong arms and thick shoulders. His smoky, spicy scent was a heavy cloud in the air around her. He invaded all her senses.

His hands unbuckled her belt, and it clattered to the floor. The rest of her clothes followed the belt in a pile near his kicked-off boots. She peeled away the rest of his clothes; then he carried her to their bed. He lavished a trail of gentle nips and kisses down her neck to her breasts. He nibbled and sucked her nipples until Fallon was wet and pushing him down her body.

His lips teased their way to her thigh. He licked and kissed his way to her pussy. Her scent and taste made his cock ache to be cradled in her warm core. Keegan's tongue found a rhythm of swirling licks and thirsty sucking. She twisted from one side to the other, her hands gathering up the blanket she lay on into knots. Her whole body was hot and strung tight as a bow. When she called out his name, he drove his tongue inside her, setting off a keening moan that made his cock ache. He kissed her stomach as she sucked in air.

"That was...wow!" She chuckled and brushed the hair back from his face.

"That's one; let's see about two." Keegan ran his hands under her sides and grabbed her buttocks, then shifted her to the center of the bed. She cradled his hips with her thighs as he kept his mouth on her, ravishing her breasts with attention. He slipped his hand between her thighs to stroke and tease her clit with a steady assault that had Fallon's back arching off the bed and her eyes rolling back in her head.

"Now, Keegan, I want you now."

The words came out with a guttural growl which made his cock spasm and his balls draw up. He positioned himself at her entrance and slowly sank into her. Fallon rocked into him, riding his cock from below. His thrusts gained a steady tempo. Her hands raked down his back and grabbed his ass, driving him further into her until their sweat-slick bodies were sliding together. The strength of what was building was staggering.

"More Keegan more," She cried. With a roar, he thrust harder, hitting her in the spot that turned her moans into one long, high-pitched keen. She shuddered against him, her legs trembling. Keegan called out her name and jerked erratically as he climaxed before collapsing against her. Later, he left the bedroom to come back with a warm towel and two mugs of cool cider. Over the next two days, they made love and counted the stars from the thermal pool.

The late afternoon fall sun warmed the cave entrance where they sat, enjoying the comfort from a sofa Keegan pulled out of the Great Room. He went back inside to get another bottle of wine.

Velli nudged Fallon's mind. ***"I found it. The H'jarta kayzaire gift."*** She transferred it to Fallon's hand. It was a pendant of a dragon in flight; its claws clasped a cut sapphire.

"It's stunning, Velli!"

"It is part of the horde I hid from Basia when she was no longer......herself........" Velli trailed off before finishing. ***"It is an old piece. It had been passed down through the ages."***

"He'll love it."

Keegan returned with wine, fruit, and cheese balanced on a small low table he placed in front of the couch. He opened the bottle and filled her glass.

"Keegan, Velli, and I want to give you this as part of the h'jarta kayzaire." She handed him the pendant.

"It's beautiful. I'll wear it always." He put it on and hugged her.

Fallon snuggled into him, sipping the sparkling spring wine. "A month ago, if someone would have told me I would be sipping wine with my dragon life mate and I would be a dragon shifter too, I would have thought they were mad."

He kissed the top of her head. "And now?"

"I couldn't see it any other way, beloved." Fallon squeezed his leg.

"Me either. I plan on loving you until the end of time, shyn h'jarta."

As she lay on his chest, she caught sight of a couple of dots in the distance. "Keegan? You see that?" She pointed to the dots.

Keegan focused on the shapes. "It's two gold dragons headed our direction....from Therus?" The figures grew in form. As they got closer, Keegan recognized them to be Haile and Revar, the dragons of Tedda Avondale, and his uncle Silvanner Varin.

They landed and shifted. Silvanner quickly spoke up. "Sorry to barge in, but there's a problem. It's Linnea and Aren. We need you both. Now"

Tedda shook her head. "I told you that crazy scheme wasn't going to work."

"It would have been fine if we didn't have to contend with the Badgers."

Helios whipped his head around. ***"Badgers! That Faction of Fetid Filth! Whatever it is, I'm in."***

420

This is the end of Book 2: Shyn Esari; A Dragon's Quest. The third book in the series will be available Christmas of 2022.

I hope you have enjoyed the tales of Therus and Valair. If you have, please leave a review.

You can keep up with the latest in the tribe or magic lands by joining my web page: rrosalisauthor.com or by following me on Facebook.

About the Author

Robbin Rosalis fell in love with the fictional genre at a young age thanks to her grandmother reading 20,000 Leagues Under the Sea to her one summer. Years later, she now has time to write. She enjoys wheel throwing pottery, horseback riding, reading, gardening, and spending time with her amazing husband when she is not writing.

Want to follow the author or Therus and Valair?
Facebook: Robbin Rosalis
Web page: http://rrosalisauthor.com